CR

Sue Graft

A is for Alibi
"Sue Grafton has created a woman we feel we know
. . . Smart, well paced and very funny."
Newsweek

B is for Burglar
"A woman to identify with . . . a gripping read."
Punch

C is for Corpse
"C is for classy, multiplex plotting, strong
characterisation and a tough-cookie heroine."
Time Out

D is for Deadbeat
"D is for deft and diverting."
Guardian

E is for Evidence
"E is for Excellent, Ms Grafton."
Sunday Times

F is for Fugitive
"Of the private investigators, Sue Grafton's Kinsey
Millhone is one of the most convincing in operation."
Independent

H is for Homicide
"S is for Super Sleuth in a scorching story."
Daily Mail

I is for Innocent
"I could also stand for incomparable . . . Riveting
throughout, cracking finale."
Observer

J is the Judgment
"Kinsey Millhone is up there with the giants of
the private eye genre, as magnetic as Marlowe, as
insouciant as Spencer. It's all exhilarating stuff."
Times Literary Supplement

K is for Killer
"*K is for Killer* is another excellent novel from the
excellent Sue Grafton."
Daily Mirror

L is for Lawless
"This is Sue Grafton at her best."
The Spectator

M is for Malice
"M is for marvellous, mesmerising and magnificent."
Manchester Evening News

N is for Noose
"Full marks to Grafton for storytelling and
stamina. No other crime writer so consistently
delivers the goods."
Literary Review

O is for Outlaw
"One of the more humane and empathic sleuths on
the block, Grafton's heroine is also genuinely
believable, full of quirks and all too human
foibles which help the reader identify with her . . .
Absolutely top form."
Time Out

Sue Grafton has become one of the most popular female crime writers, both here and in the US. Born in Kentucky in 1940, the daughter of the mystery writer C. W. Grafton, she began her career as a TV script-writer before Kinsey Millhone and the "alphabet" series took off. Her first novel, *A is for Alibi*, was inspired by Sue's own divorce: *"For months I lay in bed and plotted to kill my ex-husband, but I knew I'd bungle it and get caught so I wrote it in a book instead."*

Sue freely confesses that Kinsey is her alter ego: "I think of her as the person I might have been had I not married young and had kids; she is that stripped down piece of my personality." She writes one book a year and plans to take Kinsey all the way through the alphabet to Z when Kinsey will be forty years old.

Sue Grafton lives in Santa Barbara with her husband Steven Humphrey.

By the same author

Sue Grafton

'G' is for Gumshoe

PAN BOOKS

First published 1990 by Henry Holt and Company Inc., New York

First published in Great Britain 1990 by Macmillan

This edition published 1991 by Pan Books
an imprint of Pan Macmillan Ltd
Pan Macmillan, 20 New Wharf Road, London N1 9RR
Basingstoke and Oxford
Associated companies throughout the world
www.panmacmillan.com

ISBN 0 330 31723 7

24 26 28 27 25

A CIP catalogue record for this book is available from
the British Library.

Printed and bound in Great Britain by
Mackays of Chatham PLC, Chatham, Kent

For Molly Friedrich and Geoffrey Sanford . . . who carve a path through the jungle for me

The author wishes to acknowledge the invaluable assistance of the following people: Steven Humphrey; Eric S. H. Ching; Deputy District Attorney Harvey Giss, County of Los Angeles; Joe Driscoll, Driscoll & Associates Investigations; Noel Waters, District Attorney, Carson City, Nevada; Ms. Terry Roeser, Nevada State Public Defender; Richard and Vicki Windsor; Allen Glanze, Stano Components; Lucy Thomas, Reeves Medical Library, Cottage Hospital; Bobbie Kline, Nursing Director, Cottage Hospital Emergency Room; Karen Nelson, Pathology Department, Cottage Hospital; Lieutenant Tony Baker, Santa Barbara County Sheriff's Department; Robert Simonet, Director of Security, Four Seasons Biltmore; Sergeant Dennis Prescott and Detective Lawrence Gillespie, Santa Barbara County Coroner's Office; Pepper Breault, Santa Barbara County Court Recorder; Ken Orrock, deputy sheriff, Imperial County; Bob Hall; and Carter Blackmar.

1

▰ ▰▰ ▰▰ Three things occurred on or about May 5, which is not only Cinco de Mayo in California, but Happy Birthday to me. Aside from the fact that I turned thirty-three (after what seemed like an interminable twelve months of being thirty-two), the following also came to pass:

1. The reconstruction of my apartment was completed and I moved back in.
2. I was hired by a Mrs. Clyde Gersh to bring her mother back from the Mojave desert.
3. I made one of the top slots on Tyrone Patty's hit list.

I report these events not necessarily in the order of importance, but in the order most easily explained.

For the record, my name is Kinsey Millhone. I'm a private investigator, licensed by the State of California, (now) thirty-three years old, 118 pounds of female in a five-foot six-inch frame. My hair is dark, thick, and straight. I'd been accustomed to wearing it short, but I'd been letting it grow out just to see what it would look like. My usual practice is to crop my own mop every six weeks or so with a pair of nail scissors. This I do because I'm too cheap to pay twenty-eight bucks in a beauty salon. I have hazel eyes, a nose that's been busted twice, but still manages to function pretty well I think. If I were asked to rate my looks on a scale of one to ten, I wouldn't. I have to say, however, that I seldom wear makeup, so whatever I look like first thing in the morning at least remains consistent as the day wears on.

I'd been living since New Year's with my landlord, Henry Pitts, an eighty-two-year-old gent whose converted single-car garage apartment I'd been renting for two years. This nondescript but otherwise serviceable abode had been blown sky-high and Henry had suggested that I move into his small back bedroom while my place was being rebuilt. There is, apparently, some law of nature decreeing that all home construction must double in its projected cost and take four times longer than originally anticipated. This would explain why, after five months of intensive work, the unveiling had finally been scheduled with all the fanfare of a movie premiere. I was uneasy about the new place because I wasn't at all sure I'd like what Henry had come up with in the way of a floor plan and interior "day-core." He'd been very secretive and extremely pleased with himself since he'd gotten city approval for the blueprints. I was worried that I'd take one look at the place and not be able to conceal my dismay. I'm a born liar, but I don't do as well disguising what I feel. Still, as I'd told myself many times, it was his property and he could do anything he pleased. For two hundred bucks a month, was I going to complain? I doesn't think so.

I woke at six o'clock that Thursday morning, rolled out of bed and into my running clothes. I brushed my teeth, splashed some water on my face, did a perfunctory hamstring stretch, and headed out Henry's back door. May and June, in Santa Teresa, are often masked by fog—the weather as blank and dreary as the white noise on a TV set when the broadcast day is done. The winter beaches are stripped bare, massive boulders exposed as the tides sweep away the summer sand. We'd had a rainy March and April, but May had come in clear and mild. The sand was being returned as the spring currents shifted, the beaches restored for the tourists who would begin to pour into the town around Memorial Day and not leave again until Labor Day weekend had come and gone.

This dawn was spectacular, early morning clouds streaking the sky in dark gray tufts, sun tinting the underbelly an intense rose shade. The tide was out and the beach seemed to stretch toward the horizon in a silvery mirror of reflected sky. Santa Teresa was lush and green and the air felt soft, saturated with the smell of eucalyptus leaves and the newly cut grass. I jogged three miles and was home again thirty minutes later in time for Henry to sing "Happy birthday to yooouuu!" as he pulled a pan of freshly baked cinnamon rolls out of the oven. Being serenaded is not my favorite activity, but he did it so badly, I could only be amused and gratified. I showered, pulled on jeans, a T-shirt, and my tennis shoes, and then Henry handed me a gift-wrapped jeweler's box that contained the newly minted brass key to my apartment. He was behaving like a kid, his lean, tanned face wreathed in shy smiles, his blue eyes glinting with barely suppressed excitement. In a two-person ceremonial procession, we walked from his back door, across the flagstone patio, to the front door of my place.

I knew what the exterior looked like—two stories of cream-colored stucco with rounded corners in a style I'd have to call Art Deco. Numerous hand-crankable windows had been installed and there was new landscaping, which Henry had done himself. To tell you the truth, the outward effect was unprepossessing, which I didn't object to a bit. My prime anxiety had always been that he'd make the apartment too fancy for my taste.

We took a few minutes to survey the site, Henry explaining in detail all the hassles he'd gone through with the City Planning Commission and the Architectural Board of Review. I knew he was just dragging out the explanation to pump up

3

the suspense and, in truth, I was feeling anxious, just wanting to get the whole thing over with. Finally, he allowed me to turn the key in the lock and the front door, with its porthole-shaped window, swung open. I don't know what I'd expected. I'd tried not to conjure up fantasies of any kind, but what I saw left me inarticulate. The entire apartment had the feel of a ship's interior. The walls were highly polished teak and oak, with shelves and cubbyholes on every side. The kitchenette was still located to the right where the old one had been, a galley-style arrangement with a pint-size stove and refrigerator. A microwave oven and trash compactor had been added. Tucked in beside the kitchen was a stacking washer-dryer, and next to that was a tiny bathroom.

In the living area, a sofa had been built into a window bay, with two royal blue canvas director's chairs arranged to form a "conversational grouping." Henry did a quick demonstration of how the sofa could be extended into sleeping accommodations for company, a trundle bed in effect. The dimensions of the main room were still roughly fifteen feet on a side, but now there was a sleeping loft above, accessible by way of a tiny spiral staircase where my former storage space had been. In the old place, I'd usually slept naked on the couch in an envelope of folded quilt. Now, I was going to have an actual bedroom of my own.

I wound my way up, staring in amazement at the double-size platform bed with drawers underneath. In the ceiling above the bed, there was a round shaft extending through the roof, capped by a clear Plexiglas skylight that seemed to fling light down on the blue-and-white patchwork coverlet. Loft windows looked out to the ocean on one side and the mountains on the other. Along the back wall, there was an expanse of cedar-lined closet space with a rod for hanging clothes, pegs for miscellaneous items, shoe racks, and floor-to-ceiling drawers.

Just off the loft, there was a small bathroom. The tub was sunken with a built-in shower and a window right at tub level, the wooden sill lined with plants. I could bathe among the treetops, looking out at the ocean where the clouds were piling up like bubbles. The towels were the same royal blue as the cotton shag carpeting. Even the eggs of milled soap were blue, arranged in a white china dish on the edge of the round brass sink.

When the inspection tour was complete, I turned around and stared at him, speechless, a phenomenon that made Henry laugh aloud, tickled with himself that he'd executed his scheme so perfectly. Close to tears, I leaned my forehead against his chest while he patted at me awkwardly. I couldn't ask for a better friend.

He left me alone soon afterward and I went through every cabinet and drawer, drinking in the scent of the wood, listening to the phantom creaking of the wind in the rafters overhead. It took me fifteen minutes to move my possessions in. Most of what I owned had been destroyed by the same bomb that flattened the old place. My all-purpose dress had survived, along with a favorite vest and the air fern Henry'd given me for Christmas. Everything else had been pulverized by black powder, blasting caps, and shrapnel. With the insurance money, I'd bought a few odds and ends—jeans and jumpsuits—and then I'd tucked the rest in a money market account, where it was merrily collecting interest.

At 8:45, I locked up, looked in on Henry briefly, and fumbled my way through yet another thank-you, which he waved away. Then I headed to the office, a quick ten-minute drive into town. I wanted to stay home, circling my house like a sea captain preparing to embark on some fabulous voyage, but I knew for a fact I had bills to pay and telephone calls to return.

I dispensed with several minor items, typing up a couple of invoices for two standing accounts. The last name on the list of phone calls was a Mrs. Clyde Gersh who had left a message on my machine late the day before with a request to get in touch at my convenience. I dialed her number, reaching for a yellow pad. The phone rang twice and then a woman picked up on the other end.

5

"Mrs. Gersh?"

"Yes," she said. Her tone held a note of caution as if I might be soliciting contributions for some fraudulent charity.

"Kinsey Millhone, returning your call."

There was a split second of silence and then she seemed to recollect who I was. "Oh yes, Miss Millhone. I appreciate your being so prompt. I have a matter I'd like to discuss with you, but I don't drive and I'd prefer not to leave the house. Is there any chance you might meet with me here sometime today?"

"Sure," I said. She gave me the address and since I didn't have anything else on the books, I said I'd be there within the hour. There didn't seem to be any particular urgency to the matter, whatever it was, but business is business.

The address she'd given me was in the heart of town, not far from my office, one of the older blocks of single-family residences on a quiet tree-lined street. A tangle of shrubs formed a nearly impenetrable wall that separated the property from street view. I parked out front and let myself in through a creaking gate. The house was a shambling affair, two stories of dark green shingle set sideways on a lot dense with sycamores. I climbed pale gray wooden porch steps still fragrant with a recent repainting. The screen was open and I moved to the front door and pushed the bell, surveying the façade. The house was probably built in the twenties, not elegant by any means, but constructed on a large scale: comfortable, unpretentious, once meant for the middle class—out of reach for the average buyer in the current real estate market. A house like this would probably sell for over half a million these days and then require remodeling to bring it up to snuff.

An obese black woman, in a canary-yellow uniform with white collar and cuffs, let me in. "Mrs. Gersh's out on the upstairs porch," she said, indicating a staircase directly ahead. She lumbered off, apparently trusting me not to lift any cut-glass knickknacks from the occasional table to the right of the entranceway.

6

I had a momentary glimpse of the living room: a wide painted brick fireplace flanked by built-in bookcases with leaded-glass doors, lots of cotton shag carpeting in a much-trampled off-white. Creamy-painted wainscoting ran halfway up the wall with a pale print wallpaper above, extending across the ceiling in an inverted meadow of wildflowers. The room was shadowy and cried out for table lamps. The whole house was muffled in silence and smelled of cauliflower and curry.

I went up. When I reached the first landing, I saw that a second set of stairs branched down into the kitchen, where I could see a kettle bubbling on the stove. The maid who'd admitted me was now standing at the counter, chopping cilantro. Sensing my gaze, she turned and gave me an idle look. I moved on up.

At the top of the stairs, a screen door opened onto a broad, flat porch ringed with wooden planters filled with bright pink and orange geraniums. The main street, two blocks over, ebbed and flowed with traffic noises as sibilant as the sea. Mrs. Gersh was stretched out on a chaise longue, a plaid lap robe arranged across her legs. She might have been taking the air in a deck chair, waiting for the social director to advise her of the day's shipboard activities. She had her eyes closed, a Judith Krantz novel face-down on her lap. The branches of a weeping willow draped long, lacy limbs across one corner of the porch, which was dappled in shade.

The day was mild, but the breeze seemed faintly chilly up here. The woman was stick-thin, with the dead-white complexion of someone profoundly ill. She struck me as the sort of woman who, a hundred years ago, might have spent long years in a sanitarium with a series of misdiagnoses stemming from anxiety, unhappiness, laudanum addiction, or an aversion to sex. Her hair was an icy blond, harshly bleached, and sparse. Bright red lipstick defined the width of her mouth and she wore matching bright red polish on nails cut short. Her Jean Harlow eyebrows had been plucked to an expression of frail astonishment. Her eyes were defined by false lashes that lay against her lower lids like sutures. I judged her to be in her fifties, but she might have been younger. Disease is an aging process in itself. Her chest was sunken, with breasts as flat as the flaps on an envelope. She wore a white silk blouse, expensive-looking pale gray gabardine slacks, vivid green satin slippers on her feet.

"Mrs. Gersh?"

She was startled, eyes flying open in a blaze of blue. For a moment, she seemed disoriented and then she collected herself.

"You must be Kinsey," she murmured. "I'm Irene Gersh." She held out her left hand and clutched mine briefly, her fingers wiry and cold.

"Sorry if I frightened you."

"Don't worry about it. I'm a bundle of nerves. Please. Find a chair and sit. I don't sleep well as a rule and I'm forced to catnap when I can."

A quick survey showed three white mesh lawn chairs stacked together in one corner of the porch. I lifted the top chair, carried it over to the chaise, and sat down.

"I hope Jermaine will have the presence of mind to bring us tea, but don't count on it," she said. She shifted into a more upright position, adjusting the lap robe. She studied me with interest. It was my impression that she approved, though of what I couldn't say. "You're younger than I thought you'd be."

"Old enough," I said. "Today's my birthday. I'm thirty-three."

"Well, happy birthday. I hope I didn't interrupt a celebration."

"Not at all."

"I'm forty-seven myself." She smiled briefly. "I know I look like an old hag, but I'm relatively young . . . given California standards."

"Have you been ill?"

"Let's put it this way . . . I haven't been well. My husband and I moved to Santa Teresa three years ago from Palm

Springs. This was his parents' house. When his father died, Clyde undertook his mother's care. She passed away two months ago."

I murmured something I hoped was appropriate.

"The point is, we didn't need to move here, but Clyde insisted. Never mind my objections. He was raised in Santa Teresa and he was determined to come back."

"I take it you weren't enthusiastic."

She flashed a look at me. "I don't like it here. I never did. We used to come for visits, maybe twice a year. I have an aversion to the sea. I always found the town oppressive. There's an aura about it that I find very dark. Everybody's so smitten with the beauty of it. I don't like the attitude of self-congratulation and I don't like all the green. I was born and raised in the desert, which is what I prefer. My health has deteriorated since the day we arrived, though the doctors can't seem to find anything wrong with me. Clyde is thriving, of course. I suspect he thinks this is a form of pouting on my part, but it's not. It's dread. I wake up every morning filled with debilitating anxiety. Sometimes it feels like a surge of electricity or a weight on my chest, almost overwhelming."

"Are you talking about panic attacks?"

"That's what the doctor keeps calling it," she said.

I murmured noncommittally, wondering where this was all going to lead. She seemed to read my thoughts.

"What do you know about the Slabs?" she asked abruptly.

"The Slabs?"

"Ah, doesn't ring a bell, I see. Not surprising. The Slabs are out in the Mojave, to the east of the Salton Sea. During the Second World War, there was a Marine base out there. Camp Dunlap. It's gone now. All that's left are the concrete foundations for the barracks, known now as the Slabs. Thousands of people migrate to the Slabs every winter from the North. They call them snowbirds because they flee the harsh Northern winters. I was raised out there. My mother's still there, as far as I know. Conditions are very primitive . . . no water, no sewer lines, no city services of any sort, but it costs nothing. The snowbirds live like gypsies: some in expensive RVs, some in cardboard shacks. In the spring, most of them disappear again, heading north. My mother's one of the few permanent residents, but I haven't heard from her for months. She has no phone and no actual address. I'm worried about her. I want someone to drive down there and see if she's all right."

"How often does she usually get in touch?"

"It used to be once a month. She hitches a ride into town and calls from a little café in Niland. Sometimes she calls from Brawley or Westmorland, depending on the ride she manages to pick up. We talk, she buys supplies and then hitchhikes back again."

"She has an income? Social Security?"

Mrs. Gersh shook her head. "Just the checks I send. I don't believe she's ever had a Social Security number. All the years I remember, she supported the two of us with housework, which she did for cash. She's eighty-three now and retired, of course."

"How does mail reach her if she has no address?"

"She has a post office box. Or at least, she did."

"What about the checks? Has she been cashing those?"

"They haven't showed up in my bank statement, so I guess not. That's what made me suspicious to begin with. She has to have money for food and necessities."

"And when did you last hear from her?"

"Christmas. I sent her some money and she called to thank me. Things were fine from what she said, though to tell you the truth, she didn't sound good. She does sometimes drink."

"What about the neighbors? Any way to get through to them?"

She shook her head again. "Nobody has a telephone. You have no idea how crude conditions are out there. These people have to haul their own trash to the city dump. The only thing provided is a school bus for the children and sometimes the townspeople raise a fuss about that."

"What about the local police? Any chance of getting a line on her through them?"

"I've been reluctant to try. My mother is very jealous of her privacy, even a bit eccentric when it comes right down to it. She'd be furious if I contacted the authorities."

"Six months is a long time to let this ride."

Her cheeks tinted slightly. "I'm aware of that, but I kept thinking I'd hear. Frankly, I haven't wanted to brave her wrath. I warn you, she's a horror, especially if she's on a tear. She's very independent."

I thought about the situation, scanning the possibilities. "You mentioned that she has no regular address. How do I find her?"

She reached down and picked up a leather jewelry case she'd tucked under the chaise. She removed a small envelope and a couple of Polaroid snapshots. "This is her last note. And these are some pictures I took last time I was there. This is the trailer where she lives. I'm sorry I don't have a snapshot of her."

I glanced at the pictures, which showed a vintage mobile home painted flat blue. "When was this taken?"

"Three years ago. Shortly before Clyde and I moved up here. I can draw you a map, showing you where the trailer's located. It'll still be there, I guarantee. Once someone at the Slabs squats on a piece of land—even if it's just a ten-by-ten pad of concrete—they don't move. You can't imagine how possessive people get about raw dirt and a few creosote bushes. Her name, by the way, is Agnes Grey."

"You don't have any pictures of her?"

"Actually, I don't, but everyone knows her. I don't think you'll have a problem identifying her if she's there."

"And if I find her? What then?"

"You'll have to let me know what kind of shape she's in. Then we can decide what course of action seems best. I have to say, I chose you because you're a woman. Mother doesn't like men. She doesn't do well among strangers to begin with, but around men she's worse. You'll do it then?"

"I can leave tomorrow if you like."

"Good. I was hoping you'd say that. I'd like some way to reach you beyond business hours," she said. "If Mother should get in touch, I want to be able to call without talking to your machine. An address, too, if you would."

I jotted my home address and phone number on the back of my business card. "I don't give this out often so please be discreet," I said, as I handed it to her.

"Of course. Thank you."

We went through the business arrangements. I'd brought a standard contract and we filled in the blanks by hand. She paid me an advance of five hundred dollars and sketched out a crude diagram of the section of the Slabs where her mother's trailer stood. I hadn't had a missing persons case since the previous June and I was eager to get to work. This felt like a routine matter and I considered the job a nice birthday present for myself.

I left the Gersh house at 12:15, drove straight to the nearest McDonald's, where I treated myself to a celebratory Quarter Pounder with Cheese.

2

▰▱ ▰▱ ▰▱ By one o'clock I was home again, feeling smug about life. I had a new job, an apartment I was thrilled with . . .

The phone began to ring as I unlocked the door. I snatched up the receiver before my answering machine kicked in.

"Ms. Millhone?" The voice was female and unfamiliar. The hiss in the line suggested the call was long-distance.

"Yes."

"Will you hold for Mr. Galishoff?"

"Sure," I said, instantly curious. Lee Galishoff was an attorney in the public defender's office in Carson City, Nevada, whom I'd worked with some four years back. At the time, he was trying to track a fellow named Tyrone Patty, believed to be in this area. An armed robbery suspect named Joe-Quincey Jackson had been arrested and charged with attempted murder in the shooting of a liquor store clerk. Jackson was claiming that Tyrone Patty was the triggerman. Galishoff was very interested in talking to him. Patty was rumored to have fled to Santa Teresa, and when the local police weren't able to locate him, Galishoff had contacted the investigator for the Santa Teresa public defender's office, who in turn had referred him to me. He filled me in on the situation and then sent me the background information on Patty, along with a mug shot from a previous arrest.

I traced the subject for three days, doing a paper chase through the city directory, the crisscross, marriage licenses, divorce decrees, death certificates, municipal and superior court records, and finally traffic court. I picked up his scent when I came across a jaywalking ticket he'd been issued the week before. The citation listed a local address—some friend of his, as it turned out—and Patty answered my knock. Since I was posing as an Avon sales rep, I was fortunate I didn't have to deal with the lady of the house. Any woman in her right mind would have known at a glance I didn't have a clue about makeup. Patty, operating on other instincts, had shut the door in my face. I reported his whereabouts to Galishoff, who by then had found a witness to corroborate Jackson's claim. A warrant was issued through the Carson City district attorney's office. Patty was arrested two days later and extradited. The last I'd heard, he'd been convicted and was serving time at the Nevada State Prison in Carson City.

Galishoff came on the line. "Hello, Kinsey? Lee Galishoff. I hope I didn't catch you at a bad time." His voice was booming, forcing me to hold the receiver eight inches from my ear. Telephone voices are deceptive. From his manner, I'd always pictured him in his sixties, balding and overweight, but a photograph I'd spotted in a Las Vegas newspaper showed a slim, handsome fellow in his forties with a shock of blond hair.

"This is fine," I said. "How are you?"

"Good until now. Tyrone Patty's back in county jail, awaiting trial on a triple murder charge."

"What's the story this time?"

"He and a pal of his hit a liquor store up here and the clerk and two customers were shot to death."

"Really. I hadn't heard that."

14

"Well, there's no reason you would. The problem is, he's pissed at us, claims his life was ruined the day he was put away. You know how it goes. Wife divorced him, kids are alienated, the guy gets out and can't find a job. Naturally, he took to armed robbery again, blasting anybody in his way. All our fault, of course."

"Hey, sure. Why not?"

"Yeah, well, here's the bottom line. Apparently, couple weeks ago, he approached another inmate on a contract murder plot involving the two of us, plus the DA and the judge who sentenced him."

I found myself pointing at my chest as I squinted into the receiver. "Us, as in me?" My voice had gotten all squeaky like I was suddenly going through puberty.

"You got it. Fortunately, the other inmate was a police informant who came straight to us. The DA put a couple of undercover cops on it, posing as potential hit men. I just listened to a tape recording that would chill your blood."

"Are you serious?"

"It gets worse," he said. "From the tape, we can't tell who else he might have talked to. We're concerned he's been in touch with other people who may be taking steps we don't know about. We've notified the press, hoping to make this too hot to handle. Judge Jarvison and I are being placed under around-the-clock armed protection, but they thought I better pass the information on to you. You'd be smart to contact the Santa Teresa police to see about protection for yourself."

"God, Lee. I can't imagine they'd provide any, especially on a threat from out of state. They don't have the manpower *or* the budget for that." I'd never actually called the man by his first name before, but I felt a certain privilege, given what I'd just heard. If Patty was the plotter, Galishoff and I were fellow plottees.

"We're actually facing the same situation here," he said. "The sheriff's department can't cover us for long . . . four or five days at best. We'll just have to see how things stand after

15

that. In the meantime, you might want to hire somebody on your own. Temporarily, at any rate "

"A bodyguard?" I said.

"Well, somebody versed in security procedures."

I hesitated. "I'd have to think about that," I said. "I don't mean to sound cheap, but it would cost me a fortune. You really think it's warranted?"

"Let's put it this way—*I* wouldn't chance it, if I were you. He's got six violent priors."

"Oh."

"Oh, indeed. The insulting part is he isn't even paying that much. Five grand for the four of us. That's less than fifteen hundred bucks apiece!" He laughed when he said this, but I didn't think he was amused.

"I can't believe this," I said, still trying to take it in. When you're presented with bad news, there's always this lag time, the brain simply unable to assimilate the facts.

Galishoff was saying, "I do know a guy, if you decide that's what you want. He's a local P.I. with a background in security. At the moment, he's burned out, but I know he's excellent."

"Just what I need, somebody bored with his work."

He laughed again. "Don't let that dissuade you. This guy's good. He lived in California years ago and loves it out there. He might like the change of scene."

"I take it he's available."

"As far as I know. I just talked to him a couple days ago. His name is Robert Dietz."

I felt a little jolt. "Dietz? I know him. I talked to him about a year ago when I was working on a case."

"You have his number?"

"It's around here someplace, but you might as well give it to me again," I said.

He gave me the number and I made a note. I'd only dealt with the man by phone, but he'd been thorough and efficient, and he hadn't charged me a cent. Really, I owed him one. I heard a buzz on Galishoff's end of the phone.

He said, "Hang on a sec." He clicked off, was gone briefly, and then clicked on again. "Sorry to cut it short, but I got a call coming in. Let me know what you decide."

"I'll do that," I said. "And thanks. Keep safe."

"You, too," he said and he was gone.

I set the receiver down, still staring at the phone. A murder contract? How many times had someone tried to kill me in the last year? Well, not *that* many, I thought defensively, but this was something new. Nobody (that I knew of) had ever put out a contract on me. I tried to picture Tyrone Patty chatting up the subject with a hit man in Carson City. Somehow it seemed strange. For one thing, it was hard to imagine the kind of person who made a living that way. Was the work seasonal? Were there any fringe benefits? Was the price discounted since there were four of us to whack? I had to agree with Galishoff—fifteen hundred bucks was bullshit. In the movies, hit men are paid fifty to a hundred thou, possibly because an audience wants to believe human life is worth that. I suppose I should have been flattered I was included in the deal. A public defender, a DA, and a judge? Distinguished company for a small-town private eye like me. I stared at Dietz's number, but I couldn't bring myself to call. Maybe the crisis would pass before I had to take any steps to protect myself. The real question was, would I mention this to Henry Pitts? Naaah. It would just upset him and what was the point?

When the knock at the door came, I jumped like I'd been shot. I didn't exactly flatten myself against the wall, but I exercised a bit of caution when I peered out to see who was there. It was Rosie, who owns the tavern in my neighborhood. She's Hungarian, with a last name I don't pronounce and couldn't spell on a dare. I suppose she's a mother substitute, but only if you favor being browbeaten by a member of your own sex. She was wearing one of her muumuus, this one olive green, printed with islands, palm trees, and parrots in hot pink and chartreuse. She was holding a plate covered with a paper napkin.

When I opened the door, she pushed it toward me without preamble, which has always been her style. Some people call it rude.

"I brought you some strudel for your birthday," she said. "Not apple. It's nut. The best I ever made. You' gonna wish you had more."

"Well, Rosie, how nice!" I lifted a corner of the napkin. The strudel had a nibbled look, but she hadn't snitched very much.

"It looks wonderful," I said.

"It was Klotilde's idea," she said in a fit of candor. Rosie's in her sixties, short, top-heavy, her hair dyed the utterly faux orange-red of new bricks. I'm not certain what product she uses to achieve the effect (probably something she smuggles in from Budapest on her biannual trips home), but it usually renders her scalp a fiery pink along the part. She had pulled the sides back today and affixed them with barrettes, a style much favored in the five-year-old set. I'd spent the last two weeks helping her find a board-and-care facility for her sister Klotilde, who'd recently moved to Santa Teresa from Pittsburgh, where the winters were getting to be too much for her. Rosie doesn't drive and since my apartment is just down the street from her little restaurant, it seemed expedient for me to help her find a place for Klotilde to live. Like Rosie, Klotilde was short and heavyset with an addiction to the same hair dye that tinted Rosie's scalp pink and turned her tresses such a peculiar shade of red. Klotilde was in a wheelchair, suffering from a degenerative disease that left her cranky and impatient, though Rosie swore she'd always been that way. Theirs was a bickering relationship and after an afternoon in their presence, I was cranky and impatient myself. After checking out fifteen or sixteen possibilities, we'd finally found a place that seemed to suit. Klotilde had been settled into a ground-floor room in a former two-family dwelling on the east side of town, so I was now off the hook.

"You want to come in?" I held the door open while Rosie considered the invitation.

She seemed rooted to the spot, rocking slightly on her feet. She becomes coquettish at times, usually when she's suddenly unsure of herself. On her own turf, she's as aggressive as a Canada goose. "You might not want the company," she said, demurely lowering her eyes.

"Oh, come on," I said. "I'd love the company. You have to see the place. Henry did a great job."

She wiggled once and then sidestepped her way into the living room. She seemed to survey the room out of the corner of her eye. "Oh. Very nice."

"I love it. You should see the loft," I said. I set the strudel on the counter and quickly put some water on for tea. I took her through the place, up the spiral steps and down, showing her the trundle bed, the cubbyholes, the pegs for hanging clothes. She made all the proper noises, only chiding me mildly for the meagerness of my wardrobe. She claims I'll never get a beau unless I have more than one dress.

After the tour, we had tea and strudel, working our way through every crispy bite. I cleaned the plate of flaky crumbs with a dampened fingertip. Her discomfort seemed to fall away, though mine increased as the visit went on. I'd known the woman for two years, but with the exception of the last couple of weeks, our entire relationship had been conducted in her restaurant, which she rules like a dominatrix. We didn't have that much to talk about and I found myself manufacturing chitchat, trying to ward off any awkward pauses in the conversation. By the time we finished tea, I was sneaking peeks at my watch.

Rosie fixed me with a look. "What's the matter? You got a date?"

"Well, no. I've got a job. I have to drive down to the desert tomorrow and I need to get to the bank."

She pointed a finger and then poked me on the arm. "Tonight, you come to my place. I'm gonna buy you a glass of schnapps."

We left at the same time. I offered to drop her off, but the tavern's only half a block away and she said she preferred to walk. The last I saw of her the mild spring breezes were billowing through her muumuu. She looked like a hot-air balloon shortly before lift-off.

I headed into town, detouring by way of the automated teller machine at my bank, where I deposited Mrs. Gersh's advance and pulled a hundred bucks in cash. I circled the block and parked my car in the public lot behind my office. I confess this news about a hit man had made me conscious of my backside and I suppressed the urge to zigzag as I went up the outside stairs.

In my office, I picked up my portable typewriter, some files, and my gun, then stopped into the California Fidelity Insurance offices next door. I chatted briefly with Darcy Pascoe, who doubles as the company's secretary and receptionist. She had helped me on a couple of cases and was thinking about changing fields. I thought she'd be a good investigator and I was encouraging her. Being a P.I. beats sitting on your ass at somebody else's front desk.

I moved on to Vera Lipton's cubicle, completing my rounds. Vera's one of those women men are mad about. I swear it's not anything in particular she does. I suppose it's the air of total confidence she exudes. She likes men and they know it, even when she sasses them. She's thirty-seven, single, addicted to cigarettes and Coca-Cola, which she consumes throughout the day. You'd think that would offend the health nuts, but it doesn't seem to cause dismay. She's tall, probably a hundred and forty pounds, a redhead who wears glasses with big round lenses, tinted gray. I know none of this sounds like the girl of your dreams, but there's something about her that's apparently tough to resist. She's not in any way promiscuous, but if she goes to the supermarket, some guy will strike up a conversation with her and end up dating her for months. When the relationship's over, they usually remain such good friends that she'll match him up with someone she knows.

She was not at her desk. I can usually track her by the smell of cigarette smoke, but today I was having trouble

20

picking up the scent. I cleared a chair and sat down, taking a few minutes to flip through a handbook on insurance fraud. Wherever there's money, somebody finds a way to cheat.

"Hello, Kinsey. What are you up to?"

Vera came into the cubicle and tossed a file onto her desk. She was dressed in a denim jumpsuit with shoulder pads and a wide leather belt. She sat down in her swivel chair, reaching automatically into her bottom drawer where she keeps an insulated cold pack filled with Cokes. She took out a fresh bottle and held it up as a way of offering me one.

I shook my head.

She said, "Guess what?"

"I'm afraid to ask."

"Take a look around and tell me what you see."

I love this kind of quiz. It reminds me of that game we used to play at birthday parties in elementary school where somebody's mom would present a tray of odds and ends, which we got to look at for one minute and then recite back from memory. It's the only kind of party game I ever won. I surveyed her desk. Same old mess as far as I could see. Files everywhere, insurance manuals, correspondence piled up. Two empty Coke bottles ... "No cigarette butts," I said. "Where's the ashtray?"

"I quit."

"I don't believe it. When?"

"Yesterday. I woke up feeling punk, coughing my lungs out. I was out of cigarettes, so there I am on my hands and knees, picking through the trash for a butt big enough to light. Of course I can't find one. I know I'm going to have to throw some clothes on, grab my car keys, and whip down to the corner before I can even have my first Coke. And I thought, to hell with it. I've had it. I'm not going to do this to myself anymore. So I quit. That was thirty-one hours ago."

"Vera, that's great. I'm really proud of you."

"Thanks. It feels good. I keep wishing I could have a cigarette to celebrate. Stick around. You can watch me hyperventilate every seven minutes when the urge comes up. What are you up to?"

"I'm on my way home," I said. "I just stopped by to say hi. I'll be gone tomorrow and we'd talked about having lunch."

"Shoot, too bad. I was looking forward to it. I was going to fix you up."

"Fix me up? Like a blind date?" This news was about as thrilling to me as the notion of periodontal work.

"Don't use that tone, kiddo. This guy's perfect for you."

"I'm afraid to ask you what that means," I said.

"It means he isn't married like *someone* I could name." Her reference was to Jonah Robb, whose on-again, off-again marriage had been a source of conflict. I'd been involved with him intermittently since the previous fall, but the high had long since worn off.

"There's nothing wrong with that relationship," I said.

"Of course there is," she snapped. "He's never there when you need him. He's always off with what's-her-face at some counseling session."

"Well, that's true enough." Jonah and Camilla seemed to move from therapist to therapist, switching every time they got close to a resolution of any kind; "conflict habituated," I think it's called. They'd been together since seventh grade and were apparently addicted to the dark side of love.

"He's never going to leave her," Vera said.

"That's probably true, too, but who gives a shit?"

"You do and you know it."

"No, I don't," I said. "I'll tell you the truth. I really don't have room in my life for much more than I've got. I don't want a big, hot love affair. Jonah's a good friend and he comes through for me often enough . . ."

"Boy, are you out of touch."

"I don't want your rejects, Vera. That's the point."

"This is not a reject. It's more like a referral."

"You want to make a sales pitch? I can tell you want to make a sales pitch. Go ahead. Fill me in. I can hardly wait."

"He's perfect."

" 'Perfect.' Got it," I said, pretending to take notes. "Very nice. What else?"

"Except for one thing."

"Ah."

"I'm being honest about this," she replied righteously. "If he was totally perfect, I'd keep him for myself."

"What's the catch?"

"Don't rush me. I'll get to that. Just let me tell you his good points first."

I glanced at my watch. "You have thirty seconds."

"He's smart. He's funny. He's caring. He's competent . . ."

"What's he do for a living?"

"He's a doctor . . . a family practitioner, but he's not a workaholic. He's really available emotionally. Honest. He's a sweet guy, but he doesn't take any guff."

"Keep talking."

"He's thirty-nine, never married, but definitely interested in commitment. He's physically fit, doesn't smoke or do drugs, but he's not obnoxious about it, you know what I mean? He isn't holier-than-thou."

"Unh-hunh, unh-hunh," I said in a monotone. I made a rolling motion with my hand, meaning get to the point.

"He's good-looking too. I'm serious. Like an eight and a half on a scale of one to ten. He skis, plays tennis, lifts weights . . ."

"He can't get it up," I said.

"He's terrific in bed!"

I started laughing. "What's the deal, Vera? Is he a mouth breather? Does he tell jokes? You know I hate guys who tell jokes."

She shook her head. "He's short."

"How short?"

"Maybe five four and I'm five nine."

I stared at her with disbelief. "So what? You've dated half a dozen guys who were shorter than you."

"Yeah, well secretly, it always bothered me."

I stared at her some more. "You're going to reject this guy because of that?"

Her tone became defiant. "Listen, he's terrific. He's just not right for me. I'm not making a judgment about him. This is just a quirk of mine."

"What's his name?"

"Neil Hess."

I reached down and pulled a scrap of paper from her wastebasket. I took a pen from her desk. "Give me his number."

She blinked at me. "You'll really call him?"

"Hey, I'm only five six. What's a couple of inches between friends?"

She gave me his number and I dutifully made a note, which I tucked in my handbag. "I'll be out of town for a day, but I'll call him when I get back."

"Well, great."

I got up to leave her office and paused at the door. "If I marry this guy, you have to be the flower girl."

3

■▶ ■▶ ■▶ I bypassed my run the next morning, anxious
to hit the road. I left Santa Teresa at 6:00 A.M., my car loaded
with a duffel, my portable Smith-Corona, the information
about Irene Gersh's mother, my briefcase, miscellaneous
junk, and a cooler in which I'd tucked a six-pack of Diet
Pepsi, a tuna sandwich, a couple of tangerines, and a Ziploc
bag of Henry's chocolate chip cookies.

I took Highway 101 south, following the coastline past
Ventura, where the road begins to cut inland. My little VW
whined and strained, climbing the Camarillo grade until it
reached the crest, coasting down into Thousand Oaks. By the
time I reached the San Fernando Valley, it was nearly seven
and rush-hour traffic had crammed the road solidly from
side to side. Vehicles were changing lanes with a speed and
grace that I think of as street surfing, complete with occasional wipeouts. Smog veiled the basin, blocking out the surrounding mountains so completely that unless you knew they
were there, you might imagine the land to be flat as a plate.

At North Hollywood, the 134 splits off, heading toward
Pasadena, while the 101 cuts south toward downtown L.A.

On a map of the area, the heart of Los Angeles looks like a small hole in the center of a loosely crocheted pink shawl that spreads across Los Angeles County, trailing into Orange County to the south. Converging freeways form a tangle, with high-rise buildings caught in the knot. I've never known anyone who actually had business in downtown Los Angeles. Unless you have a yen to see Union Station, Olvera Street, or skid row, the only reason to venture into the neighborhood around Sixth and Spring is to check out the wholesale gold mart for jewelry or the Cooper Building for name-brand clothing discounted to bargain-basement prices. For the most part, you're better off speeding right on by.

You'll notice that I'm skipping right over the events of Thursday night. I will say that I did, indeed, stop by Rosie's for the drink she'd promised, only to discover that she and Henry had arranged a surprise birthday party for me. It was one of those mortifying moments where the lights come up and everybody jumps out from behind the furniture. I couldn't believe it was happening. Jonah was there, and Vera (the rat—who hadn't breathed a word of it when I'd seen her earlier), Darcy and Mac from CFI, Moza from down the block, some of the regular bar patrons, and a former client or two. I don't know why it seems so embarrassing to admit, but they had a cake and actual presents that I had to open on the spot. I don't like to be surprised. I don't like to be the center of attention. These were all people I care about, but I found it unnerving to be the object of so much goodwill. I suppose I said all the right things. I didn't get drunk and I didn't disgrace myself, but I felt disconnected, like I was having an out-of-body experience. Reflecting on it now in the privacy of my car, I could feel myself smiling. Events like this always seem better to me in retrospect.

The party had broken up at ten. Henry and Jonah walked me home and after Henry excused himself, I showed Jonah the apartment, feeling shy as a bride.

I got the distinct impression he wanted to spend the night, but I couldn't handle it. I'm not sure why—maybe it was my earlier conversation with Vera—but I felt distant and when he moved to kiss me, I found myself easing away.

"What's the matter?"

"Nothing. It's just time for me to be alone."

"Did I do something to piss you off?"

"Hey, no. I promise. I'm exhausted, that's all. The party tonight just about did me in. You know me. I don't do well in situations like that."

He smiled, his teeth flashing white. "You should have seen the look on your face. It was great. I think it's funny to see you caught off-guard." He was leaning against the door, with his hands behind his back, the light from the kitchen painting one side of his face with a warm yellow glow. I found myself taking a mental picture of him: blue eyes, dark hair. He looked tired. Jonah is a Santa Teresa cop who works the missing persons detail, which is how we'd met almost a year ago. I really wasn't sure what I felt for him at this point. He's kind, confused, a good man who wants to do the right thing, whatever that is. I understood his dilemma with his wife and I didn't blame him for his part in it. Of course, he was going to vacillate. He has two young daughters who complicate the matter no end. Camilla had left him twice, taking the girls with her both times. He'd managed to do all right without her, but the first time she crooked her little finger, he'd gone running back. It had been push-pull since then, double messages. In November, she'd decided they should have an "open marriage," which he figured was a euphemism for her screwing around on him. He felt that freed him up to get involved with me, but I was reasonably certain he'd never mentioned it to her. How "open" could this open marriage be? While I didn't want much from the relationship, I found it disquieting that I never knew where I stood. Sometimes he behaved like a family man, taking his girls to the zoo on Sunday afternoons. Sometimes he acted like a bachelor father, doing exactly the same thing. He and his daughters spent a lot of time staring at the monkeys while Camilla did God knows what. For my part, I felt like a peripheral character in a play I wouldn't have *paid* to see. I didn't need the aggravation, to tell you the truth. Still, it's hard to complain when I'd known his marital status from the outset. Hey, no sweat, I'd thought. I'm a big girl. I can handle it. Clearly, I hadn't the slightest idea what I was getting into.

"What's that expression?" he said to me.

I smiled. "That's good night. I'm bushed."

"I'll get out of here then and let you get some sleep. You've got a great place. I'll expect a dinner invitation when you get back."

"Yeah, you know how much I love to cook."

"We'll send out."

"Good plan."

"You call me."

"I'll do that."

Truly, the best moment of the day came when I was finally by myself. I locked the front door and then circled the perimeter, making sure the windows were securely latched. I turned out the lights downstairs and climbed my spiral staircase to the loft above. To celebrate my first night in the apartment, I ran a bath, dumping in some of the bubblebath Darcy had given me for my birthday. It smelled like pine trees and reminded me of janitorial products employed by my grade school. At the age of eight, I'd often wondered what maintenance wizard came up with the notion of throwing sawdust on barf.

I turned the bathroom light off and sat in the steaming tub, looking out the window toward the ocean, which was visible only as a band of black with a wide swath of silver where the moon cut through the dark. The trunks of the sycamores just outside the window were a chalky white, the leaves pale gray, rustling together like paper in the chill spring breeze. It was hard to believe there was somebody out there hired to kill me. I'm well aware that immortality is simply an illusion we carry with us to keep ourselves functional from day to day, but the idea of a murder contract was inconceivable to me.

The bathwater cooled to lukewarm and I let it galumph

away, the sound reminding me of every bath I'd ever taken. At midnight, I slid naked between the brand-new sheets on my brand-new bed, staring up through the skylight. Stars lay on the Plexiglas dome like grains of salt, forming patterns the Greeks had named centuries ago. I could identify the Big Dipper, even the Little Dipper sometimes, but I'd never seen anything that looked even remotely like a bear, a belt, or a scuttling crab. Maybe those guys smoked dope back then, lying on their backs near the Parthenon, pointing at the stars and bullshitting the night away. I wasn't even aware that I had fallen asleep until the alarm jolted me back to reality again.

I focused on the road, glancing down occasionally at the map spread open on the passenger seat. Joshua Tree National Monument and Anza-Borrego Desert State Park were blocked out in dark green, shaped like the pieces of a giant jigsaw puzzle. The national forests were tinted a paler green, while the Mojave itself was a pale beige, mountain ranges shaded in the palest brushstrokes. Much of the desert would never be civilized and that was cheering somehow. While I'm not a big fan of nature, its intractability amuses me no end.

At the San Bernardino/Riverside exit, the arms of the freeway crisscross, sweeping upward, like some vision of the future in a 1950s textbook. Beyond, there is nothing on either side of the road but telephone lines, canyons the color of brown sugar, fences of wire with tumbleweeds blown against them. In the distance, a haze of yellow suggested that the mesquite was in bloom again.

Near Cabazon, I pulled into a rest stop to stretch my legs. There were eight or ten picnic tables in a grassy area shaded by willows and cottonwoods. Rest rooms were housed in a cinderblock structure with an A-line roof. I availed myself of one, air-drying my hands since the paper towels had run out. It was now ten o'clock and I was hungry, so I pulled out my cooler and set it up on a table some ten yards from the parking lot. The virtue of being single is you get to make up all the rules. Dinner at midnight? Why not, it's just you.

Lunch at 10:00 A.M.? Sure, you're the boss. You can eat when you want and call it anything you like. I sat facing the road, munching on a sandwich while I watched cars come and go.

A kid, maybe five, was playing with an assortment of Matchbox trucks on the walkway while his father napped on a bench. Pop had a copy of *Sports Illustrated* open across his face, his big arms bared in a T-shirt with the sleeves torn out. The air was mild and warm, the sky an endless wash of blue.

On the road again, I passed the wind farms, where electricity is generated in acre after acre of turbines, arranged in rows like whirligigs. Today, gusts were light. I could watch the breezes zigzag erratically through the turbines, visible in the whimsical twirling of slender blades, like the propellers on lighter-than-air craft. Maybe, when man is gone, these odd totems will remain, merrily harvesting the elements, converting wind into power to drive ancient machines.

Approaching Palm Springs, the character of the road begins to change again. Billboards advertise fast-food restaurants and gasoline. RV country clubs are heralded as "residential communities for active adults." Behind the low hills, mountains loom, barren except for the boulders bleached by the sun. I passed a trailer park called Vista del Mar Estates, but there was no *mar* in view.

I took Highway 111 south, passing through the towns of Coachella, Thermal, and Mecca. The Salton Sea came into view on my right. For long stretches, there were only the two lanes of asphalt, powdery dirt on either side, the body of water, shimmering gray in the rising desert heat. At intervals, I would pass a citrus grove, an oasis of shade in a valley otherwise drubbed by unrelenting sun.

I drove through Calipatria. Later, I heard area residents refer to a town I thought was called Cow-pat, which I realized, belatedly, was a shortened version of Calipatria. The only landmark of note there is a building downtown with one brick column that looks like it's been chewed on by rats. It's actually earthquake damage left unrepaired, perhaps in an effort to pacify the gods.

Fifteen miles south of Calipatria is Brawley. On the outskirts of town, I spotted a motel with a VACANCY sign. The Vagabond was a two-story L-shaped structure of perhaps forty rooms bracketing an asphalt parking lot. I rented a single and was directed to room 20, at the far end of the walk. I eased my car into the space out in front, where I unloaded the duffel, the typewriter, and the cooler.

The room was serviceable, though it smelled faintly of eau de bug. The carpet was a two-toned green nylon in a shag long enough to mow. The bedspread and matching drapes were a green-and-gold floral print, flowering vines of some kind climbing up parallel trellises. The painting above the double bed showed a moose standing in lakewater up to his knees. The painted mountains were the same shade of green as the rug—just a little decorating hint from those of us in the know. I put a call through to Henry to tell him where I was. Then I dumped my belongings, christened the toilet bowl, and took off again, tracking north as far as the little hamlet of Niland.

I pulled in to what would have passed for a curb had there been a sidewalk in view. I asked a leather-faced rancher in a pair of overalls for directions to the Slabs. He pointed without a word. I took a right turn at the next corner and drove another mile and a half through flat countryside interrupted only by telephone poles and power lines. Occasionally, I crossed an irrigation canal where brown grasses hugged the banks. In the distance, to the right, I caught sight of a hillock of raw dirt, crowned by an outcropping of rock painted with religious sentiments. GOD IS LOVE and REPENT loomed large. Whatever was written under it, I couldn't read. Probably a Bible quote. There was a dilapidated truck parked nearby with a wooden house built on the back, also painted with exhortations of some fundamentalist sort.

I passed what must have served as a guard post when the original military base was still functioning. All that remained was a three-by-three-foot concrete shell, only slightly bigger than a telephone booth. I drove onto the old base. A few hundred yards down the road, a second guardhouse had been painted sky blue. Evergreens were outlined on the face of it, with WELCOME TO painted in black letters on the roof line and SLAB CITY in an arch of black letters on white, with white doves flying in all directions. GOD IS LOVE was lettered in two places, the paint job apparently left over from the sixties when the hippies came through. Nothing in the desert perishes—except the wildlife, of course. The air is so dry that nothing seems to rot, and the heat, while intense through much of the year, preserves more than it destroys. I'd passed abandoned wood cabins that had probably been sitting empty for sixty years.

Here, in the endless stretch of gravel and dirt, I could see numerous vans, a few automobiles, many with doors hanging open to dispel the heat. Trailers, RVs, tents, and pickup trucks with camper shells were set up in makeshift neighborhoods. The wide avenues were defined by clumps of creosote and mesquite. Only one roadway was marked and the sign, propped up against a stone, read 18TH ST.

Along the main road, one of the world's longest flea markets had been laid out. The tables were covered with odds and ends of glass, used clothing, old tires, used car seats, defunct television sets, which were being sold "cheep." A hand-lettered sign announced HOLES DUG & ODD JOBS. There was not a buyer in sight. I didn't even catch sight of any residents. A United States flag flew from a hand-rigged pole and I could see state flags as well, all snapping in a hot wind that whipped up the dust. Here, there were no TV antennas, no fences, no telephone poles, no power lines, no permanent structures of any kind. The whole place had a gypsy air, varicolored awnings offering protection from the midday sun. The silence was broken by an occasional barking dog.

I pulled over to the side of the road and parked my car, getting out. I shaded my eyes and scanned the area. Now that my eyes had adjusted to the harsh light, I could see that there were actually people in view: a couple sitting in the open doorway of their mobile home, a lone man passing from one aisle of vehicles to the next. No one seemed to pay any attention to me. The arrival and departure of strangers was apparently so commonplace that my presence elicited no interest whatever.

About fifty yards away, I spotted a woman sitting in a rectangle of shade formed by a bright red and orange parachute that had been strung up between two campers. She was nursing a baby, her face bent to the sight of the infant. I approached, stopping about fifteen feet away. I wasn't sure what constituted personal turf out here and I didn't want to trespass.

"Hi," I said. "I wonder if you could give me some help."

She looked up at me. She might have been eighteen. Her dark hair was pulled up in a ragged knot on top of her head. She wore shorts and a cotton shirt, unbuttoned down the front. The baby worked with such vigor that I could hear the sucking noise from where I stood. "You lookin' for Eddie?"

I shook my head. "I'm trying to find a woman named Agnes Grey. Do you happen to know her?"

"Nunh-unh. Eddie might. He's been out here a lot longer than me. Is she permanent?"

"I understand she's been out here for years."

"Then you might check at the Christian Center down here on the left. Trailer with a sign out listing all the activities. Lot of people register with them in case of emergency. What'd you want her for?"

"She has a daughter up in Santa Teresa who hasn't heard from her for months. She asked me to find out why her mother hasn't been in touch."

She squinted at me. "You some kind of detective?"

"Well, yeah. More or less. I'm a friend of the family and I was down in this area anyway so I said I'd check it out." I took out the two snapshots Irene Gersh had given me. I moved over and held them out so she could see. "This is her trailer. I don't have a picture of her. She's an old woman, in her eighties."

The girl tilted her head, looking at the photographs. "Oh,

yeah, that one. I know her. I never heard her real name Everybody calls her Old Mama."

"Can you tell me where to find her?"

"Not really. I can tell you where her trailer's at, but I haven't seen her for a while."

"Do you remember when you saw her last?"

She thought about it briefly, screwing up her face. "I never paid much attention so I can't really say. She goes stumping up and down out here when she needs a ride into town. Everybody's real good about that, if your car's broke or something and you gotta have a lift. She's kinda weird though."

"Like what?"

"Uh, well, you know, she has these spells when she talks to herself. You see people like that jabbering away, making gestures like they're in the middle of an argument. Eddie took her into Brawley couple times and he said she was all right then. Smelled bad, but she wasn't out of her head or anything like that."

"You haven't seen her lately?"

"No, but she's probably still around someplace. I been busy with the baby. You might ask somebody else. I never talked to her myself."

"What about Eddie? When do you expect him back?"

"Not till five, I think he said. If you want to check her trailer, go down this road about a quarter mile? You'll see this old rusted-out Chevy. That's called Rusted-Out Chevy Road. Turn right and drive till you pass these concrete bunker things on the left. They look like U's. I don't know what they are, but her trailer's in the next lot. Just bang on the door loud. I don't think she hears good from what Eddie said."

"Thanks. I'll do that."

"If you don't find her, you can come on back here and wait for him, if you like. He might know more."

I glanced at my watch. It was just 12:25. "I may do that," I said. "Thanks for the help."

4

▰▰▰ ▰▰▰ ▰▰▰ The trailer on Rusted-Out Chevy Road was a sorry sight, bearing very little resemblance to the snapshot I had in my possession, which showed an old but sturdy-looking travel trailer, painted flat blue, sitting on four blackwall tires. From the picture, I estimated that it was thirty-some years old, built in the days when it might have been hitched to the back of a Buick sedan and hauled halfway across the country. Now, spray paint had been used to emblazon the siding with the sort of words my aunt urged me to hold to a minimum. Some of the louvres on the windows had been broken out and the door was hanging on one hinge. As I drove by, I saw a unisex person, approximately twelve years of age, sitting on the doorsill in ragged cutoffs, hair in dreadlocks, finger up its nose, apparently mining the contents. I passed the place, did a U-turn and doubled back, pulling over to the side of the road in front. By the time I got out, the doorsill was deserted. I knocked on the doorframe.

"Hello?" I sang. Nothing. "Heellloo."

I peered in. The place was empty, at least the portion I could see. The interior, which had probably never been clean, was littered now with trash. Empty bottles and cans were discarded in a heap where a fold-down table should have been. Dust coated most surfaces. The banquette on the right looked like it had been chopped up for firewood. The doors on the kitchen cabinets had all been removed. Cupboards were empty. The tiny four-burner butane-fueled stove looked like it hadn't been used for months.

I glanced to my left, moving down a short passage that led to a small bedroom in the back. A door on the right opened onto a bathroom, which consisted of a defunct chemical toilet, a ragged hole in the wall where a basin had once been attached, and a length of pipe sticking out above a shower pan filled with rags. The bedroom contained a bare mattress and two sleeping bags zipped together and left in a wad. Someone was living here and I didn't think it was Irene Gersh's mom. I peered through the window, but all I saw outside was a buff-colored stretch of desert with a low range of mountains ten or fifteen miles away. Distances are deceptive out here because there aren't any reference points.

I picked my way back to the front door and stepped out, circling the trailer. Around the corner, a bucket lined with a plastic bag served as a makeshift outhouse. There were several bags like it, tied at the top and tossed together in a pile, a black fly manufacturing plant. Across the road, there was a concrete pad where a Winnebago was moored. Beside the RV, there was a pickup truck mounted with a camper shell. The pad itself was cracked, weeds growing up through the crevices. A Weber grill had been set out and the smell of charcoal lighter and smoking briquettes drifted across the road to me. Near the grill, there was a folding table surrounded by mismatched chrome chairs. As I crossed the road, a woman emerged from the trailer carrying a tray loaded with a foil-covered plate, condiments, and utensils. She was in her forties, slim, with a long, weathered face. No makeup, salt-and-pepper hair cropped short. She wore blue jeans and a flannel shirt, both faded to a pale gray. She went about her business, ignoring my approach. I watched her put five fat hamburger patties on the grill. She moved over to the table and began to set it with forks and paper plates.

"Excuse me," I said. "Do you know the woman who lives over there?"

"You related?"

"I'm a friend of the family."

"About time somebody took an interest," she said snappishly. "What's going on over there is a low-down disgrace."

"What *is* going on over there?"

"Kids moved in. You can see they trashed the place. Loud parties, loud arguments, fights breaking out. We all make it a point to mind our own business out here, but there's limits."

"What about Agnes? What happened to her? Surely, she's not still living there."

The woman cocked a head toward the Winnebago. "Marcus? You want to come out here, please? Woman's asking about Old Mama."

The door to the Winnebago opened and a man peered out. He was of medium height, small-boned, with warm skin tones suggesting Mediterranean origins. His hair was dark, combed back from his face. His nose was short and straight, his lips very full. His dark eyes were fringed with black lashes. He looked like a male model in an Italian menswear ad. He stared at me for a moment, his expression neutral.

"Who're you?" he asked. No accent. He wore pleated pants and the sort of ribbed undershirt old men wear.

"I'm Kinsey," I said. "Agnes Grey's daughter asked me to drive out here and check on her. Do you have any idea where she is?"

He surprised me by holding out his hand to introduce himself. We shook. His palm was soft and hot, his grip firm.

"I'm Marcus. This is my wife, Faye. We haven't seen Old Mama for a long time. Like, months. We heard she got sick, but I don't know for sure. Hospital in Brawley. You might see if she's there."

"Wouldn't somebody have notified her relatives?"

Marcus stuck his hands in his pockets with a shrug. "She might not've told them. This's the first I knew she had family. She's a real private person. Like a recluse almost. Minds her own business as long as you mind yours. Where's this daughter live?"

"Santa Teresa. She's been worried about Agnes but she didn't have a way to get in touch."

Neither of them seemed impressed with the sincerity of Irene's concern. I changed the subject, looking back at the trailer across the road. "Who's the little gremlin I saw sitting on the front step?"

Faye spoke up, her tone sour. "There's two of them. Boy and a girl. They came by a few months ago and staked the place out. They must have heard it was empty because they moved in pretty quick. Runaways. Don't know how they survive. Probably stealing or whoring, whichever comes first. We asked them to clean up the sewage, but of course they don't."

Clearly, *sewage* was a euphemism for the bags of sewage. "The kid I saw couldn't have been twelve years old," I said.

Faye answered. "They're fifteen. Boy is, at any rate. They act like wild animals and I know they do drugs. They're always picking through our garbage, looking for food. Sometimes, other kids come by and camp out with them. Word must be out they have a place to crash."

"Can't you report 'em to the cops?"

Marcus shook his head. "Tried that. They vamoose the minute anybody shows up."

"Could there be a connection between Agnes's disappearance and their moving in?"

"I doubt it," he said. "She'd been gone a couple months by the time they got here. Somebody might have told them the trailer was empty. They never seemed to worry about her showing up. I know they've torn the place apart, but there's not much we can do."

I gave him my card. "This is my number in Santa Teresa. I'll be down here a couple of days seeing if I can get a line on her. After that, you can reach me at this 805 area code.

38

Would you give me a call if she gets in touch? I'll try to check back with you before I leave town, in case you've heard from her. Maybe you'll think of something that might be of help."

Faye peered over his shoulder at the card I'd given him. "A private detective? I thought you said you were a family friend."

"A hired friend," I said. I had started back to my car when he called my name. I turned and looked at him.

"There's a sheriff's substation in Niland, right next to the old jail on First. You might check with the deputy. There's always a possibility she's dead."

"Don't think it hasn't occurred to me," I said. His gaze held mine briefly and then I moved on.

I headed back toward the township of Niland, 145 feet below sea level, population twelve hundred. The old jail is a tiny stucco structure with a shake roof and an ornamental iron wheel attached to the wooden porch rail. Next door, not ten feet away, is the new jail, housed in the sheriff's substation, also stucco and not much wider than the width of one door and two windows. An air conditioner hung out of a window around on the side. I parked out in front. A note was taped to the front door. "Back at 4:00 P.M. In emergency or other business talk to Brawley deps." Not a clue about how to contact the Brawley sheriff's department.

I stopped at a gas station and while the tank was being filled, I found a pay phone and checked the dog-eared directory that was chained to the wall, looking up the telephone number of the Brawley sheriff's department. From the address listed, I had to guess it wasn't far from my motel on Main. In a quick call, I learned that Sergeant Pokrass, the deputy I should be talking to, was presently at lunch and would be back at one o'clock. A glance at my watch showed it was 12:50.

The sheriff's substation is a one-story stucco building with a red tile roof, located right across the street from the Brawley Police Department. There were two white sheriff's cars parked in the narrow lot. I went in through a glass door. A

Pepsi machine dominated the corridor. To the left of the entrance was a closed door that, according to the sign, led to a courtroom. On the other side of the hallway were two small offices with an open door between them. The interior was polished brown linoleum, Formica countertops, light wood desks, metal file cabinets, swivel chairs. There were two deputies and a civilian clerk in sight, the latter on the telephone. The low murmur of conversation was underscored by the steady, low ratchet of the police radio.

Deputy Pokrass turned out to be a woman in her thirties, tall and trim, with sandy hair cut short, glasses with tortoiseshell rims. The tan uniform seemed designed for her: all function, no frills. There was very little animation to her face. Her eyes were a penetrating brown, rather cold, and her manner, while not actually rude, was on the abrupt side of businesslike. We didn't waste a lot of time on pleasantries. I stood at the short counter and filled her in on the situation, keeping my account brief and to the point. She listened intently, without comment, and when I finished she picked up the telephone. She called the local hospital, Pioneers Memorial, and asked for the patient billing and accounting department, her voice warming only slightly in her conversation with someone named Letty on the other end. She pulled a yellow legal pad closer and picked up a pencil sharpened to a perfect point. She made a note, her handwriting full of angular downstrokes. I was sure that, even at the age of twelve, she'd never been the type to make a little happy face when she dotted an *i*. She hung up the phone and used a straightedge to tear off the strip of paper on which she'd written an address.

"Agnes Grey was admitted to Pioneers on January 5, through emergency after the paramedics picked her up outside a downtown coffee shop where she collapsed. Diagnosis by the admitting physician was pneumonia, malnutrition, acute dehydration, and dementia. On March 2, she was transferred to Rio Vista Convalescent Hospital. This is the address. If you locate her, let us know. Otherwise you can come back in and fill out a missing persons report. We'll do what we can."

I glanced at the paper, then folded it and put it in my jeans pocket. "I appreciate your help." By the time I got the sentence out, she'd turned away, already back at work on the report she was typing. I used my proffered hand to scratch my nose, feeling the way you do when you wave back at someone who turns out to be waving happily at someone else.

On the way to my car, it occurred to me that the admissions officer at the convalescent home might be reluctant to give me information on Agnes Grey. If she was still a patient, I could probably get a room number and whip right in. If she'd been released, things might get trickier. Medical personnel aren't as chatty as they used to be. Too many lawsuits over the right to privacy. Best not blow my chances, I thought.

I went back to the Vagabond, where I unzipped the duffel and removed my all-purpose dress. I gave it a shake. This faithful garment is the only dress I own, but it goes anyplace. It's black, collarless, with long sleeves and a zipper down the back, made of some slithery, miracle fabric that takes unlimited abuse. You can smush it, wad it up, sit on it, twist it, or roll it in a ball. The instant you release it, the material returns to its original state. I wasn't even sure why I'd brought it— hoping for a hot night on the town, I suppose. I tossed it on the bed, along with my (slightly scuffy) low-heeled black shoes and some black panty hose. I took a three-minute shower and redid myself. Thirteen minutes later I was back in the car, looking like a grown-up, or so I hoped.

The Rio Vista Convalescent Hospital was set in the middle of a residential area, an old two-story stucco building painted a tarnished-looking Navajo white. The property was surrounded by chain-link fence, wide gates standing open onto a parking lot. The place didn't look like any hospital I'd ever seen. The grounds were flat, unlandscaped, largely sealed over in cracked asphalt on which cars were parked. As I approached the main entrance, I could see that the brittle blacktop was limned with faded circles and squares of some obscure sort. It wasn't until I'd passed through the main doors and was standing in the foyer that I knew what I'd been looking at. A playground. This had once been a grade school. The lines had been laid out for foursquare and tetherball. The interior was nearly identical to the elementary school I'd attended. High ceilings, wood floors, the sort of lighting fixtures that look like small perfect moons. Across from me, a water fountain was still mounted on the wall, white porcelain with shiny chrome handles down low at kiddie height. Even the air smelled the same, like vegetable soup. For a moment, the past was palpable, laid over reality like a sheet of cellophane, blocking out everything. I experienced the same rush of anxiety I'd suffered every day of my youth. I hadn't liked school. I'd always been overwhelmed by the dangers I sensed. Grade school was perilous. There were endless performances: tests in spelling, geography, and math, homework assignments, pop quizzes, and workbooks. Every activity was judged and criticized, graded and reviewed. The only subject I liked was music because you could look at the book, though sometimes, of course, you were compelled to stand up and sing all by yourself, which was death. The other kids were even worse than the work itself. I was small for my age, always vulnerable to attack. My classmates were sly and treacherous, given to all sorts of wicked plots they learned from TV. And who would protect me from their villainy? Teachers were no help. If I got upset, they would stoop down to my level and their faces would fill my field of vision like rogue planets about to crash into earth. Looking back on it, I can see how I must have worried them. I was the kind of kid who, for no apparent reason, wept piteously or threw up on myself. On an especially scary day, I sometimes did both. By fifth grade, I was in trouble almost constantly. I wasn't rebellious—I was too timid for that—but I did disobey the rules. After lunch, for instance, I would hide in the girls' rest room instead of going back to class. I longed to be expelled, imagining somehow that I could be free of school forever if they'd just kick me out. All my behavior netted me were trips to the office, or endless hours in a little chair placed in the hall. A public scourging, in effect. My aunt would swoop down on the principal, an avenging angel, raising six kinds of hell that I should be subjected to such abuse. Actually, the first time I got the hall penalty, I was mortified, but after that, I liked it pretty well. It was quiet. I got to be alone. Nobody asked me questions or made me write on the board. Between classes, the other kids hardly looked at me, embarrassed on my behalf.

"Miss?"

I glanced up. A woman in a nurse's uniform was staring at me. I focused on my surroundings. I could see now that the corridor was populated with wheelchairs. Everyone was old and broken and bent. Some stared dully at the floor and some made mewing sounds. One woman repeated endlessly the same quarrelsome request: "Someone let me out of here. Someone let me up. Someone let me out of here . . ."

"I'm looking for Agnes Grey."

"Patient or employee?"

"A patient. At least she was a couple of months back."

"Try administration." She indicated the offices to my right. I collected myself, blanking out the sight of the feeble and infirm. Maybe life is just a straight shot from the horrors of grade school to the horrors of the nursing home.

The administration offices were housed in makeshift quarters where the principal's office had probably been once upon a time. A portion of the large central hallway had been annexed and was now enclosed in glass, providing a small reception area, which was furnished with a wooden bench. I waited at the counter until a woman emerged from the inner office with an armload of files. She caught sight of me and veered in my direction with a public-relations smile. "May I help you?"

"I hope so," I said. "I'm looking for a woman named Agnes Grey. I understand she was a patient here a few months ago."

The woman hesitated briefly and then said, "May I ask what this is in connection with?"

I took a chance on the truth, never guessing how popular I was going to be as a consequence. I gave her my card and then recited my tale of Irene Gersh and how she'd asked me to determine her mother's whereabouts, ending with the oft-repeated query: "Do you happen to know where she is at this point?"

She blinked at me for a moment. Some interior process caused a transformation in her face, but I hadn't the faintest idea how it related to my request. "Would you excuse me, please?"

"Sure."

She moved into the inner office and emerged a moment later with a second woman, who introduced herself as Mrs. Elsie Haynes, administrator of the facility. She was probably in her sixties, rotund, with a hairstyle that was whisker-short along the neck and topped by a toupee of ginger-colored curls. This made her face appear too large for her head. She was, however, smiling at me most pleasantly. "Miss Millhone, how very nice," she said, holding out her hands. The handshake consisted of her making a hand sandwich with my right hand as the lunch meat. "I'm Mrs. Haynes, but you must call me Elsie. Now how can we be of help?"

This was worrisome. I usually don't get such receptions in my line of work. "Nice to meet you," I said. "I'm trying to locate a woman named Agnes Grey. I understand she was transferred here from Pioneers."

"That's correct. Mrs. Grey has been with us since early March. I'm sure you'll want to see her, so I've asked the floor supervisor to join us. She'll take you up to Mrs. Grey's room."

"Great. I'd appreciate that. Frankly, I didn't expect to find her here. I guess I thought she'd be out by now. Is she doing okay?"

"Oh my, yes. She's considerably better . . . quite well . . . but we *have* been concerned about continued care. We can't release a patient who has noplace to go. As nearly as we can tell, Mrs. Grey doesn't have a permanent address and she's never admitted to having any next of kin. We're delighted to

44

hear that she has relatives living in the state. I'm sure you'll want to notify Mrs. Gersh and make arrangements to have her transferred to a comparable facility in Santa Teresa."

Ahh. I felt myself nodding. Her Medi-Cal benefits were running out. I tried a public-relations smile of my own, unwilling to commit Irene Gersh to anything. "I'm not sure what Mrs. Gersh will want to do. I told her I'd call as soon as I found out what was going on. She'll probably need to talk to you before she makes any decisions, but I'm assuming she'll ask me to drive Agnes back to Santa Teresa with me."

She and her assistant exchanged a quick look.

"Is there a problem with that?"

"Well, no," she said. Her gaze shifted to the doorway. "Here's Mrs. Renquist, the ward supervisor. I think she's the person you should properly discuss this with."

We went through another round of introductions and explanations. Mrs. Renquist was perhaps forty-five, thin and tanned, with a wide, good-natured mouth and the dusky, lined complexion of a smoker. Her dark auburn hair was pulled back in a knot shaped like a doughnut, probably supported by one of those squishy nylon devices they sell at Woolworth's. The three women seemed to hover about me like secular nuns, full of murmurs and reassurances. Within minutes, Mrs. Renquist and I were out in the corridor, heading toward the ward.

5

I heard Agnes Grey before I ever laid eyes on her. Mrs. Renquist and I had climbed the wide curving stairs to the second floor. We proceeded down the upper hallway without saying much. The character of the grade school was still oddly evident, in spite of the fact that extensive remodeling had been done to accommodate current use. The former classrooms had been quite large, with wide, multipaned windows stretching almost ceiling to floor. Light streamed in through glass embedded with chicken wire. The woodwork had been left in its original state, varnished oak aged to a glossy russet shade. Up here, the worn wood floors had been covered with mottled white vinyl tiles and the once spacious rooms had been partitioned into cubicles, containing two beds each. The walls were painted in shades of pale green and blue. The place was clean, if impersonal, the air perfumed with intimate body functions gone sour. Old people were visible everywhere, in beds, in wheelchairs, on gurneys, huddled on hard wooden benches in the wide corridor; idle, insulated from their surroundings by senses that had shut down over the years. They seemed as motionless as plants, resigned to infrequent watering. Anyone would wither under such a regimen: no exercise, no air, no sunlight. They had outlived not only friends and family, but most illnesses, so that at eighty and ninety, they seemed untouchable, singled out to endure, without relief, a life that stretched into yawning eternity.

We passed a crafts room where six women sat around a table, making potholders out of nylon loops woven on red metal frames. Their efforts were as misshapen as mine had been when I was five. I never liked doing that shit the first time around and I didn't look forward to having to do it again at the end of my days. Maybe I'd get lucky and be struck down by a beer truck before I was forced into such ignominy.

The recreation room was evidently just ahead, as I'd picked up the blast of a television set turned up loud enough for failing ears, a PBS documentary by the sound of it. The banging and shrieking suggested tribal rites somewhere in a culture not given to quietude. We turned left into a six-bed ward where a series of curtains were all that separated one patient from the next. At the far end of the room, like the origins of the Nile, I could see the source of the uproar. It wasn't a television set at all. Without even asking, I knew this was Agnes. She was stark naked, dancing a dirty boogie on the bed while she accompanied herself by banging on a bedpan with a spoon. She was tall and thin, bald everyplace except her bony head, which was enveloped in an aureole of wispy white fuzz. Malnutrition had distended her belly, leaving her long limbs skeletal.

The lower portion of her face had collapsed on itself, jaw drawn up close to her nose in the absence of intervening teeth. She had no visible lips and the truncated shape of her skull gave her the look of some long-legged, gangly bird with a gaping beak. She was squawking like an ostrich, her bright, black eyes snapping from point to point. The minute she caught sight of us, she fired the bedpan in our direction like a heat-seeking missile. She seemed to be having the time of her life. A nurse's aide, maybe twenty years old, stood by helplessly. Clearly, her training had never prepared her for the likes of this one.

Mrs. Renquist approached Agnes matter-of-factly, pausing only once to pat the hand of the woman in the next bed who seemed to be praying feverishly for Jesus to take her very soon. Meanwhile, Agnes, having asserted herself, was content to march around on the bedcovers saluting the other patients. To me, it looked like a wonderful form of indoor exercise. Her behavior seemed far healthier than the passivity of her wardmates, some of whom simply lay in moaning misery. Agnes had probably been a hell-raiser all her life, and her style, in old age, hadn't changed a whit.

"You have a visitor, Mrs. Grey."

"What?"

"You have a visitor."

Agnes paused, peering at me. Her tongue crept into view and then disappeared again. "Who's this?" Her voice was hoarse from screeching. Mrs. Renquist held out a hand to her, helping Agnes down off the bed. The nurse's aide took a clean gown from the nightstand. Mrs. Renquist shook it out and draped it around Agnes's scrawny shoulders, pushing her arms into the sleeves. Agnes submitted with the complaisance of a baby, her rheumy-eyed attention still focused on me. Her skin was speckled with color: pale brown maculae, patches of rose and white, knotty blue veins, crusty places where healing cuts formed fiery lines of red. The epidermal tissue was so thin I half-expected to see the pale gray shapes of internal organs, like those visible on a newly hatched bird. What is it about aging that takes us right back to birth? She smelled sooty and dense, a combination of dried urine and old gym socks. Right away, I started revising the notion of driving back to Santa Teresa in the same tiny car with her. The aide excused herself with a murmur and made a hasty getaway.

I held out a hand politely. "Hello, Agnes. I'm Kinsey Millhone."

"Hah?"

Mrs. Renquist leaned close to Agnes and hollered my name so loud that two other old ladies on the ward woke up and began to make quacking sounds. *"Kinsey Millhone. She's a friend of your daughter's."*

Agnes drew back, giving me a suspicious look. "Who?"

"Irene," I yelled.

"Who asked you?" Agnes shot back, peevishly. She began to work her lips mechanically, as if tasting something she'd eaten fifty years before.

Mrs. Renquist repeated the information, enunciating with care. I could see Agnes withdraw. A veil of simplicity seemed to cover her bright gaze and she launched abruptly into a dialogue with herself that made no sense whatever. "Keep hush. Do not say a word. Well, I can if I want. No, you can't. Danger, danger, ooo hush, plenty, plenty. Don't even give a *hint* . . ." She began a warbling rendition of "Good Night, Irene."

Mrs. Renquist rolled her eyes and a short, impatient sigh escaped. "She pulls this when she doesn't feel like doing what you want," she said. "She'll snap out of it."

We waited for a moment. Agnes had added gestures and her tone was argumentative. She'd adopted the quarrelsome air of someone in a supermarket express line when the customer at the register tries to cash a paycheck. Whatever universe she'd been transported to, it did not include us.

I drew Mrs. Renquist aside and lowered my voice. "Why don't we leave her alone for the time being," I said. "I'm going to have to put a call through to Mrs. Gersh anyway and ask her what she wants done. There's no point in upsetting her mother any more than we have to."

"Well, it's whatever you want," Mrs. Renquist said. "She's just being ornery. Do you want to use the office phone?"

"I'll call from the motel."

"Be sure we know how to get in touch with you," she said, with a faint note of uneasiness. I could see a hint of panic in her eyes at the notion that I might leave town without making arrangements for Agnes's removal.

"I'll leave the motel number with Mrs. Haynes."

I drove back to the Vagabond, where I put in a call first to Sergeant Pokrass at the sheriff's department, advising her that Agnes Grey had indeed turned up.

Then I placed the call to Irene Gersh and filled her in on her mother's circumstances. My report was greeted with dead silence. I waited, listening to her breathe in my ear.

"I suppose I better talk to Clyde," she said finally. She did not sound happy at having to do this and I could only imagine what Clyde's reaction would be.

"What do you want me to do in the meantime?" I asked.

"Just stay there, if you would. I'll give Clyde a call at the office and get back to you as soon as possible, but it probably won't be till around suppertime. I'd appreciate it if you'd drive back out to the Slabs and put a padlock on Mother's door."

"What good is that going to do?" I said. "The minute I'm gone, the little turds will break in. The louvres in one window are already gone. Frustrate these kids and they'll tear the place apart."

"It sounds like they've already done *that*."

"Well, true, but there's no point making life any more difficult."

"I don't care. I hate the idea of trespassers and I won't abandon the place. She may still have personal belongings on the premises. Besides, she might want to go back when she's feeling like herself again. Did you talk to the sheriff? Surely there's some way to patrol the area."

"I don't see how. You know the situation better than I do. You'd have to have an armed guard to keep squatters out and what's the point? That trailer's already been trashed."

"I want it locked," she said with an unmistakable edge.

"I'll do what I can," I said, making no attempt to disguise my skepticism.

"Thank you."

I gave her the telephone number at the Vagabond and she said she'd get in touch with me later on. I changed back into jeans and tennis shoes, hopped in the car, and headed over to a hardware store where I bought an oversize padlock of cartoon proportions that weighed about three pounds. The clerk assured me it would take a blasting cap to pop it off the hasp. What hasp, I thought? While I was at it, I bought the whole mechanism—hinged metal fastening and the corresponding staple—along with the tools to install the damn thing. Nothing was going to keep those kids out. I'd seen at least two holes punched into the trailer shell. All they'd have to do was enlarge one and they could crawl in and out like rats. On the other hand, I was getting paid to do this, so what did I care? I picked up some nails and a couple of pieces of scrap lumber and returned to my car.

I drove north on 111, doing the eighteen-mile return trip to the Slabs. Offhand, I couldn't recall the name of the road I was looking for so I kept my speed down and spent a lot of time peering off to my right. I passed a grove of date palms on my left. Beyond, in the far distance, I could see the vivid green of fields under cultivation. Somehow the countryside looked different, but it wasn't until I spotted the sign reading SALTON SEA RECREATION AREA that I realized how far I'd overshot the mark. The road to the Slabs had to be ten miles back. I spotted a gravel side road ahead on the left and I figured it was as good a place as any to make the turnaround. An old high-sided truck was approaching, kicking up a trail of dust in spite of the fact it was only moving ten miles an hour.

I slowed for the turn, checking my rearview mirror. A red pickup truck was barreling down on me, but the driver must have noted my change in speed. He veered right, cutting around me as I gunned the engine, scooting out of his path. I heard the faint pop of a rock being crushed under my wheel, but it wasn't until I'd done the U-turn and was back on 111, that I felt the sudden roughness in the ride. The flap-flap-flapping sound warned me that one of my back tires was flat.

"Oh great," I said. Clearly, I'd run over something more treacherous than a rock. I pulled over to the side of the road and got out. I circled my car. The rim of my right rear wheel was resting on the pavement, the tire forming a flabby rubber puddle underneath. It must have been five or six years since I'd changed a tire, but the principles probably hadn't changed. Take the jack out of the trunk, crank the sucker till the weight is lifted off the wheel, remove the hubcap, struggle with the lug nuts, pull the bad wheel off and set it aside while you heft the good one into place. Then replace all the lug nuts and tighten them before you jack the car down again.

I opened my trunk and checked my spare, which was looking a bit soggy in itself. I wrestled it out and bounced it on the pavement. Not wonderful, but I decided it would get me as far as the nearest service station, which I remembered seeing a few miles down the road. This is why I jog and bust my hump lifting weights, so I can cope with life's little inconveniences. At least I wasn't wearing heels and panty hose and I didn't have glossy fingernails to wreck in the process.

Meanwhile, the flatbed had turned out onto the highway and had come to a stop a hundred yards behind me. A dozen male farmworkers hopped off the back of the truck and rearranged themselves. They seemed amused at my predicament and called out suggestions in an alien tongue. I couldn't really translate, but I got the gist. I didn't think they were giving any actual pointers on how to change a flat. They seemed like a good-natured bunch, too weary from the short hoe to do me any harm. I rolled my eyes and waved at them dismissively. This netted me a wolf whistle from a guy grabbing his crotch.

I tuned them out and set to work, cussing like a stevedore as the flatbed pulled away. At times like this, I tend to talk to myself, coaching myself through. It was midafternoon and the sun was beating down on me. The air was dry, the quiet unbroken. I don't know the desert well. To my untutored eye, the landscape seemed unpopulated. At ground level, where I sat wielding my crescent wrench, all I could see was a dead mesquite tree a few feet away. I've been told that if you listen closely, you can hear the clicks of the wood-boring beetles that tunnel through the dead wood to lay their eggs.

I settled down to work, letting the isolation envelop me. Little by little, I became accustomed to the stillness in the same manner that eyes become accustomed to the dark. I picked up the drone of an occasional insect and noticed then the foraging warblers catching bugs on the fly. The true citizens of the Mojave emerge from their lairs by night: rattlesnakes and lizards, jackrabbits, quail, the owl and the Harris hawk, the desert fox and the ground squirrel, all searching for prey, angling to eat each other in a relentless predatory sequence that begins with the termites and ends with the coyote. This is not a place I'd want to unroll my sleeping bag and lay my little head down. The sun spiders alone will scare you out of ten years' growth.

By 3:20, I'd successfully completed the task. I rolled the flat tire around to the front of the car so I could hoist it into my trunk. I could hear a foreign body rattle around inside, a rock or a nail by the sound of it. I checked for the puncture, running my fingers around the circumference of the tire. The hole was in the sidewall—a ragged perforation not quite the size of my little fingertip. I blinked at it, feeling chilled, not wanting to believe my eyes. It looked like a bullet hole. An involuntary sound escaped as I was overtaken by one of those rolling shudders you experienced as a kid on leaving a dark room. I lifted my head. I surveyed the countryside. No one. Nothing. Not another car in sight. I wanted out of there.

I hoisted the tire and shoved it into my trunk. Swiftly, I gathered the jack and my crescent wrench, moved around to the driver's side and got in. I started the engine and rammed into gear, pulling back onto the highway. I drove faster than I should have, given the condition of my spare, but I didn't like the idea of being out there by myself. It had to have been the guy in the pickup truck. He'd passed me just as the blowout occurred. Of course, a rock might have caused the damage, but I couldn't think how it could have penetrated the sidewall, leaving such a nice neat hole in its wake.

The first service station I passed was out of business. The gas pumps were still standing, but the windows were broken and graffiti, in a garland, had been sprayed along the foundation. Local advertisers were using the supporting columns for their poster art and a real estate company announced in bold print that the property could be leased. Fat chance.

On the outskirts of Niland, at the intersection of Main Street and the Salton Highway, I found a small station selling one of those peculiar brands of gasoline that make your car engine burp. I put some air in the spare tire and dropped off the flat.

"I've got some business to take care of at the Slabs," I said. "Any way you can do this in the next hour and a half?"

He studied the tire. The look he gave me suggested that he'd come to the same conclusion I had, but he made no comment. He said he'd pull the tire off the rim and have it patched by the time I returned. I was guessing I'd be back by five o'clock. I didn't want to imagine myself out in the desert once the sun went down. I gave him a ten for his trouble and told him I'd pay for the repair when I got back. I hopped in my car and then leaned my head out in his direction. "Where's the road to the Slabs?"

"You're on it," he said.

I took Main to the point where it becomes Beal Road, approaching Slab City this time with a sense of familiarity. I felt safer out here. There seemed to be more people about at this hour: an RV pulling into a site, kids being dropped off in a snub-nosed yellow school bus. Now the dogs were out, leaping joyously at the sight of all the children home from school. When I reached Rusted-Out Chevy Road, I turned right and soon Agnes Grey's blue trailer appeared just ahead. I parked short of the place and pulled my tools out of the backseat. Thoroughly paranoid by now, I took out my little Davis semi-automatic and tucked it into the waistband of my blue jeans at the small of my back. I grabbed an old cotton shirt and pulled it on over my T-shirt, gathered up the lumber, the padlock, and the latch, and approached the trailer on foot.

The gremlins were in residence. I could hear the murmur of their voices. I reached the front door, unable to avoid the gravel crunching underfoot. The voices were silenced instantly. I leaned against the frame, peering in at an angle. For all I knew, I'd get whacked with a two-by-four. Instead, I found myself face-to-face with the dreadlocked creature I'd spied earlier that day. A second scummy face appeared beside the first. I'd been informed by the neighbors that one was the boychick and one was the girl. I was guessing this one to be male, but I truly couldn't discern any sex-based differences. Neither had facial hair. Both were young, with the unformed features of cherubs, tatty mops on top, ragged clothes below. Neither smelled any better than Agnes had.

The boy and I eyed each other and swelled up in the manner of apes. So ludicrous. We were both the same size— five six, neither one of us over a hundred and twenty pounds. Little banty-weight toughs. One possible difference was that I was willing to kick the shit out of him and I didn't think he was prepared to do likewise. With a glance at his companion, he rocked back on his heels, hands in his pockets as if he had all day. He said, "Hey, Poopsie. What the fuck are you doin' here?"

I felt my temper flash. My nerves were already on edge and I didn't need any aggravation from a little punk like him. "I own this place, ass eyes," I said snappishly.

"Oh really? Let's see you prove it."

"No problem, *Poopsie.* I've got the deed of trust." I pulled the gun out of my waistband and held it with the barrel up. It wasn't loaded, but it looked good. If I'd had my old Colt, I could have cocked it for effect. I freely confess—while I can intimidate little boys, I'm not that good with the grown ones. "Get lost," I said.

The two of them fell all over each other trying to scramble out the back. The trailer shook with their trampling feet and then they were gone. I ambled down the passageway and peered into the bathroom. As I suspected, they were using a hole in the wall as an emergency exit.

The first thing I did was board up their escape route, pounding nail after nail into the flimsy bathroom wall. Then I used a handheld drill to set the screw holes for the hasp I was mounting. I can't say I worked with any astonishing skill, but I got the job done and the physical labor improved my mood. It felt good to smash things. It felt good to sweat. It felt good to be in control of one small corner of the universe. As long as I was here, I did a quick search, looking to see if there was anything of Old Mama's left. I couldn't find a thing. The cupboards were bare, closets stripped, the various nooks and crannies emptied of her possessions. Most of them had probably been sold at the flea market on the road coming in.

I went out to the VW and snagged the 35-millimeter camera I keep in the rear well. I had part of a roll of film left and I snapped off as many photos of the place as I could. I didn't think Irene Gersh was going to "get it" otherwise. She had talked as if her mother might retire here in her golden years.

Before I popped the padlock into place, I bundled up the gremlins' sleeping bags and miscellaneous belongings and left them by the front step. Then I went across the road and told Marcus what I'd done. As I returned to the trailer, I spotted a slice of crawl space underneath, makeshift storage, where a few items had been crammed. I got down on my hands and knees, reaching back among the bugs and spiders, and pulled out a couple of dilapidated cardboard boxes. One was open and contained a motley collection of rusted garden tools: trowels, a spade, a short hoe. The second box had the top flaps closed, sections interlocked to secure the contents without anything actually being sealed shut. I pulled the flaps back and checked inside. The box contained numerous pieces of china wrapped in newspaper, a child's tea set. It didn't even look like a full set to me, but I thought Irene or her mother might like to take a look. Certainly, I wasn't eager to leave the dishes for the gremlins to raid. I closed the box up again. I snapped the padlock shut on the trailer door. I had no hope whatever of keeping the little buggers at bay, but I'd tagged the necessary bases. I toted the box to my car and shoved it in the backseat. It was still light when I left the Slabs, but by the time I picked up my tire and headed back into Brawley, it was fully dark.

·In my pocket was the .38 slug the mechanic had removed from the tire. I really wasn't sure what it signified, but as I'm keenly aware of the obvious, I had a fair idea.

6

◖▬◗ ◖▬◗ ◖▬◗ I went back to the Vagabond and got cleaned up. I made a wad of my overshirt and tucked it in the duffel, pulled on a fresh T-shirt and buckled on my shoulder rig. I put my briefcase on the bed beside me while I took out a box of PMC cartridges and loaded my .32, which I tucked snugly under my left arm. A threat on your life is a curious thing. It seems, at the same time, both abstract and absurd. I didn't have any reason to disbelieve the facts. I was on Tyrone Patty's hit list. Some guy in a pickup had shot out my tire on an isolated stretch of road. Now, it could have been a wholly unrelated prank, but I suspect if the flatbed full of farm-workers hadn't pulled up behind me, the guy in the pickup might have circled back and plugged me. God. Saved by a truckload of Mexicans making obscene digital remarks. I might have been abducted or killed outright. Instead, prov-identially, I was still in one piece. What I was having trouble with was figuring out what to do next. I knew better than to go to the local cops. I couldn't tell them the make, the model, or the license number of the truck itself and I hadn't gotten a good look at the driver's face. Under the circumstances, the cops might sympathize, but I didn't see what they could offer in the way of help. Like the Santa Teresa police, they'd be long on concern and short on solutions.

What then? One alternative was to pack my car and head back to Santa Teresa "toot sweet." On the other hand, it didn't seem smart to be out on the road at night, especially in territory like this, where it was possible to drive for ten miles without seeing a light. My friend in the pickup had already tried for me once. Better not offer him a second opportunity. Another possibility was to put a call through to the Nevada private eye and ask for some help. The community of private investigators is actually a small one and we're protective of one another. If anyone could offer me assistance, it would be someone who played the same game I did with the same kind of stakes. While I pride myself on my independence, I'm not a fool and I'm not afraid to ask for backup when the situation calls for it. That's one of the first things you learn as a cop.

In a curious way, this still didn't feel like an emergency. The jeopardy was real, but I couldn't seem to make it connect to my personal safety. I knew in my head the danger was out there, but it didn't feel dangerous—a distinction that might prove deadly if I didn't watch my step. I knew I'd be wise to take the situation seriously, but I couldn't for the life of me work up a sweat. People in the early stages of a terminal illness must react the same way. "You're kidding . . . who, me?"

After the phone call from Irene Gersh, I'd have to come up with a game plan. In the meantime, as I was starving, I decided I might as well grab a bite of supper. I zipped on a windbreaker, effectively concealing the shoulder holster and the gun.

On the far side of the road was a café with a blinking neon sign that said EAT AND GET GAS. Just what I needed. I crossed the highway carefully, looking to both sides like a kid. Every vehicle I saw seemed to be a red pickup truck.

The café was small. The lighting was harsh, but it had a comforting quality. After years of horror movies, I'm inclined to believe bad things only happen in the dark. Silly me. I elected to sit against the rear wall, as far from the plate-glass window as I could get. There were only six other patrons and they all seemed to know one another. Not one of them seemed sinister. I studied a clear plastic menu with a slip-in mimeographed sheet reproduced in a blur of purple ink. The items seemed equally divided between cholesterol and fat. This was my kind of place. I ordered a Deluxe Cheeseburger Platter, which included french fries and a lily pad of lettuce with a slice of gas-ripened tomato laid over it. I had a large Coke and topped it all off with a piece of cherry pie that made me moan aloud. This was the cherry pie of my childhood, tart and gluey with a lattice top crust welded in place with blackened sugar. It looked like it had been baked with an acetylene torch. The meal left me in a chemical stupor. I figured I'd just consumed enough additives and preservatives to extend my life by a couple of years . . . if I didn't get killed first.

On the way back to my room, I stopped by the motel office to see if there were any messages. There were two from the convalescent home and a third from Irene, who had called about ten minutes before. All three were marked URGENT. Oh, boy. I tucked the slips into my pocket and headed out the door. Once out on the walkway, I stopped dead in my tracks, struck by the eerie sensation that I was being watched. A silvery feeling traveled my body from head to toe, as chilling as a trickle of melting snow down the back of my neck. I was acutely aware of the glowing windows behind me. I eased out of range of the exterior lights and paused in the shadows. The parking lot was poorly illuminated and my motel room was at the far end. I listened, but all I could hear were the noises from the highway—the whine of trucks, the sonorous blast from a speeding semi warning vehicles in its path. I wasn't sure what had alerted me, if anything. I peered into the dark, turning my head from side to side, eyes averted as I tried to pinpoint discreet sounds against the obliterating fog of background noise. I waited, heart thumping in my ears. I didn't like what this business was doing to my head. Faintly, I picked up the musical tinkling of a little kid giggling somewhere. The tone was impish, high-pitched, the helpless snuffling of someone being tickled unmercifully. I sank down on my heels beside a wall of thick shrubbery.

A man appeared from the far end of the parking lot, walking toward me through the shadows with a kid perched on his shoulders. He had his arms raised, in part to secure the child, in part to torment him, digging the fingers of one hand into his ribs. The kid clung to the man, laughing, fingers buried in his hair, his body swaying in a tempo with his father's walking pace, like a rider mounted on a camel. The man ducked as the two of them turned into a lighted passageway, an alcove where I'd seen the soft drink and ice machines. A moment later, I heard the familiar clunking sound of a can of soda plummeting down the slot. The two emerged, this time hand in hand, chatting companionably. I let my breath out, watching them round the corner to the exterior stairs. They appeared again on the second floor where they entered the third room from the end. End of episode. I wasn't even aware that I'd taken my gun out, but my jacket was unzipped and it was in my hand. I stood upright, tucking my gun away. My heartbeat slowed and I shook some of the tension out of my arms and legs, like a runner at the end of an arduous race.

I returned to my room along the narrow drive that ran behind the motel. It was very dark, but it felt safer than traversing the open parking lot. I cut around the end of the building and unlocked my door, reaching around to flip the light on before I slipped inside. The room was untouched, everything exactly as I'd left it. I locked the door behind me and closed the drapes. When I sat down beside the bedtable and picked up the telephone, I realized my underarms were damp with sweat, the fear like the aftershock of an earthquake. It took a moment for my hands to quit shaking.

I called Irene first. She picked up instantly, as if she'd been hovering by the telephone. "Oh, Kinsey. Thank God," she said when I identified myself.

"You sound upset. What's going on?"

"I got a call from the convalescent home about an hour ago. I had a long chat with Mrs. Haynes earlier this afternoon and we've made arrangements to have Mother flown up by air ambulance. Clyde has gone to a great deal of trouble to get her into a nursing home up here. Really, it's a lovely place and quite close to us. I thought she'd be thrilled, but when Mrs. Haynes told her about it, she went berserk . . . absolutely out of control. She had to be sedated and even so, she's raising hell. Somebody's got to go over there and get her calmed down. I hope you don't mind."

Hell, I thought. "Well, I don't want to argue, Irene, but I can't believe I'd be of any help. Your mother hasn't the faintest idea who I am and, furthermore, she doesn't care. When she saw me this afternoon, she threw a bedpan across the room."

"I'm sorry. I know it's a nuisance, but I'm at my wit's end. I tried talking to her myself by phone, but she's incoherent. Mrs. Haynes says sometimes the medication has that effect; instead of calming these older patients down, it just seems to rev them up. They have a private-duty nurse driving up from El Centro for the eleven-o'clock shift, but meanwhile, the ward's in an uproar and they're begging for help."

"God. All right. I'll do what I can, but I don't have any training in this kind of thing."

"I understand," she said. "I just don't know who else to ask."

I told her I'd head on over to the hospital and then I hung up. I couldn't believe I'd been roped into this. My presence on a geriatric ward was going to prove about as effective as the padlock on the trailer door. All form, no content. What really bugged me was the suspicion that nobody would have even *suggested* that a boy detective do likewise. I didn't want to see that old lady again. While I admired her spunk, I didn't want to be in *charge* of her. I had my own ass to worry about. Why does everybody assume women are so nurturing? My maternal instincts were extinguished by my Betsy Wetsy doll. Every time she peed in her little flannel didies, I could feel my temper climb. I quit feeding her and that cured it, but it did make me wonder, even at the age of six, how suited I was for motherhood.

It was in this charitable frame of mind that I proceeded to the Rio Vista. I drove with an eye to my rearview mirror to see if anyone was following. I watched for pickup trucks of every color and size. I thought the one I'd seen was a Dodge, but I hadn't been paying close attention at the time and I couldn't have sworn to it.

Nothing untoward occurred. I reached the convalescent hospital, parked my car in a visitors' slot, walked back through the front entrance and headed for the stairs. It was ominously quiet. No telling what Agnes was up to. It was only 8:00 P.M. but the floor lights had already been dimmed and the facility was bathed in the muted rustle and hush of any hospital at night. The old sleep restlessly, pained limbs crying out. Nights must be long, filled with fretful dreams, the fear of death, or, worse perhaps, the certainty of waking to another interminable day. What did they have to hope for? What ambitions could they harbor in this limbo of artificial light? I could sense the hiss of oxygen in the walls, the pall of the pharmaceuticals with which their bodies were infused. Hearts would go on beating, lungs would pump, kidneys filtering all the poisons from the blood. But who would diagnose their feelings of dread, and how would anyone provide relief from the underlying malady, which was despair?

When I reached the ward, I could see that Agnes's bed was the only one with a light. A male aide, a young black, set his magazine aside and tiptoed in my direction with a finger to his lips. We spoke briefly in low tones. The medication had finally kicked in and she was dozing, he said. Now that I was here, he had his regular duties to attend to. If I needed anything, I could find him at the nurses' station down the hall. He moved out of the room.

62

I crossed quietly to the pool of bright light in which Agnes slept. The counterpane on her bed was a heavyweight cotton, harsh white, her thin frame scarcely swelling the flat coverlet. She snored softly. Her eyes seemed to be opened slightly, lids twitching as she tracked some interior event. Her right hand clutched at the sheet, her arthritic knuckles as protuberant as redwood burls. Her chest was flat. Coarse whiskers sprouted from her chin, as if old age were transforming her from one sex to the other. I found myself holding my breath as I watched her, willing her to breathe, wondering if she'd sail away right before my eyes. This afternoon, she'd seemed sassy and energetic. Now, she reminded me of certain old cats I've seen whose bones seem hollow and small, who seem capable of levitating, so close are they to fairylike.

I glanced at the clock. Twelve minutes had passed. When I looked back, her black eyes were pinned on my face with a surprising show of life. There was something startling about her sudden watchfulness, like a visitation from the spirit world.

"Don't make me go," she whispered.

"It won't be so bad. I hear the nursing home is lovely. Really. It'll be much better than this."

Her gaze became intense. "You don't understand. I want to stay here."

"I do understand, Agnes, but it's just not possible. You need help. Irene wants you close so she can take care of you."

She shook her head mournfully. "I'll die. I'll die. It's too dangerous. Help me get away."

I felt the hair stiffen along my scalp. "You'll be fine. Everything's fine," I said. My voice sounded too loud. I lowered my tone, leaning toward her. "You remember Irene?"

She blinked at me and I could have sworn she was debating whether to admit to it or not. She nodded, her voice tremulous. "My little girl," she said. She reached out and I took her shaking hand, which was bony and hot, surprisingly strong.

"I talked to Irene a little while ago," I said. "Clyde's found a place close by. She says it's very nice."

She shook her head. Tears had leaped into her eyes and they trickled down her cheeks, following deeply eroded lines in her face. Her mouth began to work, her face filled with a pleading she couldn't seem to articulate.

"Can you tell me what you're afraid of?"

I could see her struggle, and her voice, when it came, was so frail that I had to rise slightly from my chair to catch what she was saying. "Emily died. I tried to warn her. The chimney collapsed in the earthquake. The ground rolled. Oh, I could see . . . it was like waves in the earth. Her head was bashed in by a brick. She wouldn't listen when I told her it was dangerous. Let it be, I said, but she had to have her way. Sell the house, sell the house. She didn't want roots, but that's where she ended up . . . down in the ground."

"When was this?" I asked, trying to keep the conversation afloat.

Agnes shook her head mutely.

"Is that why you're worried? Because of Emily?"

"I heard the niece of the owner of that old house across the street died several years ago. She was a Harpster."

Oh, boy. We were really on a roll here. "She played the harp?" I asked.

She shook her head impatiently. Her voice gathered strength. "Harpster was her maiden name. She was big in the Citizens Bank and never married. Helen was an ex-girlfriend of his. She left because of his temper, but then Sheila came along. She was so young. She had no idea. The other Harpster girl was a dancer and married Arthur James, a professional accordion player who owned a music shop. I knew him because we girls at the Y used to go over to his place and he would play for us after he locked the door," she said. "It's a small world. The girls said their uncle's house was their second home. She might still be there if he left it to her. She'd help."

I watched her carefully, trying to understand what was going on. Was there really something she was too frightened to talk about? "Was Emily the one who married Arthur James?"

"There was always some story . . . always some explanation." She waved a hand vaguely, her tone resigned.

"Was this in Santa Teresa? Maybe I could help you if I understood."

"Santa came over special and gave us all a stockingful of goodies. I let her have mine."

"Who, Emily?"

"Don't talk about Emily. Don't tell. It was the earthquake. Everyone said so." She extracted her hand and a veil of cunning dropped over her eyes. "My arthritis is in my shoulder and knee. My shoulder has been broken two times. The doctor didn't even touch it, just X-rayed. I had two cataract operations at least, but I never had to have a tooth filled. You can see for yourself." She opened her mouth.

Sure enough, no fillings, which is not that big a deal when you have no teeth.

"You look like you're in pretty good shape for someone your age," I said gamely. The subject was careening around like conversational pinball.

"Lottie was the other one. She was a simpleton, but she always had a big smile on her face. She didn't have the brains God gave a billy goat. She'd go out the back door and then she'd forget how to get back in. She'd sit on the porch steps and howl like a pup until someone let her in. Then she'd howl to get back out again. She was the first. She died of influenza. I forget when Mother went. She had that stroke, you know, after Father died. He wanted to keep the house and Emily wouldn't hear of it. I was the last one and I didn't argue. I wasn't really sure until Sheila and then I knew. That's when I left."

I said, "Unh-hunh," and then tried another tack. "Is it the trip that worries you?"

She shook her head. "The smell when it's damp," she said. "Never seemed to bother anyone else."

"Would you prefer to have Irene fly down and travel back with you?"

"I worked cleaning houses. That's how I supported Irene

all those years. I watched Tilda and I knew how it was done. Of course, she was dismissed. He saw to that. No financial records. No banks. She was the only casualty. It was the only time her name was ever in the papers."

"Whose name?"

"You know," she said. Her look now was secretive.

"Emily?" I asked.

"Time wounds all heels, you know."

"Is this your father you're talking about?"

"Oh dear, no. He was long gone. It would be in the footing if you knew where to look."

"What footing?"

Her face went blank. "Are you talking to me?"

"Well, yes," I said. "We've been talking about Emily, the one who died when the chimney fell."

She made a motion as if to lock her lips and throw away the key. "I did it all to save her. My lips are sealed. For Irene's sake."

"Why is that, Agnes? What is it you're not supposed to tell?"

She focused a quizzical look on me. I was suddenly aware that the real Agnes Grey was in the room with me. She sounded perfectly rational. "Well, I'm sure you're very nice, dear, but I don't know who you are."

"I'm Kinsey," I said. "I'm a friend of your daughter's. She was worried when she didn't hear from you and she asked me to come down and find out what was going on."

I could see her expression shift and off she went again. "Well, no one knew that. No one even guessed."

"Uh, Agnes? Do you have any idea where you are?"

"No. Do you?"

I laughed. I couldn't help myself. After a moment, she began to laugh, too, the sound as delicate as a cat sneezing. Next thing I knew, she'd drifted off to sleep again.

7

I did not sleep well. I found myself thinking about Agnes, whose fears were contagious and seemed to set off worries of my own. The reality of the death threat had finally filtered down into my psyche, where it was beginning to accumulate an energy of its own. I was sensitive to every noise, to changes in room temperature as the night wore on, to shifting patterns of light on venetian blinds. At 1:00 A.M., a car pulled into a parking slot near my room and I found myself instantly on my feet, peering through the slats as a couple emerged from a late-model Cadillac. Even in heavy shadow, I could tell they were drunk, clinging to one another in a hip-grinding embrace. I moved away from the window, my senses heightened by anxiety as the two of them fumbled their way into the room next to mine. Surely, if they were killers they wouldn't postpone my demise for the noisy grappling that started up the minute the bolt shot home. The bedframe began to thump relentlessly against the adjoining wall like a kid drumming his heels. There were occasional lulls while the woman offered up suggestions to her hapless companion. "Hop on up here like a puppy dog," she would say. Or "Get that old bald-headed thing over here."

On my side of the wall, the picture of the moose would start to rattle out another little tap dance. I had to reach up and hold it, lest the frame jounce right off the hook and smack me in the face. She was a screamer, sounding more like a woman in labor than one in love. The tempo picked up. Finally, she uttered a little yelp of astonishment, but I couldn't tell if she came or fell off the bed. After a moment, the smell of cigarette smoke wafted through the walls and I could hear their murmured postmortem. Twelve minutes later, they were at it again. I got up and took the picture off the wall, stuffed a sock in each cup of my bra and tied it across my head like earmuffs, with the ends knotted under my chin. Didn't help much. I lay there, a cone over each ear like an alien, wondering at the peculiarities of human sex practices. I would have much to report when I returned to my planet.

At 4:45, I gave up any hope of getting back to sleep. I took a shower and washed my hair, returning to the room wrapped in a motel towel the size of a place mat. As I pulled on my clothes, she was beginning to yodel and he was yipping like a fox. I had never heard so many variations on the word *oh*. I locked the door behind me and headed out across the parking lot on foot.

The smell of desert air was intense: sweet and cold. The sky was still an inky black with strands of dark red cutting through the low clouds at the horizon. I was nearly giddy from lack of sleep, but I felt no sense of endangerment. If someone were waiting in the bushes with an Uzi, I would leave this world in a state of sublime innocence.

The lights in the café were just blinking on, vibrant green neon spelling out the word CAFE in one convoluted loop, like a squeeze of tooth gel. I could see a waitress in a pale pink uniform scratch at her backside at the height of a yawn. The highway was empty and I crossed at a casual pace. I needed coffee, bacon, pancakes, juice, and I wasn't sure what else, but something reminiscent of childhood. I sat at the far end of the counter, my back against the wall, still mindful of the plate-glass window and the gray wash of dawn light outside. The waitress, whose name turned out to be Frances, was probably my age, with a country accent and a long tale to tell about some guy named Arliss who was systematically unfaithful, most recently with her girlfriend, Charlene.

"He has really tore himself with me this time," she said, as she plunked down a bowl of steaming oatmeal in front of me.

By the time I finished eating, I knew everything there was to know about Arliss and she knew a lot about Jonah Robb.

"If it was me, I'd hang on to him," she said, "but now not at the expense of meeting this doctor fella your friend Vera wants to fix you up with. I'd jump right on that. He sounds just real cute to me, though personally I've made it a practice not to date a man knows more about my insides than I do. I went out with this doctor once? Actually he's a medical student, if the truth be known. First time we kissed, he told me the name of some condition arises when you get a pubic hair caught down in your throat. Tacky? Lord God. What kind of person did he think I was?" She leaned on the counter idly swiping it with a damp rag so she'd look like she was busy if the boss stopped in.

"I never heard of a doctor dating a private eye, have you?" I said.

"Honey, I don't even know any private eyes, except you. Maybe he's tired of nurses and lab technicians and lady lawyers and like that. He's been dating Vera, hasn't he? And what is she, some kind of *insurance* adjuster . . ."

"Claims manager," I said. "Her boss got fired."

"But that's my point. I bet they never sat around having long heart-to-heart chats about medical malpractice, for God's sake. He's bored with that. He's looking for someone new and fresh. And think of it this way, he probably doesn't have any communicable diseases."

"Well, now there's a recommendation," I said.

"You better believe it. In this day and age? I'd insist on a blood test before the first lip lock."

The front door opened and a couple of customers came in. "Take my word for it," she said, as she moved away. "This guy could be it. You could be Mrs. Doctor Somebody-or-other by the end of the year."

I paid my check, bought a newspaper from the vending machine out front, and went back to my room. All was quiet next door. I propped myself up in bed and read the *Brawley News*, including a long article about "palm gardens," which I learned was the proper term for the groves of date palms strung out on both sides of the Salton Sea. The trees, exotic transplants brought in from North Africa a century ago, transpire as much as five hundred quarts of water a day and have to be pollinated by hand. The varieties of dates—the Zahid, the Barhi, the Kasib, the Deglet Noor, and the Medjool—all sounded like parts of the brain most affected by stroke.

As soon as it seemed civilized, I called the convalescent hospital and talked to Mrs. Haynes about Agnes Grey. Apparently, she'd been as docile as a lamb for the remainder of the night. Arrangements for her transport to Santa Teresa by air ambulance had been finalized and she was taking it in stride. She claimed she couldn't even remember what had so upset her the day before.

After I hung up, I put a call through to Irene and passed the information on to her. Agnes's outburst still felt unsettling to me, but I didn't see what purpose my apprehension might serve.

"Oh, Mother's just like that," Irene said when I voiced my concern. "If she's not raising hell, she feels she's somehow remiss."

"Well, I thought you should know how fearful she was. She sure raised the hair on the back of my neck."

"She'll be fine now. Don't be concerned. You've done a wonderful job."

"Thanks," I said. As there didn't seem to be any reason to

remain in the area, I told her I'd be taking off shortly and would give her a call as soon as I got back to town.

I packed my duffel, gathered up my briefcase, the portable typewriter, and miscellaneous belongings, and locked everything in the car while I went up to the front office to settle my bill.

When I returned, the lovers were just emerging from the room next door. They were both in their fifties, a hundred pounds overweight, dressed in matching western-cut shirts and oversize blue jeans. They were discussing interest rates on short-term Treasury securities. The slogan painted on the Cadillac's rear window read: JUST MERGED. I watched them cross the parking lot, arms around each other's waists, or at least as far as they would go. While the car warmed up, I pulled my little .32 out of the briefcase where I'd tucked it the night before and transferred it to my handbag on the passenger seat.

I cut over to Westmorland, taking 86 north. I drove the first ten miles with a constant check on the rearview mirror. The day was sunny and the number of cars on the road was reassuring, though traffic began to thin some by the time I reached Salton City. I fiddled with the car radio, trying to find a station with more to offer than static or the price of soybeans, alfalfa, and sugar beets. I caught a flash of the Beatles and focused briefly on the radio while I did some fine-tuning.

It was when I glanced up again, with an automatic reference to the traffic behind me, that I spotted the red Dodge pickup bearing down on me. He couldn't have been more than fifty yards back, probably driving eighty miles an hour to my fifty-five. I uttered a bark of surprise, jamming my foot down on the accelerator in a futile attempt to get out of his path. The engine nearly stalled out with the unexpected surge, shuddering a hop, skip, and a jump before it leaped ahead. The front grill of the pickup appeared at my rear window, completely filling the glass. It was clear the guy meant to crawl right up my tailpipe, crushing me in the process. I jerked the steering wheel to the right, but not fast enough. The Dodge caught my rear fender with a smashing blow, spinning me in a half circle that left me facing south instead of north. I slammed on the brakes and the VW skittered along the shoulder, throwing up a spray of gravel. My handbag seemed to leap into my lap of its own accord. The engine died. I turned the key in the ignition and willed the car to start. Dimly, I registered the now empty highway. No help in sight. Where had everybody gone? Just up ahead on my left, a soft-packed dirt road followed the curve of an irrigation canal that bordered a fallow field, but there was no ranch house visible and no signs of life.

Behind me, the Dodge had made a U-turn and was now accelerating as it headed straight at me again. I ground at the starter, nearly singing with fear, a terrified eye glued to my rearview mirror where I could see the pickup accumulating speed. The Dodge plowed into me, this time with an impact that propelled the VW forward ten yards with an ear-splitting *BAM.* My forehead hit the windshield with a force that nearly knocked me out. The safety glass was splintered into a pattern of fine cracks like a coating of frost. The seat snapped in two and the sudden liberation from my seat belt slung me forward into the steering wheel. The only thing that saved me from a half-rack of cracked ribs was the purse in my lap, which acted like an air bag, cushioning the blow.

The other driver threw the pickup into reverse, then punched on the gas. The truck lurched back, then forward, ramming into me like a bumper car. I felt the VW leave the ground in a short flight that ended in the irrigation ditch, plumes of runoff water splatting out in all directions. I narrowly avoided biting my tongue in half as I bounced against the headliner and then off the dashboard. I put a hand on my mouth and checked my teeth automatically, making sure I hadn't lost any. The car seemed to float briefly before it settled against the muddy bottom. The runoff water in the ditch was only three feet deep, but both doors had popped open and silty water flooded in.

On the shoulder of the road, my assailant got out of the pickup and moved around to the rear, a tire iron in his right hand. Maybe he thought a death by bludgeoning was more consistent with a car wreck than a bullet in the brain. He was a big man, white, wearing sunglasses and a baseball cap. Mewing in panic, I fumbled in my handbag for my gun and rolled out of the VW. I crouched, shielded by the car as I jacked a shell into the chamber. I propped the barrel of the gun on the roof and steadied the sites with both hands.

Miraculously, I saw the guy toss the tire iron in the bed of the pickup as he slid back under the steering wheel and slammed the door. The window was rolled up on the passenger side, where a sheet of paper had been affixed. Like an eye test, I made out the top line of print which read AS IS, with several lines of print below; the temporary sticker from a used car lot. I thought I saw a face peering out at me briefly as the engine roared to life and the truck peeled out. I felt a jolt of recognition, which I didn't have time to process. The pain descended and I felt the blackness close in, narrowing my vision to a long, dark barrel with a glinting bull's-eye of daylight at the far end. I took a deep breath to clear my head and looked up in time to catch one last glimpse of the pickup as it headed north toward Mecca. The license plate had been caked with mud. No numbers were visible.

Two cars went by on the road, heading south. The driver in the second car, a vintage Ford sedan, seemed to do a double take, catching sight of the VW, which sat in the canal partially submerged. He braked to a stop and began to back up, transmission whining in reverse. The adrenaline surging through my system crested like a wave and I began to shake. It was over. I found myself weeping audibly, from pain, from fear, from relief.

"Need some help?" The old man had angled his car onto the shoulder of the road and rolled his window down. Dimly, I realized he was probably obscuring any tire tracks left by the Dodge, but the gravel shoulder seemed too hard-packed to take a print. To hell with it. I was safe and that's all I cared about. I shoved the gun in my bag and staggered to my feet, wading across the canal toward the road. I scrambled up the embankment, tennis shoes slipping in the mud. As I approached the sedan, the old man studied the knot on my forehead, my disheveled hair, my blood-streaked face, my blue jeans sopping wet. I wiped my nose on my sleeve, registering the streak of blood that I'd mistaken for tears. I swayed on my feet. I could feel the goose egg protruding from the middle of my forehead like I was suddenly sprouting a horn. Pain thundered in my head, and for the first time, nausea stirred. I crossed to his car, watching his concern mount when he saw how shaky I was. "Sister, you're a mess."

"Is there any way you can get the highway patrol out here? Somebody just ran me off the road."

"Well, sure. But don't you want a lift somewhere first? You look like you could use some medical attention. I just live up the road a piece."

"I'm fine. I just need a tow truck . . ."

"Young lady, you listen here. I'll give the sheriff a call and get a tow truck out, too, but I'm not going to leave you standin' here by the road."

"I don't want to leave my car."

"That car's not going to budge and I'm not either unless you do as I say."

I hesitated. The VW was totaled. The entire back end appeared foreshortened, the right rear fender crushed. The car had been suffering from countless dings and dents anyway, the beige paint oxidized to a chalky hue, highlighted with rust. I'd had the car nearly fifteen years. With a pang of regret, I turned back to the sedan, hobbling around to the passenger side. I felt like I was leaving a much-loved pet behind. I'd apparently banged my left leg from the knee right up my thigh and it was already stiffening up. When I finally dared to pull my jeans down, I was going to find a bruise the size and color of an eggplant. The old man leaned across and opened the door for me.

"I'm Carl LaRue," he said.

"Kinsey Millhone," I replied. I slid in, slouching down on the base of my spine so I could rest my head against the seat. Once I closed my eyes, the nausea subsided somewhat.

The sedan eased out into the highway again, heading south about a quarter of a mile before we made a left turn onto a secondary road. I sincerely hoped this was not part of some elaborate ruse, the old man in cahoots with the guy in the pickup truck. I flashed on the AS IS sticker in the window, the glimpse I'd had of someone peering out at me. Gingerly, I sat up, remembering where I'd seen the face. It was at the rest stop where I'd eaten lunch on the way down to the desert. There'd been a kid there, a boy maybe five, playing with a Matchbox toy. His father had been napping with a magazine laid across his face . . . a white guy, with big arms, in a T-shirt with the sleeves ripped out. Once I made the connection, I knew I'd actually seen them twice. The same man had crossed the darkened motel parking lot with the kid perched up on his shoulders as they headed for the Coke machine. I felt a chill ripple through me at the recollection of how he'd tickled the kid. What sang in my memory was the peal of impish laughter, which seemed now as dainty and evil as a demon's. What kind of hit man would bring his kid along?

8

While Mr. LaRue put a call through to the county sheriff's department, I found myself folding up like a jackknife on the lumpy couch in his living room, overwhelmed by sleepiness. My head was pounding. My neck was stiff from whiplash, my rib cage bruised. I felt cold and little, as I had just after the accident in which my parents were killed. In a singsong voice, inexplicably, my brain began feeding back to me the text I'd read in the morning paper. "Palms grow to 70 feet and can produce 300 pounds of dates. A mature palm will grow 15 to 18 bunches of dates. Each cluster, when the fruit has reached the size of a pea, must be protected with brown paper covers to ward off birds and rain. . . ." What I couldn't remember anymore was where I was or why I hurt so bad.

Carl was shaking me persistently. He'd apparently placed a call to the hospital emergency room and had been told to bring me in. His wife, whose name kept slipping away, had soaked a washcloth in ice water so she could dab the dirt and crusted blood off my face. My feet had been elevated and I'd been wrapped in a down comforter. At their urging, I roused myself and shuffled out to the car again, still wrapped in the puffy quilt like a bipedal worm.

By the time we reached the emergency room, I had come out of my stupor sufficiently to identify myself and make the correct answers to "How many fingers am I holding up?" and similar neurological pop quizzes I took while lying flat on my back. The ceiling was beige, the cabinets royal blue. Portable X-ray equipment was wheeled in. They X-rayed my neck first, two views, to make sure it wasn't broken, and then did a skull series, which apparently showed no fractures.

I was allowed to sit up then while a young doctor peered at me eye to eye, our breaths intermingling with a curious intimacy as he checked my corneal reflexes, pupil size, and reaction to light. He might have been thirty, brown curly hair receding from a forehead creased with fine horizontal lines. Under his white jacket, he wore a buff-colored dress shirt and a tie with brown dots. His aftershave lotion smelled of newly cut grass, though his electric mower had missed a couple of hairs just under his chin. I wondered if he realized I was noting his vital signs while he was noting mine. My blood pressure was 110 over 60, my temperature, pulse, and respirations normal. I know because I peeked every time he jotted anything down. In a box at the bottom of the page, he scrawled the words "postconcussional syndrome." I was happy to realize the accident hadn't impaired my ability to read upside down. Various forms of first aid were administered and most of them hurt, including a tetanus shot that nearly made me pass out.

"I think we should keep you overnight," he said. "It doesn't look like you sustained any major damage, but your head took quite a bump. I'd be happier if we could keep an eye on you for the next twelve hours, at any rate. Anybody you want notified?"

"Not really," I murmured. I was too battered to protest and too scared to face the outside world anyway. He moved out to the nurses' station, which I could see through an interior window shuttered for privacy by partially closed rust-red venetian blinds. In the corridor, a sheriff's deputy had appeared. I could see horizontal slats of him chatting with the young female clerk who pointed over her shoulder to the room where I sat. The other cubicles in the emergency room were empty, the area quiet. The deputy conferred with the doctor, who evidently decided I was fit enough to answer questions about how my car came to be sitting in an irrigation ditch.

The deputy's name was Richie Windsor, one of those baby-faced cops with an uptilted nose and plump cheeks reddened by sunburn. He had to be a rookie, barely twenty-one, the minimum age for a sheriff's deputy. His eyes were hazel, his hair light brown and cut in a flattop. He hadn't been at it long enough to adopt the noncommittal, paranoid expression that most cops assume. I described the incident methodically, sparing no details, while he took notes, interjecting occasional enthusiastic comments in a borrowed Mexican accent. "Whoa!" he would say, or "Get real, kemosabe!" He seemed nearly envious that someone had tried to kill me.

When I finished my recital, he said he'd have the dispatcher broadcast a "be on the lookout" in case the Dodge was still somewhere in the area. We both knew the chances of intercepting the man were slim. If the guy was smart, he'd abandon the vehicle at the first opportunity. As the deputy turned to leave, I found myself snagging impulsively at his uniform sleeve.

"One thing," I said. "The doctor wants me here overnight. Is there any way we can keep my admission under wraps? This is the only hospital in the area. All the guy has to do is call Patient Information and he'll know exactly where I am."

"Good point, *amigo*. Let me see what I can do," he said. He tucked his pen away.

Within minutes, the admissions office had sent a young female clerk over with a wheelchair, a clipboard full of forms to be completed, and a patient identification strip in a cloudy plastic band, which she affixed to my wrist with a device that looked like a hole punch.

Carl LaRue and his wife had been sitting patiently in the corridor all this time. They were finally ushered in to see me while last-minute arrangements were being made for a bed. The deputy had apparently cautioned the old couple about the situation.

"Your whereabouts is safe with us," Carl said. "We won't say a word."

His wife patted my hand. "We don't want you to worry now. You just get you some rest."

"I appreciate everything you've done," I said. "Really. I can't thank you enough. I'd probably be dead if you hadn't come along."

Carl shifted uncomfortably. "Well, now. I don't know about that. I'm happy to be of help. We got kids of our own and we'd want somebody helping them under similar circumstances."

His wife tucked her arm in his. "We best get a move on. They'll want to put you to bed."

As soon as they departed, I was whisked up to the second floor by freight elevator to a private room, probably on the contagious-disease ward where no visitors were allowed. It was only three in the afternoon and the day looked like it'd be a long one. I didn't get zip for painkillers because of the head injury, and I wasn't allowed to sleep lest I slip into some coma from which I might never wake. My vital signs were checked every hour. The meal carts were long gone, but a kindly nurse's aide found me a cup of muscular cherry Jell-O and a packet of saltines. I pictured the ward clerk filling out a charge slip for twenty-six dollars. I could probably hold my hospital bill down to seven or eight hundred bucks, but only if I didn't need a Band-Aid or a safety pin. I had insurance, of course, but it offended me to be charged the equivalent of the down payment on a car.

My eye lighted on the telephone. There was a telephone book in the bottom of the nightstand. I looked up the area code for Carson City, Nevada (702 all locations, in case you really want to know), dialed Information, and got the listing for Decker/Dietz Investigations, which I dialed in turn. The phone rang five times. I half-expected a service to pick up or a machine to kick in, but someone picked up abruptly on the sixth ring, sounding brusque and out of sorts. "Yes?"

"May I speak to Robert Dietz?"

"I'm Dietz. What can I do for you?"

"I'm not sure if you remember me," I said. "My name is Kinsey Millhone. I'm a friend of Lee Galishoff's and he suggested I get in touch. I called you about a year ago from Santa Teresa. You helped me locate a woman named Sharon Napier . . ."

"Right, right. I remember now. Lee said you might call."

"Yeah, well it looks like I'm going to need some help. I'm in Brawley, California, at the moment in a hospital bed. Some guy ran me off the road—"

He cut in. "How bad are you hurt?"

"I'm okay, I guess. Cuts and bruises, but no broken bones. They're just keeping me for observation. The car was totaled, but a passing motorist came along before the guy could finish me off—"

Dietz broke in again. "Where's Brawley? Refresh my memory."

"South of the Salton Sea, about ninety minutes east of San Diego."

"I'll come down."

I squinted, unable to repress a note of surprise. "You will?"

"Just tell me how to find you. I have a friend with a plane. He can fly me into San Diego. I'll rent a car at the airport and be there by midnight."

"Well, God, that's great. I mean, I appreciate your efficiency, but tomorrow morning's fine. They're probably not going to let me out before nine A.M."

"You haven't heard about the judge," he said flatly.

"The judge?"

"Jarvison. They got him. First name on the list. He was gunned down this morning in the driveway of his house."

"I thought he had police protection."

"He did. From what I understand, he was supposed to be sequestered with the other two but he wanted to be at home. His wife just had a baby and he didn't want her left alone."

"Where was this, in Carson City?"

"Tahoe, fourteen miles away."

Jesus, I thought, it must have happened just about the same time the guy here was after me. "How many people did Tyrone Patty hire?"

"More than one from the sound of it."

"How's Lee doing? Is he okay?"

"Don't know. I haven't talked to him. I'm sure security on him is tight."

"What about the killer? Did he get away?"

"She. Woman posing as a meter reader in a little truck across the street."

I could feel outrage flash through me like a fever. "Dietz, I hate this. What the hell is going on? The guy who tried to kill me brought his *kid* along." I took a few minutes then to fill in the details. He listened intently, asking questions now and then to clarify a point. When I finished, a short gap in the conversation suggested he had paused to light a cigarette. "You have a gun?" he asked. I could almost smell the smoke drifting through the line.

"In my handbag. A little thirty-two. It's not much of a weapon, but I can hit where I aim."

"They let you keep that?" he said with disbelief.

"Hey, sure. Why not? When you check into a hospital, you get quizzed about meds. Nobody thinks to ask about your personal firearms."

"Who knows you're there?"

"I'm not sure. It's a small town. I asked the deputy to keep it quiet, but word gets around. Actually, I was feeling secure until I talked to you."

"Good. Stay nervous. I'll get there when I can."

"How will you find me? They're not going to let you roam around up here in the dead of night."

"Don't worry about it. I got ways," he said.

"How will I know it's you and not another one of Tyrone Patty's little friends?"

"Pick a code word."

"Dill pickle."

He laughed. "What's that supposed to mean?"

"Nothing. That just popped into my head."

"Dill pickle. Around midnight. Be careful with yourself."

After I hung up, I eased out of bed and crept out to the nurses' station, clutching my hospital gown shut with one hand behind my back. Three nurses, a ward clerk, and an aide sat behind the counter. All five looked up at me, eyes straying then to a spot just behind me. I turned. The rookie deputy was sitting on a bench against the wall. Sheepishly, he lifted a hand, a blush creeping up his face.

"You caught me. I'm burnt," he said. "I thought maybe somebody oughta keep an eye on you in case this dude comes back. I hope you don't mind."

"Are you kidding? Not at all. I appreciate your concern."

"This's my girlfriend, Joy . . ."

The nurse's aide flashed a smile at me and I was introduced to the other four women in turn. "We've alerted security," one of the nurses said. "If you want, you can get some sleep now."

"Thanks. I could use some. There's a private eye named Robert Dietz, who said he'd be here later on. Let me know when he gets here and make sure he's alone." I told them the code word and his estimated time of arrival.

"What's he look like?"

"I don't know. I never met the man."

"Don't worry about it. We'll take care of it," Richie said.

I slept until dinnertime, sat up long enough to eat a plate of hospital food concealed under an aluminum hubcap. My vital signs were checked and I slept again until 11:15 that night. At intervals, I was aware of someone taking my pulse, fingers cool as an angel's pressed against my wrist. By the time I woke, someone had retrieved some of my belongings from the car. The portable typewriter and my duffel were tucked against the wall. I clenched my teeth and slid out of bed. When I bent over to unzip the duffel, my head pounded like a hangover. I pulled out fresh jeans and a turtleneck and laid them on the bed. The drawer in my bedtable held soap, toothbrush, toothpaste, and a small plastic bottle of Lubriderm. I went into the bathroom and brushed my teeth, grateful that all of them were present and accounted for. I took a long, hot bath in a tub with handholds affixed to the wall at every conceivable point. I needed them. Getting in and out of the bathtub only made me aware of multi-hurt places distributed randomly all up and down my bod.

While I dried myself off, I checked myself in the mirror, disheartened by the sight. In addition to the bruise on my forehead, my eyes were now dark along the orbital ridge and streaked with red underneath, perfect for Halloween only six months away. My left knee was purple, my torso sooty-looking with bruises. Combing my hair made me wince, sucking air through my teeth. I moved into the other room and took my time getting dressed, resting between articles of clothing. The process was exhausting, but I plugged on doggedly. Whatever damage I'd sustained in the accident was taking its toll.

I stretched out on the bed again with a glance at the clock. Midnight straight up. I figured Dietz would arrive any minute now. Somehow I assumed he'd want to hit the road right away, which suited me fine. If I'd suffered a concussion, it must have been mild. I wasn't even sure I'd lost consciousness and I wasn't aware of any post-trauma amnesia— though, of course, if I'd forgotten something that thoroughly, how would I really know? My head still hurt, but so what? That might go on for weeks and in the meantime, I wanted out. I wanted someone in charge—preferably someone with a big gun and no hesitation about using it. I noticed I was skipping right past the notion of Judge Jarvison.

The next thing I was aware of was the soft pinging of the hospital paging system and the rattle of the breakfast carts out in the corridor. It was morning and some female was addressing me. It took me a minute to remember where I was.

"Miss Millhone? Time to take your temperature . . ." I automatically opened my mouth and she slipped a cold, wet thermometer under my tongue. I could taste lab alcohol that hadn't been rinsed off properly. She took my blood pressure, holding my right arm against her body while she secured the Velcro cuff. She placed the silver dollar of the stethoscope against the crook of my arm and began to pump the cuff. I opened my eyes. She was not one I'd seen before: a slender Chicana with bright red lipstick on a plump mouth, her long brown hair pulled up in a ponytail. Her eyes were pinned to the gauge as the needle descended counterclockwise. I assumed my blood pressure was normal, as she didn't gasp aloud. It would help if they'd tell you things about yourself now and then.

I turned my head toward the window and saw a man leaning against the wall, arms folded across his chest. Dietz. Late forties. Five ten, maybe 170, in jeans, cowboy boots, and a tweed sport coat with a blue toothbrush protruding from the breast pocket like a ballpoint pen. He was clean-shaven, his hair medium length and showing gray around the ears. He was watching me with expressionless gray eyes. "I'm Dietz." Husky voice in the middle range.

With a ripping sound, the aide removed the blood-pressure cuff and made a note in my chart. With my free hand, I took the thermometer out of my mouth. "What time'd you get in?"

"One fifteen. You were out like a light so I let you sleep."

The aide took the thermometer and studied it with a frown. "You didn't keep this in long enough."

"I don't have a fever. I was in an accident," I said.

"The charge nurse is gonna fuss at me if I don't get a temp."

I tucked the thermometer in the corner of my mouth like a cigarette, talking to Dietz while it bobbled between my lips. "Did you get any sleep?"

"In this place?"

"As soon as the doctor comes, we can get the hell out of here," I said. "The guy with the kid was in the same motel. I think we ought to go back and see what we can find out from the desk clerk. Maybe we can pick up the license number of his truck."

"Sir, I'm gonna have to ask you to wait in the hall."

"They found the truck. I called the county sheriff from a pay phone when I got in. The vehicle was abandoned outside San Bernardino. They'll go over it for prints, but he's probably too smart for that."

"What about the local car lots?"

"We can try it, but I think you're going to find out the truck's a dead end."

The aide was getting restless. "Sir . . ."

He flicked a look at her. I started to object, but Dietz pushed away from the wall at that point. "I'll go down to the lounge and grab a cigarette," he said.

9

■▶ ■▶ ■▶ By 10:35, he was helping me ease my battered bones into the passenger seat of a bright red Porsche. I watched him move around the front of the car and slide in on the driver's side.

"You rented this?"

"It's mine. I drove down. I didn't want to wait for my buddy with the plane. He couldn't leave soon enough."

I snapped on the seat belt and settled into the low, black leather seat. He fired the engine up with a rumble and pulled out of the parking lot, adjusting the air conditioner. The compact interior of the car smelled of leather and cigarette smoke. With the tinted windows rolled up against the desert heat, I felt insulated from the harsh realities of the spare countryside.

"Where we headed?"

"The body shop where your car was towed."

"Will it be open on Sunday?"

"Now it is."

"How'd you manage that?"

"I called the emergency number. The guy's meeting us there."

We headed into Brawley to an auto body shop that was housed in a converted gas station just off the main street. My VW was parked in a side lot, surrounded by chain-link fence. As we pulled into the service area, the owner emerged from the office with a set of keys in hand. He unlocked the padlock on the chain-link fence and rolled the gate back. Dietz pulled into the lot and parked the car, placing a restraining hand on my arm as I moved to open the door.

"Wait till I come around," he said. From his tone, I didn't think good manners were at stake. I did as I was told, watching the way he positioned himself as he opened the car door for me, shielding my exit. The owner of the station didn't seem to notice anything unusual in the interaction between us. Dietz handed him a folded bill, but I couldn't see what denomination it was. Large enough, apparently, that the man had agreed to meet us here on a day when the place was ordinarily closed.

We circled my car, surveying the damage. There was scarcely a spot on it that wasn't affected in some way.

"Looks like she got banged up pretty good," the owner said to Dietz. I didn't know if he was referring to me or the vehicle. I wrenched open the buckled door on the passenger side and emptied the glove compartment, tucking the registration in my purse, tossing out the collection of ancient gasoline receipts. I still had some personal belongings in the backseat: law books, a few hand tools, my camera equipment, odds and ends of clothing, a pair of shoes. Many items had tumbled onto the floor in the course of the attack and were now sodden with the muddy water from the ditch. I checked the much-abused box of old china and was gratified to find that nothing had been broken. I loaded what I could into the trunk of Dietz's Porsche. What I didn't immediately toss, I packed in a large cardboard box that the shop owner obligingly rustled up out of the shop. I tucked the box of dishes into the larger box. I wrote a check for the towing, arranging at the same time to have everything shipped to me in Santa Teresa. I'd file a claim with my insurance company as soon as I got back, though I couldn't believe the car would net me much.

Ten minutes later, we were heading north on 86. As soon as we were under way, Dietz put a cigarette between his lips and flicked open a Zippo. He hesitated, glancing over at me. "My smoking going to bother you?"

I thought about being polite, but it didn't make much sense. What's communication for if it isn't to convey the truth? "Probably," I said.

He lowered the window on his side and tossed the lighter out, flipped the cigarette out after it, and followed both with the pack of Winstons from his shirt pocket.

I stared at him, laughing uncomfortably. "What are you *doing*?"

"I quit smoking."

"Just like that?"

He said, "I can do anything."

It sounded like bragging, but I could tell he was serious. We drove ten miles before either of us said another word. As we approached Salton City, I asked him to slow down. I wanted him to see the place where the guy in the Dodge had caught up with me. We didn't stop—there wasn't any point—but I didn't feel I could pass the spot without some reference to the event.

At Indio, we pulled into the parking lot of a small strip shopping mall where a Mexican restaurant was tucked between a VCR repair shop and a veterinarian.

"I hope you're hungry," Dietz said. "I don't want to stop once we hit the outskirts of Los Angeles. Sunday traffic is the pits."

"This is fine," I said. The truth was I felt tense and needed the break. Dietz handled the car well, but he drove aggressively, impatient every time he found himself behind another vehicle. The highway was only two lanes wide and his passing style had me clinging to the chicken stick. His attention was constantly focused on the road ahead and behind, watching (I surmised) for suspicious vehicles. He kept the radio off and the dead quiet in the car was broken only by the thump of his fingers tapping out a beat on the steering wheel. He had the kind of energy that set me on edge. It might not have been objectionable in the open air, but in the confines of the car, I felt crowded to the point of claustrophobia. The idea of having him at my side twenty-four hours a day for any length of time at all was worrisome.

We pushed through glass doors into a long, blank rectangular space that had evidently been designed for retail sales. A clumsy partition separated the kitchen from the dining area where a few tables had been arranged. Through the doorway, I could see a stove and battered refrigerator that might have come from a garage sale. Dietz told me to wait while he strolled through to the rear, where he checked the back door. The place was chilly and echoed when we scraped back our chairs to sit down. Dietz angled himself so he could keep an eye on the car through the plate-glass windows in the front.

Someone peered out of the kitchen at us with uncertainty. Maybe they thought we were from the health department inspecting for rat turds. There was some sort of whispered consultation and then a waitress appeared. She was short and heavyset, a middle-aged Mexican in a white wraparound apron decorated with stains. Shyly, she tried out her language skills. My Spanish is limited to (approximately) three words, but I could swear she offered to serve us squirrel soup. Dietz kept squinting and shaking his head. Finally, the two of them rattled at each other in Spanish for a while. He didn't seem fluent, but he managed to make himself understood.

I studied him casually while he fumbled with his vocabulary. He had a battered look, his nose slightly flattened, with a knot at the bridge. Mouth wide and straight, turning lopsided when he smiled. His teeth were good, but my guess was that some of them weren't his. Looked too even to me and the color was too white. He turned back to me.

"The place just opened yesterday. She recommends the menudo or the combination plate."

I leaned toward him, avoiding her bright gaze. "I don't eat menudo. It's made with tripe. Have you ever seen that stuff?

It's white and spongy-looking . . . all these perforations and bumps. It's probably some internal organ human beings don't even have."

"She'll have the combination plate," he said to her blandly. He held up two fingers, ordering one for himself.

She shuffled away in huaraches that she wore with white socks. She returned moments later with a tray that held glasses, two beers, a small dish of salsa, and a basket of tortilla chips still sizzling with lard.

We snacked on chips and salsa while we waited for our lunch.

"How do you know Lee Galishoff?" I asked. The beer bottle had a little piece of lime resting on the top and I squeezed some in. Both of us ignored the glasses, which were still hot from a recent washing.

Dietz reached for his cigarettes before he remembered that he'd thrown them out. He caught himself and smiled, shaking his head. "I did some work for him, hunting down a witness on one of his first trials. After that, we started playing racquetball and became good friends. What about you?"

I told him briefly the circumstances through which I'd ended up tracking Tyrone Patty for him. "I take it you've done security work before."

He nodded. "It's a lucrative sideline, especially in this day and age. Tends to limit your personal life, but at least it's relief from straight private-eye work, which is a yawn, as you know. Last week I sat for six hours looking at microfiche in the tax assessor's office. I can't stand that stuff."

"Lee told me you were feeling burned out."

"Not burned out. I'm bored. I've been doing it for ten years and it's time to move on."

"To what?" I asked. The beer was very cold and made a nice contrast to the fiery salsa, which was making my nose run. I kept dabbing surreptitiously with a paper napkin, looking like a junkie in need of a fix.

"Don't know yet," he said. "I got into the business in the first place by default. Started out doing repos, serving papers, stuff like that for a guy who eventually took me into his agency. Ray hated doing fieldwork—too rough for his taste—so he did all the paperwork and I dealt with the deadbeats. He was the cerebral type, really had it up here." He tapped his temple.

"You're using past tense. What happened to him?"

"He dropped dead of a heart attack ten months ago. The guy jogged, worked out lifting weights. He married this gal, gave up alcohol and cigarettes, gave up dope, gave up staying out all night. Bought a house, had a baby, happy as a pig eating shit, and then he died. Forty-six. A month ago, his widow started talking like she expected me to step in and fill the gap. It's bullshit. No thanks. I had her cash me out."

"You've lived in California?"

He gestured dismissively. "I've lived everywhere. I was born in a van on the outskirts of Detroit. My mother was in labor and the old man didn't want to stop. I got hauled all over hell and gone as a kid. Pop worked the oil rigs so we spent a lot of time in L.A. . . . this was in the late forties, early fifties when the big boom was on. Texas, Oklahoma. It was dangerous damn work, but the money was good. Pop was a brawler and a bully, very protective of me as long as I was tough myself. He was the kind of guy who'd get in a bar fight and tear the place apart . . . just for the hell of it. If he had a clash with the boss or decided he didn't like what was going on, we'd pack up and hit the road."

"How'd you manage to go to school?"

"I didn't if I could help it. I hated school. I couldn't see the point. To me, it all looked like preparation for something I didn't want to do anyway. I was never going to work in a feed store so why did I have to know how many bushels in a peck? Is that an issue that comes up for you? Two trains leaving different cities at sixty miles an hour? I couldn't sit still for junk like that. Nowadays they call kids like me hyperactive. All those rules and regulations, just for the sake of it. I couldn't stand it. I never did graduate. I ended up with an equivalency degree. Took some kind of written test that I aced without ever cracking a book. The system's not designed for transients. I liked phys ed and shop, woodworking, auto mechanics ... stuff like that. But nothing academic. Doesn't make any sense unless you start at the beginning and work straight through. I always showed up in the middle and had to leave before the end. Story of my life."

Lunch arrived and we paused to study our food, trying to figure out what it was. Rice and a puddle of refrieds, something folded with cheese leaking out, something flat. I recognized a tamale because it was wrapped in a corn husk. This was real basic fare—no parsley, no orange slice twisted open and resting on the top. My plate was so hot, I could have used it to iron a shirt. The cook appeared from the kitchen shyly bearing a stack of steaming flour tortillas wrapped in a cloth. The two hospital meals had left my taste buds craving astonishment. I wolfed the food, slowing only long enough to suck down another cold beer. Everything was excellent, the sort of flavors that make you whimper. I reached the finish line slightly in advance of Dietz and wiped my mouth on a paper napkin. "What about your mother? Where was she all this time?"

He shrugged, mouth full, waiting till he could speak. "She was there. My granny, too. The four of us traveled in an old station wagon with our gear shoved in the back. Everything I know my mom or my granny taught me in a moving vehicle. Geography, geology. We'd buy these old textbooks and work our way through. Usually, they'd be drinking beers and cutting up, laughing like lunatics. I thought that was neat and learning was a hoot. Put me in a classroom, I withered from the quiet."

I smiled. "You were probably the kind of kid I was afraid of in school. Boys mystified me. I never understood where they were coming from. When I was in fifth grade, we used to give these plays every Friday afternoon. Improvisational stuff we'd rehearse in the cloak room. The girls would always do love stories full of tragedy and self-sacrifice. The boys had sword fights ... lots of mouth noises and bumping. They'd stagger against the wall and then fall down dead. I couldn't figure out why that was fun. I didn't much like what the girls did, but at least people weren't getting stabbed with imaginary rapiers."

He smiled. "Were you raised in Santa Teresa?"

"I've lived there all my life."

He shook his head in mock amazement. "I couldn't even list all the places I've been."

"Were you in the service?"

"I was spared that, thank God. I was too young for Korea and too old for Vietnam. I'm not sure I could have passed the physical in any event. I had rheumatic fever as a kid . . ."

The waitress returned and started clearing our plates.

"Can you tell me where the ladies' room is?" I said to her.

"*Gracias,*" she said, smiling at me happily while she loaded the tray.

"*El cuarto de damas?*" Dietz supplied.

"Oh *sí, sí!*" She laughed at herself when she understood her mistake. She gestured toward the kitchen. I pushed back my chair. Dietz made a move as though to accompany me, but I stopped him. "God, Dietz. There are limits here, you know?"

He let it pass, but I noticed that he watched me carefully as I moved toward the back door. The *damas* did their business in a mop closet in the rear. While I was washing my hands afterward, I caught sight of myself in a shard of mirror that was propped up on the sink. I looked worse than I had the night before. My forehead was black and blue, my eye sockets smudged now with lavender. The red streaks beneath my eyes made it look like I had conjunctivitis. The dry desert climate had affected my hair, causing it to look like something I'd swept up from under the bed. I couldn't believe I'd been out in public without having people shriek and point. My head was starting to pound again.

By the time I reached the table, Dietz had paid the bill. "You okay?" he asked.

"You don't happen to have any pain pills, do you?"

"I have some Darvocet in the car."

He bought a can of Coke and we took it with us when we left. I watched him scan the parking lot as he unlocked the car. He opened the door for me, waiting until I was safely tucked in before he moved around to the driver's side. Once in his seat belt, he searched the glove compartment for the vial of pills.

"Let me know if this doesn't do the job. I've got prescriptions for everything." He checked a label or two, found what he was looking for, and shook a pill out onto his palm. I murmured a thank-you. He popped the can of Coke open for me and I washed the medication down. Within minutes, the pain began to recede. Shortly after that, I fell asleep.

I woke as we crossed the Ventura County line. I could smell the ocean before I even opened my eyes. The air was moist and briny, the surrounding countryside lush with green, a peculiar juxtaposition of junipers and palms. After the lean monotony of the desert, the coastal vegetation seemed lavish and strange. I could feel every cell in my body respond, drinking in the damp. Dietz glanced over at me. "Better?"

"Much." I sat up and ran my hands through my hair, scratching at the flattened strands. The medication had erased the pain, but I was feeling slightly out of it. I leaned my head back again and slouched down on my tail bone. "How's the traffic been?"

"We're through the worst of it."

"If I don't get a shower soon, I'll have to kill myself."

"Twenty-five miles to go."

"No sign of a tail?"

His gaze crept up to the rearview mirror. "Why follow us? He probably knows where you live."

"A happy thought," I said. "How long is this whole thing likely to go on?"

"Hard to say. Until he gives up or gets caught."

"And who's doing that?"

He smiled. "Not me. My job's to look after you, not catch bad guys. Let's leave that to the cops."

"And what's my responsibility in all of this?"

"We'll talk about that in the morning. Most of what I want is 'obedience without whining.' Very few women master it."

"You don't know me very well."

He peered over at my face. "I don't know you at all."

"Well, here's a hint," I said dryly. "I was raised by my mother's sister. My folks were killed in an accident and I went to live with her when I was five. This is the first thing she ever said to me . . . 'Rule number one, Kinsey . . . rule number one . . .'—and here she pointed her finger right up in my face—'No sniveling.' "

"Jesus."

I smiled. "It wasn't so bad. I'm only slightly warped. Besides, I got even. She died ten years ago and I sniveled for months. It all came pouring out. I'd been a cop for two years and I gave that up. Turned in my uniform, turned in my nightstick . . ."

"Symbolic gesture," he interjected.

I laughed. "Right. Six months later, I was married to a bum."

"At least the story has a happy ending. No babies?"

I shook my head. "Not a one."

"With me, it's just the opposite. I never had a wife, but I've got two kids."

"How'd you manage that?"

"I lived with a woman who refused to marry me. She swore I'd leave her in the end and sure enough that's what I did."

I stared at him for a while, but he subsided into silence. Soon afterward, the outskirts of Santa Teresa began to speed into view and I felt an absurd rush of joy at the notion of home.

10

We found a parking spot for the Porsche two doors down from my place and unloaded the trunk. By the time we pushed through the gate and rounded the corner to the rear, Henry had emerged from his back door to welcome me home. He stopped in his tracks, his smile faltering as his eyes shifted from my face to Dietz's. I introduced the two of them and they shook hands. Belatedly, I remembered what my battered visage must look like.

"I was in an accident," I said. "A guy ran me off the road. I had to leave the car in Brawley and Dietz gave me a ride back."

Henry was visibly dismayed, especially as he was in possession of only half the tale. "Well, who was the fellow? I don't understand. Didn't you file a report with the police down there?"

I hesitated, uncertain how much detail to get into at this point. Dietz settled the matter for me. "Let's go inside and we'll fill you in on the rest of it." He was clearly uneasy about standing around in the open air, exposed to view.

I unlocked the door and pushed it open, moving into the

apartment with Henry behind me and Dietz at the rear, herding us like a sheepdog.

"I'll just be a second. I want to get things squared away," I said to Henry. And then to Dietz, "Henry designed the place. It was just finished two days ago. I've spent exactly one night here."

I set my duffel down and cranked open a window to let in some fresh air. The apartment still smelled of sawdust and new carpeting. The space felt like a Barbie-doll penthouse in its own carrying case: scaled-down furniture, built-ins, spiral staircase, the loft visible above.

"I brought your mail in," Henry said, his eyes on my guest. He sat down on the couch, perplexed at the liberties Dietz seemed to take. The contrast between the two men was interesting. Henry was tall and lean, the blue eyes in his narrow, tanned face giving him the look of an ascetic; someone otherworldly, aged and wise. Dietz was compact, more muscular, a pit bull of a man with a thick chest and a brazen manner, his face marked by life, as if he'd had lessons hammered into him since birth. Henry had a stillness about him where Dietz was restless and energetic, the air around him charged with a curious tension.

Dietz circled the place without comment, automatically checking security, such as it was. I had latches on the windows, but not much else. He pulled the shutters closed, checked closets, peered into the downstairs bath. He snapped his fingers, idly popping them against his palms in a gesture that suggested some inner agitation. His manner was authoritative and Henry shot a look at me to see how I was taking it. I made one of those faces that said, Your guess is as good as mine, pal. It's not like I enjoyed someone taking over like this, but I wasn't fool enough to protest with my life on the line.

I turned my attention to the mail. Most of it looked like junk, but before I could sort it properly Dietz removed the stack from my hands and set it on the counter.

"Let it be till I can take a look at it," he said.

Henry couldn't stand it. "What's going on here? I don't understand what this is about."

"Someone's been hired to kill her," Dietz said unceremoniously. I don't think I would have been so blunt, but Henry didn't fall backward on the couch in a faint so maybe he's not as easily upset as I assume. Dietz filled in the picture, laying out the circumstances by which the Carson City DA's office had first gotten wind of Tyrone Patty's assassination plot. "The police in Carson City are doing what they can to control the situation up there. Obviously, Kinsey's position is a little bit more perilous . . ."

"Why's she here at all?" Henry burst out. "Why not take her someplace out of town?"

"I was out of town," I said, "and what good did it do? Three people knew where I was going and the guy was right there. Hell, he even managed to get there before I did at the first rest stop on the road." I told him briefly about spotting my assailant at the rest area near Cabazon.

"There has to be someplace," Henry said stubbornly.

"Frankly, I think we're better off right here as long as we take a few elementary precautions," Dietz said. "I've got a portable alarm system with me . . . receiver, siren, 'panic button' for her in case someone tries to break in and I'm not actually on the premises. If it seems useful, we can wire in pressure mats for selected doorways, both here and at your place. I want us all to keep an eye out for strangers. And that includes the mailman, gas man, delivery people, meter readers . . . anyone." He turned to look at me. "We'll vary your schedule as much as possible. Take a different route to and from the office every day. I'll be with you for the most part, but I want you to understand the basic strategy. Stay away from public places and public events. By the same token, I don't want you anyplace isolated or remote."

"What about jogging, or going to the gym?"

"Stow that for now. Any guy with a canvas bag could probably walk into the gym."

"Should I have a gun?" Henry asked, moving right into cops-and-robbers mode.

"Henry, you hate guns!"

"It may come to that, but I doubt it," Dietz said to Henry, ignoring me completely. "We're looking at prevention. With luck, we won't have anybody to shoot at."

"Hey. Excuse me. Do you guys mind if I voice an opinion?" Dietz turned to me.

I said, "If the guy in the truck wants to kill me, he'll kill me. I'm willing to be careful, but let's don't go nuts here."

Dietz shook his head. "I disagree. He'll do it if you're foolish and give him the chance, but he's not getting paid enough to stick his neck out."

I turned to Henry, filling him in. "He's a cut-rate killer. Fifteen hundred bucks."

Dietz amplified. "For that kind of money, he's not going to hang around for long. If he's quick about it, it may be worth it to him. Otherwise forget it. It's not cost-effective."

"Yeah," I said. "We don't want him to get chewed out by his accountant."

Dietz said, "Listen. The guy's trying to make a buck. Every day he's in Santa Teresa, it's costing him something. Food, lodging, gasoline. If he has a kid with him, the expenses mount up." He was rattling his car keys. "I'm going over to the police station and have a chat with the cops. You have any plans for tonight?"

I started to answer when I realized he was talking to Henry. I raised my hand like a schoolkid. "I don't mean to be argumentative, but could I have a vote?" I hated being so obnoxious, but this was driving me nuts. These guys were riding right over me.

Dietz smiled at me briefly. "Sorry. You're right. I have a tendency to overorganize."

I murmured something, backing down of course. The truth was I didn't have any idea what to do. I just didn't want to be pushed around.

Dietz put his keys in his pocket. "What about groceries? Let me know what we need and I can stop by a supermarket on my way back."

I didn't even have to look. The refrigerator was empty and my cupboards were bare.

"Any requests?"

"Whatever you want. I don't really cook."

"Me neither. We'll have to fake it. I want us eating in whenever possible. While I'm gone, please stay here and keep the door locked. We'll set up the alarm in the morning first thing. I don't want you going out. And no answering the telephone. You have a machine on it?"

I nodded.

"Let the machine pick up."

"I can stay with her if you think it's wise," Henry said.

Dietz looked at me to check my reaction. The guy was a quick study. I'd have to give him that.

"I'd like to have some time by myself," I said. Who knew when I'd ever get to be alone again?

Dietz was apparently willing to honor the request. Henry offered to cook for us, but I really didn't feel up to it. I was tired. I was sore. I was irritable. I just wanted to grab a quick supper and go to bed. My culinary repertoire was limited to peanut-butter-and-pickle sandwiches and hot sliced hard-boiled egg with lots of mayonnaise and salt. I'd have to quiz Dietz later on his specialties. Surely, he could do something.

I showered while Dietz was gone, remembering numerous items I wished I'd asked him to pick up. Wine for one. I gave my hair a quick shampooing, feeling antsy and distracted. The sound of running water masked other sounds in the apartment. Someone could be breaking one of my windows out and I wouldn't hear it. I should have had Henry baby-sit. I cut the shower short, wrapped myself in a towel, and peered over the loft railing. Everything looked just as it had before—no broken window, no bloodied hand reaching through to turn the latch.

I put on jeans and a fresh shirt, found clean sheets in the linen closet and made up the sofa bed. It was odd to have a houseguest even in the guise of a bodyguard. I wasn't used to living in the place by myself, let alone with a guy I'd only met that day.

I unpacked the duffel and tidied up the living room. Dietz had told me not to answer the telephone, but he hadn't said anything about phoning out. It was only 6:15. I needed the comfort of business as usual.

I put a call through to Mrs. Gersh. "Irene? This is Kinsey Millhone. I just wanted to touch base and check on your mother. Is she up here yet?"

"How nice of you. Yes, she is. Mother arrived about three this afternoon," she said. "We had an ambulance meet her at the airport and take her right to the nursing home. I just got back from seeing her, as a matter of fact, and she seems fine. Tired, of course."

"The trip must have been hard on her."

Irene's voice dropped slightly. "They must have sedated her, though nobody said as much. I expected her to be raising Cain, but she was very subdued. At any rate, I can't tell you how grateful I am you were able to locate her, and so quickly, too. Even Clyde seems relieved."

"Good. I'm glad. I hope everything works out."

"What about you, dear? I heard about your accident. Are you all right?"

I squinted at the phone with puzzlement. "You heard about that?"

"Well, yes. From your associate. He called here this afternoon, wondering when you'd be home."

All of my internal processes came to a dead halt. "What associate?"

"I don't know, Kinsey. I thought you'd know that. He said he was a partner in your agency. I really didn't catch the name." A note of doubt had crept into her voice, probably in response to the chilly note in mine.

"What time was this?"

"About an hour ago. I told him I hadn't heard from you, but I was certain you'd be driving back this afternoon. That's when he mentioned that you'd had an accident. Is something wrong?"

"Irene . . . I don't have a partner. What I have is some guy hired to kill my ass. . . ."

I could practically hear her blink. "I don't understand, dear. What does that mean?"

"Just what it sounds like. A hit man. Someone hoping to murder me for money."

There was a pause, as if she were having to translate from a foreign tongue. "You're joking."

"I wish I were."

"Well, he seemed to know all about you and he sounded very nice. I never would have said a word if he hadn't seemed so familiar."

"I hope you didn't give him my home address or phone number," I said.

"Of course not. If he'd asked me that, I'd have known something was amiss. This is awful. I feel terrible."

"Don't worry about it. It's not your fault. If you hear from the guy again, or from anyone else, please let me know."

"I will. I'm so sorry. I had no idea . . ."

"I understand. There was no way you could know. Just get in touch with me if you hear from him again."

After I hung up, I went into the downstairs bathroom and stood in the tub, looking out the window at the street. It was not quite dark, that hazy twilight hour when light and shadow begin to merge. Lights in the neighborhood were beginning to come on. A car passed slowly along the street and I found myself pulling back. I didn't actually whimper, but that's how I felt. It was amazing to me how quickly I was losing my nerve. I consider myself a capable person (*ballsy* is the word that comes to mind), but I didn't like the idea of this guy breathing down my neck. I returned to the living room, where I circled restlessly in a space scarcely bigger than a nine-by-twelve rug.

At 6:45 there was a tap at the door. My heart volunteered an extra beat just to speed the adrenaline along. I peered through the porthole. Dietz was standing on the doorstep, his arms loaded with groceries. I unlocked the door and let him in. I took one bag of groceries while he put the other on the kitchen counter. I'm not sure what expression I had on my face, but he picked up on it. "What's wrong?"

My voice sounded abnormal, even to my own ears. "Some guy called the woman I was working for and asked about me. He told her about the accident and asked if I was back in town yet."

Dietz's hand moved toward the pocket where he'd kept his cigarettes. He flashed a look of annoyance, apparently meant for himself. "How'd he know about her?"

"I have no idea."

"Shit!"

"What'd the cops have to say?"

"Not much. At least they know now what's going on. They'll have the beat car cruise by at intervals."

"Whoopee-do."

"Cut the sarcasm," he said irritably.

"Sorry. I didn't know it would come out like that."

He turned back to one of the grocery bags, pulling out a garment that looked like the blue vests we'd worn in high school sports to distinguish one team from another. "Lieutenant Dolan suggested you wear this. It's a bulletproof vest, a man's, but it should do the job. Some rookie left it behind when he quit the force."

I took the thing, holding it up by one Velcro strap. It was heavier than it looked and it had all the sex appeal of an ace bandage. "What about you? Don't you need one of these?"

Dietz was taking his jacket off. "I've got one in the car. I'm going to clean up. We'll talk about supper in a bit."

I put groceries away while he showered in the downstairs bathroom. Judging from the items he'd bought, he must have snagged two each from every department he passed. I hadn't been in the apartment long enough to decide where anything should go, so I amused myself with paper goods and staples, cans, condiments, spices, and household cleaners. Fortunately, he'd had the presence of mind to buy a bottle of Jack Daniel's, two bottles of white wine, and a six-pack of beer. I'm ashamed to say how cheered I was by the sight. Given my current level of anxiety, I wasn't above a nip of alcohol. I put the beer away and got out the corkscrew.

The bathroom door opened and Dietz came out, dressed in jeans and a dress shirt, his feet bare, the scent of aftershave wafting toward me in a cloud. He was toweling his hair dry and it stood out around his head like straw. The gray in his eyes was as clean as ice. He spotted the radio on the kitchen counter and turned it on, tuning in a country-western song with lots of major chords and a rocking-horse rhythm that would probably drive me mad. My problem with country music is that I try to avoid the very situations the lyrics lament. However, having objected to his cigarettes, I didn't feel comfortable protesting his taste in music as well. He probably wasn't any happier with the proximity than I was.

I poured wine in a glass. "Want some?"

"Of course!"

I handed him the glass of wine and poured a second for myself. I felt like we should drink a toast to something, but I couldn't think what. "Are you hungry? I notice you picked up some bacon and eggs. We could have that if you like."

"Fine. I wasn't sure what else to get. I hope you're not a vegetarian. I should have asked."

"I eat anything . . . well, except tripe," I said. I set the wineglass on the counter so I could get out the eggs. "Scrambled all right? I'm terrible at fried."

"I can cook 'em."

"I don't mind."

"It shouldn't be your responsibility. I'm not here as a guest."

I hate bickering about who's going to be nicer. I got out the skillet and tried a new subject. "We never talked about money. Lee didn't mention your hourly rate."

"Let's not worry about that. We'll work something out."

"I'd feel better if we came to some agreement."

"What for?"

I shrugged. "I don't know," I said. "It's just more business-like."

"I don't want to charge you. I'm doing this for fun."

I turned and stared at him. "You think this is fun?"

"You know what I mean. I've chucked the business anyway so this one's on me."

"I don't like that," I said. "I know you mean well, and believe me, I appreciate the help, but I don't like to feel indebted."

"There's no debt implied."

"I'm going to pay you," I said, testily.

"Great. You do that. My rates just went up. Five hundred bucks an hour."

I stared at him and he stared back. "That's bullshit."

"That's *my* point. It's bullshit. We'll work something out. Right now I'm hungry so let's quit arguing."

I turned back to the skillet with a shake of my head. The joy of being single is you always get to have your own way.

I went up to bed at nine, exhausted. I slept fitfully, aware that Dietz was up and prowling restlessly well into the night.

11

▬ ▬ ▬ I woke automatically at 6:00 A.M. and rolled
out of bed for my early morning run. Oh, wow, shit, hurt. I
was sucking air through my teeth, on my hands and knees,
staring at the floor when I remembered Dietz's advisory. No
jogging, no lifting weights. He hadn't said a word about getting out of bed. I was clearly in no condition to work out
anyway. The second day of anything is always the worst. I
staggered to my feet and hobbled over to the loft rail, peering down at the living room. He was up. The sofa bed had
been remade. I caught the smell of fresh coffee and a glimpse
of him sitting at the kitchen counter with the L.A. *Times* open
in front of him, probably wishing he could have his first
cigarette of the day. From my perspective, foreshortened, his
face seemed to be dominated by his furrowed brow and jut-
ting chin, his body topheavy with bulky shoulders and biceps.
He reversed the pages, flipping to the middle of the metro
section, which is where all the juicy Los Angeles crime is
detailed. I eased out of his line of sight, climbed into bed
again, and spent a few minutes staring up through the skylight. A marine layer had blanketed the Plexiglas dome with

white. Impossible to tell yet what kind of day it would be. It seldom rains here in May. Chances were the clouds would lift and we'd have sunshine, mild breezes, the usual lush green. Sometimes perfection ain't that easy to bear. Meanwhile, I couldn't lie here all day, though I was tempted, I confess.

If I went downstairs, I'd have to be polite and interact with Dietz, making small talk of some as yet undetermined sort. New relationships are daunting, even when they're short-term. People have to trade all those tedious details about their previous lives. It made me tired to consider the sheer weight of the exchange. We'd touched on the preliminaries in the car coming home, but we had reams of data to cover yet. Chitchat aside, Dietz might turn on the radio again . . . more Roy Orbison. I couldn't face that at 6:05 A.M.

On the other hand, it was my house and I was hungry, so why shouldn't I go downstairs and eat? I didn't have to talk to him. I pushed the covers back and got up, limped into the bathroom and brushed my teeth. My face was still a Technicolor wonder, a rainbow of bruises after a shower of blows. I wiggled my eyebrows and studied myself. The contusion on my forehead was shifting subtly from dark blue to gray, my blackened eyes lightening from lavender to an eerie green. I've seen eye shadow in the same shade and it always puzzles me why women want to look like that. "I got belted in the chops last night," is what it says. My hair was, as usual, mashed from the night's sleep. I'd showered the night before but I hopped in again, not for the sake of cleanliness, but hoping to improve my mood. Having Dietz under the same roof was making my skin itch.

Once I pulled on jeans and an old sweatshirt, I dumped my dirty clothes in the hamper, tucked the empty duffel in the closet, and made the bed. I went downstairs. Dietz murmured a good morning without lifting his eyes from the sports page. I helped myself to some coffee, poured a bowl of cereal with milk, grabbed the funnies, and toted it all into the living room, where I sat, bowl in hand, spooning cereal into my mouth absentmindedly while I read the comic page. The funnies never make me laugh, but I read them anyway in hopes. I caught up with Rex Morgan, M.D., the girls in Apartment 3G, and Mary Worth. It's comforting how slowly life moves in a comic strip. I hadn't read the paper in maybe four days and the professor was just now looking startled at something Mary'd said to him. What a wag she was. I could tell he was disconcerted by the wavy lines around his head.

Dimly, I was aware that Dietz had opened the front door and stepped out into the backyard. When I finished my cereal, I washed my bowl and spoon and left them in the dish rack. Hesitantly, I moved to the front door and peered out, feeling like a housebound cat discovering that a door has inadvertently been left ajar. Was I allowed outside?

The marine layer was already beginning to dissipate, but the yard had that bleached look that a mist imparts. The foghorn was bleating intermittently—a calf separated from its mother—in the still morning air. The strong scent of seawater saturated the yard. Sometimes I half expect the surf to be lapping at the curb out front.

Dietz was hunkering near the flower beds. Henry had put in some bare root roses the year before and they were in full bloom: Sonia, Park Place, Lady X, names giving no clue about the final effect. "Aphids," he said. "He should buy some ladybugs."

I leaned against the doorframe, too paranoid to venture all the way out into the yard. "Are we going to talk about security again or did we cover it last night?"

He got to his feet, turning his attention to me. "We should probably discuss your schedule. Any standing appointments? Massage, beauty salon?"

"Do I look like someone with a standing appointment at a beauty salon?"

He studied my face with curiosity, but refrained from comment. "The point is, we don't want your movements predictable."

I rubbed my forehead, which was still smarting to the touch. "I gathered as much. Okay, so I cancel my masseuse, bikini wax, and the weekly pedicure. Now what?"

He smiled. "I appreciate your cooperation. Makes my job easier."

"Believe me, I'm not interested in being killed," I said. "I do need to go in to the office."

"What time?"

"Doesn't matter. I want to pick up my mail and get some bills paid. Minor stuff really, but I don't want to put it off."

"No problem. I'd like to see the place."

"Good," I said, turning to go back inside.

"Kinsey? Don't forget the body armor."

"Right. Make sure you wear yours, too."

Upstairs, I dutifully stripped off my sweatshirt and slipped on the bulletproof vest, pressing the Velcro straps into place. Dietz had told me this particular vest offered threat-level-one protection, which was good against a .38 Special or less. Apparently, he was assuming a hit man wouldn't use a 9-millimeter automatic. I tried not to think about garrotes, head wounds, blasted kneecaps, the penetrating power of ice picks—any one of a number of assaults not covered by the oversize bib I wore.

"Make sure it's tight enough," Dietz had called up from below.

"Got it," I said. I had pulled the sweatshirt on over the vest and checked myself in the mirror. I looked like I was eleven years old again.

At 8:45, we moved through the front gate. Dietz had gone out first to check the car and scan the street. He returned, motioning me forward. He walked slightly in front of me, his stride brisk, his eyes alert as we traversed the fifty paces to his Porsche. The whole maneuver had an urgency about it that made me feel like a rock star. "I thought a bodyguard was supposed to be inconspicuous," I said.

"That's one theory."

"Won't everybody guess?"

He looked over at me. "Let's put it this way. I'm not in-terested in advertising what I do, but if this guy's watching us, I want him to understand just how hard his job is going to be. Most attacks occur suddenly and at very close range.

I'll try not to be obnoxious, but I'm sticking to you like glue."

Well, that answered that.

Dietz drove with his usual determination. He was a real A-type personality, one of those guys who lives like he's always late for some appointment, irritated at anybody who slows him down. Bad drivers caught him by surprise, as though they were the exception instead of the rule. I directed him to the downtown area, which, fortunately, was only ten minutes away. If he noticed I was bracing myself between the dashboard and the door frame, he didn't mention it.

At the entrance to the parking lot, he slowed the car, surveying the layout. "Is this where you usually park?"

"Sure, the office is right up there."

I watched him calculate. He was clearly hoping for a way to change my routine, but parking farther away was only going to make the walk longer, thus exposing us for an extended period. He pulled in, handed me the ticket, and found a parking space. "Anything looks weird," he said, "speak up right away. Any sign of trouble, we'll get the fuck out."

"Right," I said. It was amazing what this "we" business was doing to my head. I wasn't famous for letting guys tell me what to do and I was hoping I wouldn't get used to it.

Again, he came around to the passenger side and opened the door, his gaze sweeping the lot as I emerged into the open air. He took my elbow, walking me rapidly across the lot to the back stairs. I wanted to laugh. It felt like having a parent march you up to your room. He entered the building first. The second-floor corridor was deserted. California Fidelity offices weren't open yet. I unlocked my office door. Dietz stepped in ahead of me and took a quick look around, making sure there weren't any goons lurking behind the furniture.

He scooped up the mail that had piled up on the floor just under the slot. He sorted through it quickly. "Let me tell you what we're looking for, in case I'm not here to do this. An unfamiliar return address, or one done by hand. Anything marked personal, extra postage due to weight, oil stains . . ."

"A bulky package with a fuse hanging out the side," I said.

He handed me the stack, his expression bland. It's hard to warm to somebody who looks at you that way. Apparently, he didn't think I was as funny as I thought I was. I took the stack of mail and sorted through it as he had. Much of it was third-class, but I did have a few checks coming in—all with return addresses I could identify on sight. Together we listened to the few messages on my machine. None were threatening. Dietz wanted time to acquaint himself with the building and its environs, so he went off to inspect the premises while I put on a pot of coffee.

I opened the French doors and paused, suddenly reluctant to step out on the balcony. Across the street, I could see the tiers of the parking garage and it occurred to me that anyone could drive up two levels, park, and get a bead on me. I wasn't even sure a high-powered rifle would be required. You could almost throw a rock from there and pop me in the noggin. I stepped away from the doors, withdrawing into the shadowy safety of the office. I really hated this.

At 9:05, I put a call through to my insurance agent and reported the accident. She said there was no blue book on the VW because of its age. It looked like I was going to be lucky if I picked up two hundred bucks on the claim, so there was no point in having the car towed. Finding an adjuster in Brawley who would go out and take a look was almost more trouble than the car was worth. She said she'd check into it and get back to me. This conversation failed to fill me with happiness. I have a savings account, but the purchase of a car would seriously deplete my funds.

Dietz returned to the office in time to intercept Vera, who had stopped in to say hello on her way into the office next door.

"My God, what happened to you?" she said when she saw my face.

"My car ended up in an irrigation ditch down in Brawley," I said. "This is Robert Dietz. He was nice enough to drive me back. Vera Lipton, from the offices next door."

They shook hands briefly. She was wearing a black leather miniskirt that fit her like automobile upholstery and made a creaking sound when she eased into one of my client chairs. Dietz moved over and parked a hip on the edge of my desk. It was amusing to watch them size each other up. Unknown to Vera, Dietz was viewing her as a potential assassin while I suspect she was evaluating his qualifications for a roll in the hay—whether hers or mine, I couldn't say. From her expression, she assumed he'd picked me up hitchhiking and since she considers me hopelessly conservative when it comes to men, I thought the possibility might lend me a certain stature in her eyes. I tried to look like the kind of woman who'd flag down a stranger on the road, but she wasn't interested in me—she was studying him. I was going to have to call this doctor friend of hers so we could double-date.

She reached into her handbag automatically and pulled a cigarette from a pack of Virginia Slims. "I'm not smoking this. I just need to hold it," she said when she caught my look. "I quit last week," she added in an aside to him.

I glanced at Dietz to see what his reaction would be. He hadn't had a cigarette now for over twenty-four hours, a personal best perhaps. Fortunately, he seemed to be sidetracked by the pheromones wafting through the air like perfume. Vera didn't actually drape one long leg across the chair arm, but there was something provocative about the way she sat. As often as I've seen her operate, I've still never figured out exactly what she does. Whatever the behavior, most men will begin to sit, lie down, and fetch like trained pups.

"I hope you're not forgetting the dinner tomorrow night," she said. She knew from my face I hadn't the faintest idea what she was talking about. "For Jewel. Retirement," she said, keeping it simple for those of us who'd suffered brain damage.

"Oh, that's right! I completely forgot. Really, I'm sorry, but I just don't see how I can make it," I said, with visual reference to Dietz. He was never going to permit my attendance at a public affair. Vera caught the look and said to Dietz, "You're invited, of course. Jewel's leaving the company after twenty-five years. Attendance is mandatory . . . no ifs, ands, or buts."

"Where's it being held?" he asked.

"The Edgewater Hotel. A private dining room. Should be very elegant. It's costing enough."

"How many people are we talking about?"

Vera shrugged. "Maybe thirty-five."

"Invitation only?"

"Sure. It's California Fidelity employees and guests. Why?"

"Can't do it," I said.

"I think we can manage it," Dietz said at the same time. "It will help if there's been no advance publicity."

Vera looked from one of us to the other. "What's going on?"

Dietz filled her in.

I waited, feeling oddly irritated, while they went through the catechism of disbelief and assurances. Vera expressed all the requisite attitudes. "God, that's awful. I can't believe things like that actually go on. Listen, if you guys don't want to risk it, I'll understand."

"I'll want to check it out, but we'll see how it looks. Can we let you know in the morning?" Dietz said.

"Of course. As long as I know by noon, it shouldn't be any problem."

"What time's the dinner?"

"No-host cocktails at seven. The dinner's at eight." Vera glanced at her watch. "Oops. I gotta scoot. It's been nice meeting you."

"You, too."

She moved toward the door.

"Oh, and Vera . . . ," he said. "We'd prefer to keep this quiet."

She pulled her glasses down on her nose, looking at him over the rims. There was an elegant pause while she raised a brow. "Of course," she said—the word *asshole* implied. There was something flirtatious in the very way she left the room. Lord, she was really going all out for this guy.

Dietz seemed to color. It was the first time I'd seen him disconcerted by anything. The most unlikely men turn out to be suckers for abuse.

When the door closed behind her, I turned on Dietz with an outraged tone. "I thought you said no public events!"

"I did. I'm sorry. I can see I caught you by surprise. I don't want to interfere any more than I have to. If this is something you want, then let's find a way to do it."

"I'm not going to risk my life for something like that!"

"Look. There's no way we can eliminate every possibility of attack. I'm here to reduce the likelihood, that's all. The *president* goes out in public, for God's sake," he said. His tone shifted. "Besides, I'm not convinced the guy we're dealing with is a pro. . . ."

"Oh, great. He might be a lunatic, instead."

Dietz shrugged matter-of-factly. "If we play our cards right, you'll be safe enough. The guest list is restricted and these are people you know. Once we scope it out, the question boils down to, do you want to go or not? You tell me. I'm not here to dictate the terms of your life."

"I don't know yet," I said, somewhat mollified. "The dinner's no big deal, but it might be nice to be out."

"Then let's see what it looks like and we'll decide after that."

By noon, I'd wrapped up my business and locked my files again. The phone rang just as Dietz and I were heading out the door. I started to answer, but he held a hand up, stopping me. He picked it up. "Millhone Investigations." He listened briefly. "Hold on." He passed the phone to me.

"Hello?"

"Kinsey, this is Irene Gersh. I'm sorry to be a bother. You're busy I know . . ."

"No problem. What's up?"

"Mother's disappeared. I don't suppose she's been in touch with you."

"Well, no, but I'm not sure she'd know who to call if she wanted to. I only saw her twice. How long's she been gone?"

"Nobody really knows. The supervisor at the nursing home swears she was there at breakfast time. An aide took her to the dining room in a wheelchair and then went off to take care of someone else. She told Mother she'd just be a minute, but when she turned around Mother'd left her wheelchair and had taken off on foot. Nobody dreamed she could get very far. I guess they scoured the building and grounds and now they've started searching the neighborhood. I'm on my way over but I thought I'd check with you first, just in case you knew anything."

"I'm sorry, but I haven't heard from her at all. You need some help?"

"No, no. There's really no need at this point. The police have been notified and they have a patrol car cruising the area. So far there's no sign of her, but I'm sure she'll turn up. I just didn't want to overlook the possibility that she might be with you."

"I wish I could be more help. We've got an errand to run, but we can check with you later and see what's going on. Give me the address and telephone number at the nursing home." I tucked the phone against my shoulder while I made a note on a piece of scratch paper. "I'll give you a call when we get back."

"Thank you. I appreciate your concern."

"In the meantime, don't worry. I'm sure she's somewhere close."

"I hope so."

I told Dietz what was going on as we headed down the back steps. I was half-tempted to have him take me over to the nursing home, but it didn't feel like a real emergency. He wanted to see the Edgewater and check the arrangements for the banquet. He suggested I call Irene from the hotel as soon as he was done. It made sense and I agreed, though I knew for a fact if I were on my own, I'd have done it the other way. I was feeling distracted and, for once, his driving style didn't bother me. It was hard to imagine where Agnes could have gone. I knew she was capable of raising hell when it suited her, but Irene had made it sound like she was resigned to the move. I had to shrug to myself. Surely, she'd turn up.

12

▶▶ ▶▶ ▶▶ I leaned my head back on the seat, staring out
the car window while Dietz circled the area surrounding the
hotel. I could see that he was committing various routes to
memory, getting a sense of the sections of the road where we
might be vulnerable to attack. I wasn't that interested in attending the dinner. Now that I thought about it, what the
hell did I care? Jewel was a nice lady, but I really didn't know
her well. I wasn't feeling that good and—just to get basic—I
didn't have a thing to wear. The all-purpose dress—the only
one I owned—had been in my car at the time of the accident.
In the auto body lot down in Brawley, I remembered packing
soggy items in a cardboard box, which hadn't arrived in Santa
Teresa yet. When the dress did get here, it was probably
going to smell like a swamp, complete with primordial life
forms wiggling out of the wet. I could always ask Vera to lend
me some rags. She towered over me, outweighing me by a
good twenty pounds, but I'd seen her wearing a sequined
tunic cut right to her crotch. It would probably hit me at the
knee. Not that I could wear a skirt in my current condition,
of course. I was sporting a bruised leg that made me look like

116

spoiled fruit. On a more optimistic note, once I strapped on my body armor, what difference would it make that her bazookas were twice the size of mine?

Dietz had apparently satisfied himself with the general layout of the neighborhood and we were getting down to the particulars. He pulled into the Edgewater parking lot and turned his Porsche over to a parking attendant, passing the guy a folded bill. "Keep the car up here close and let me know if anyone takes an interest."

The attendant glanced down at the bill. "Yessir! Hey, sure!"

Dietz and I moved toward the entrance.

"Why so quiet?" he asked as he steered me through the lobby by the elbow like the rudder of a boat.

I pulled my arm away automatically. "Sorry," I murmured. "I've been thinking about the banquet and it's put me in a bad mood."

"Anything I can help with?"

I shook my head. "What's this feel like to you?"

"What, the job?"

"Yeah. Trailing around with me everywhere. Doesn't it get on your nerves?"

"I don't have nerves," he said.

I turned and scanned his face, wondering if that was really true.

He hunted down the hotel manager and had a long talk with him about the banquet room, the closest medical facility, and matters of that ilk. I would have jettisoned the whole plan, but by now we'd invested so much time and energy, I felt I was obligated to follow through. Meanwhile, Dietz was triggering all the disagreeable aspects of my personality. I was beginning to remember certain personal traits that had probably contributed to my divorces. I prefer to believe it was all *their* fault, but who are we trying to kid here . . .

I left Dietz in the manager's office and wandered down the corridor. Just off the hotel lobby, there were little shops where rich people browsed, looking for ways to spend money without having to leave the premises. I went into a clothing boutique and circled the place. The merchandise seemed unreal to me, outfits laid out with all the color-coordinated accessories. My notion of accessories is you wear your gym socks with matching rims. The air smelled of one of those movie-star perfumes that cost a hundred and twenty bucks an ounce. Just for laughs, I checked the sale rack. Even marked down, most items cost more than my monthly rent. I crossed to the section where the evening wear was arranged: long skirts in brocade, tops stiff with sequins, everything embroidered, hand-stitched, hand-painted, appliquéd, beaded and otherwise bejeweled. The saleswoman glanced over at me with a practiced smile. I could see her expression falter slightly and I was reminded, yet again, how unnerving my appearance must be to those unprepared for it. I was hoping I looked like I'd just had cosmetic surgery. A little nose bob, eye tucks. For all she knew I was holing up here with some sugar daddy until the swelling went down.

Dietz appeared in the doorway and I moved in his direction. As usual, he grabbed me by the elbow without ceremony and marched me down the hall. He was brusque, distracted, probably mentally several moves ahead. "Let's have lunch."

"Here?" I said, startled. I'm more the Burger King type myself.

"Sure, why not? It'll cheer you up."

We'd reached the entrance to the hotel restaurant, a vast room enclosed in glass, with polished red tile floors and white wicker furniture. The room was dense with greenery: palms and rubber plants, potted ficuses lending an air of tropical elegance. The patrons were actually very casually dressed: tennis outfits, golf shirts, and designer sweats. Dietz was wearing the same jeans and tweed sport coat he'd worn for two days, while I was in my jeans and tenny-bops. No one seemed to pay the slightest attention to us, except for the occasional look of curiosity that flickered to my face.

He spotted a sheltered table near a fire exit with a sign

prominently displayed above it: THIS DOOR MUST BE KEPT UNLOCKED DURING BUSINESS HOURS. Perfect if needed to make a fast getaway. The service area nearby was being used as a station for linen and flatware. A waitress had been sentenced to folding napkins into cloth boats.

"How about that one," he said. The hostess nodded and led the way, showing us to our seats without questioning his taste.

She handed us two oversized menus bound in leather. "Your waiter will be right with you," she said and moved away. I'll admit I checked the menu with a certain curiosity. I'm used to fast-food chains where the menus feature glossy photos of the food, as if the reality itself is bound to disappoint.

The edibles here were itemized on a quarto of parchment, handwrit by some kitchen scribe who had mastered Foodspeak. ". . . lightly sauced pan-smoked filets of free range veal in a crib of fresh phyllo, topped with squaw bush berries, and accompanied by hand-formed gaufrettes of goat cheese, wild mushrooms, yampa root, and fresh herbs . . ." $21.95. I glanced at Dietz, who didn't seem at all dismayed. As usual, I could tell I was completely out of my element. I hardly ever eat squaw bush berries and yampa root.

I checked the other patrons. My view was actually half-obscured by a Boston fern. Next to the plant stand was a cylindrical cage in which finches were twittering. There were small bamboo baskets affixed to the wire sides and the little birds hopped in and out with strips of newspaper, making nests. There was something charming about their bright-eyed busyness. Dietz and I watched them idly while we waited for our waiter.

"You know anything about crows?" he asked.

"I'm not much on birds."

"I wasn't either until I met one personally. I used to have a crow named Albert. Bertie, when I got to know him better. I got him when he was just a little guy and had him for years. A young crow doesn't navigate well and they'll sometimes crash-land. They're called branchers at that age—that's about all they can do, lumber awkwardly from branch to branch. Sometimes they get stuck and they wail like babies until you get 'em down. Bertie must have bitten off a bit more than he could chew and he'd tumbled to the ground. I had a cat named Little John who brought him in, squawking hellishly. LJ and I had a tussle to see who was going to take possession. Fortunately for Bertie, I won the contest. He and the cat became friends later, but it was touch-and-go for a while there. LJ was pissed off because he thought this was Thanksgiving dinner and I was getting in his way . . ."

Dietz looked up. The waiter was approaching, dressed like an usher at a wedding, complete with white gloves.

"Good afternoon. Something to drink before lunch?" The waiter's manner was circumspect and he avoided making eye contact.

Dietz turned to me. "You want a drink?"

"White wine," I said.

"Chardonnay, sauvignon blanc?" the waiter asked.

"Chardonnay."

"And you, sir?"

"I'll have a beer. What do you have imported?"

"Amstel, Heineken, Beck's dark, Beck's light, Dos Equis, Bohemia, Corona . . ."

"Beck's light," Dietz said.

"Are you ready to order?"

"No."

The waiter stared at Dietz, then nodded and withdrew.

Dietz said, "We probably won't see him for half an hour, but I hate being bullied into ordering."

He picked up his story again about Bertie the crow, who liked to take long walks on foot and lived on a diet of M&M's, hard-boiled eggs, and dry cat food. While Dietz talked, his gaze shifted restlessly around the room. He seldom looked at faces, always at hands, checking for concealed weapons, sudden movements, signals perhaps. Some underling arrived, bearing our drinks, but the waiter didn't return. Dietz scanned the dining room, but there was no sign of him. Twenty minutes passed. I could see Dietz take note and in a surge of uneasiness, he finally tossed a bill on the table and got up. "Let's get out of here. I don't like this."

"Do you see everything as part of some plot?" I asked, trotting after him.

"That may be all that keeps the two of us alive."

I shrugged to myself and let it go at that. When we reached the front entrance, the Porsche was parked right up against the shrubs. He snagged the keys off the board himself and helped me into the car. He got in on his side and fired up the engine.

We drove home along the beach. I was exhausted and my head was starting to pound. When we got to my apartment, Dietz hauled out his portable alarm system, which he showed me how to arm and disarm. He affixed it to the door.

"I'll tell Henry to keep an ear tuned while I'm out . . ."

"You're going off somewhere?" I felt a little bubble of panic arise, testimony to how quickly I'd come to depend on him for my sense of personal safety.

"I want to have another chat with Lieutenant Dolan. He said he'd talk to the Carson City DA and try to get an ID on this guy with the kid. Somebody must have heard of him. Maybe we can pick up a mug shot and at least figure out what he looks like. I'll be back in half an hour. You'll be fine here. Get some rest. You look beat."

He took off while I downed a pain pill and headed up to the loft. I had promised to call Irene and I could feel the tiny voice of my conscience whining deep within. The phone rang just as I was pulling off my shoes. Dietz had told me not to answer it if he wasn't there, but I couldn't help myself. I leaned across the bed and picked up the receiver.

It was Irene Gersh. "Oh good, it's you. I'm calling from the nursing home. I'm so glad you're there. I was afraid you were still out."

"We just got in. I was thinking I should call you, but I hadn't worked up the energy."

"Is this a bad time?"

"It's fine. Don't worry about it. What's happening?"

"Nothing. That's the point. I'm sorry to be such a pest, but I'm just beside myself. Mother's been gone now for eight hours and there's simply no sign of her. Clyde feels maybe we should get out and check the neighborhood ourselves."

"Sounds smart," I said. "You need any help knocking on doors?" In that split second my concern for Agnes's safety overrode my worries about myself.

"Thank you. We'd appreciate it. The longer Mother's on the loose, the more frightened I get. Somebody must have seen her."

"You'd think so," I said. "When do you need me there?"

"Soon if you could. Clyde called from work and he's on his way over now. If it's not too much trouble . . ." She gave me an address in the eleven hundred block of Concorde.

"I'm on my way," I said and hung up. I put a quick call through to Lieutenant Dolan's office and left word for Dietz to meet me at the nursing home, reiterating the address. That done, I picked my way carefully down the stairs. I craved action. My whole body was seizing up in the wake of the accident and my joints felt stiff with rust. Certain postures caused excruciating pains to shoot through my neck, causing me to murmur, "Ow, ow, ow." I was hoping the painkiller would do its work before long.

I found a jacket and my handbag, checked to make sure my little .32 was accounted for, and headed for the door, searching for my car keys in the outside leather pouch. Where the hell were they? I stopped dead, perplexed, and then it dawned on me. I didn't *have* transportation. My VW was still down in Brawley at the auto body shop. Well, hell, I thought.

I turned on my heel, picked up the phone again, and called a cab. By that point, I had already begun to internalize some of Dietz's precautions. I knew better than to loiter outside on the curb in plain sight. I waited, dutifully standing in the tub in the downstairs bathroom, where I could look out the window until the cab appeared in front. For the second time, I snatched up my jacket and my handbag. When I opened the front door, the alarm system went off, scaring me so badly that I nearly wet my pants.

Henry's back door banged open and he came running out with a meat cleaver in his hand. All he had on was a pair of turquoise briefs and his face was pale as bread dough. "My God, what happened? Are you all right?"

"Henry, I'm fine. I accidentally set off the alarm."

"Well, get back inside. You scared the hell out of me. I was about to take a shower when that damn thing went off. Why are you out here? Dietz said you were napping. You look awful. Go to bed." His panic had rendered him a little cranky, I thought.

"Would you quit worrying? There's no cause for hysteria. Irene Gersh called me and I'm on my way over to the nursing home to help look for her mom. I've got a cab waiting out in front."

Henry grabbed my jacket. "You'll do no such thing," he said snappishly. "You can wait till Dietz gets back and go over there with him."

I could feel my temper climb in response to his. I grabbed the jacket back, the two of us tugging like kids in a school-yard. The cleaver he was holding made it treacherous work.

The second time he reached for the jacket, I held it up and away from him. "Henry," I said warningly. "I'm a free human being. Dietz knows I'm going over there. I called Dolan's office and talked to him myself. He's on his way."

"You did not. I know you. You're lying through your teeth," Henry said.

"I *did* call!"

"But you didn't *talk* to him."

"I left a message. That's just as good."

"What if he never gets it?"

"Then you can tell him where I am! I'm going."

"No, you're not!"

I had to argue for five minutes before I was allowed to leave the premises. Meanwhile, the cab driver had already tooted twice and he appeared from around the corner looking for his fare. I don't know what he must have thought when he caught sight of us . . . me with my battered face, Henry in his Calvin Klein skivvies with a cleaver in his mitt. Fortunately, Henry knew the guy and after earnest reassurances on all sides, he finally consented to my departure. He didn't like the idea, but there wasn't much he could do.

The cabbie was still shaking his head with mock disgust. "Get some pants on, Pitts. You could get arrested like that."

By the time I reached the nursing home on the Upper East Side, it was nearly two o'clock. I realized as the cab pulled up that I knew the neighborhood. Rosie and I had combed the entire area, looking for a board-and-care for her sister, Klotilde. The houses, for the most part, were built on a grand scale: rambling interiors with high ceilings, oversize windows, wide porches, surrounded by massive oaks and old, shaggy palms.

In contrast, the nursing home from which Agnes had disappeared was a two-story Victorian structure with a carriage house in the rear. The frame siding was a pale gray, with the trim done in fresh white. The steeply pitched roof was made of slate tiles, overlapping like fish scales. At the second-story level, a raw-looking L of decking and a set of wooden stairs had been added as a fire escape. The house sat on a large corner lot, the property shaded by countless trees, dotted with flower beds, and bordered with shrubs, which were pierced by the protruding upright arrows of an ornamental iron fence. There were several cars visible in the small parking lot in the rear.

Irene had apparently been watching for my arrival. I paid the driver and emerged from the cab in time to see her moving toward me down the front walk, followed by a gentleman I assumed was Clyde Gersh. Again, I was struck by the aura of illness that surrounded her. She was stick-thin and seemed unsteady on her feet. The shirtwaist dress she wore was a jade-green silk that only emphasized the unearthly pallor of her skin. She'd clearly gone to some trouble with her appearance, but the effect was stark. Her foundation makeup was too peachy a shade, and the false lashes made her eyes jump out of her face. A swath of blusher high on each cheek gave her the look of someone in the throes of a fever. "Oh, Kinsey. God bless you." She reached for me with trembling hands that were cold to the touch.

"How are you, Irene? Is there any sign of her?"

"I'm afraid not. The police have taken the report and they've issued one of those . . . oh, what do you call them . . ."

Clyde spoke up. "A 'be on the lookout' bulletin."

"Yes, that's it. Anyway, they'll have a patrol car cruising the neighborhood. I'm not sure what else they can do for the time being. I'm just sick."

Clyde spoke up again, extending his hand. "Clyde Gersh."

Irene seemed flustered. "Oh, I'm sorry. This is Miss Millhone. I don't know what I was thinking of."

Clyde Gersh was probably in his late fifties, some ten years older than his wife. He was tall and stooped, wearing an expensive-looking suit that seemed to hang on his frame. He had a thinning head of gray hair, a lined face, his brow knotted with concern. His features had the droopy quality of a man resigned to his fate. His wife's state of health, whether real or self-induced, must have been a trial to him. He'd adopted an air of weary patience. I realized I had no idea what he did for a living. Something that entailed a flexible schedule and wingtip shoes. A lawyer? Accountant?

The two of us shook hands. He said, "Nice to meet you, Miss Millhone. I'm sorry for the circumstances."

"Me, too. I prefer 'Kinsey,' if you would. What can I do to help?"

He glanced apologetically at his wife. "We were just discussing that. I'm trying to talk Irene into staying here. She can hold down the fort while we get out and bump doors. I told the director of this two-bit establishment he'll have a lawsuit on his hands if anything's happened to Agnes. . . ."

Irene shot him a look. "We can talk about this later," she

said to him. And to me, "The nursing home has been wonderful. They feel Mother was probably confused. You know how willful she is, but I'm sure she's fine. . . ."

"Of course she is," I said, though I had my doubts.

Clyde's expression indicated he had about as much faith as I did. "I'm just heading out if you'd care to join me," he said. "I think we should check the houses along Concorde as far as Molina and then head north."

Irene spoke up. "I want to come, Clyde. I won't stay here by myself."

An expression of exasperation flickered briefly in his face, but he nodded agreement. Whatever opposition he may have previously voiced, he now set aside, perhaps in deference to me. He reminded me of a parent reluctant to discipline a kid in front of company. The man wanted to look good. I glanced along the street for some sign of Dietz.

Irene caught my hesitation. "Something wrong, dear? You seem worried."

"Someone's meeting me here. I don't want to take off without leaving word."

"We can wait if you like."

Clyde gestured impatiently. "You two do what you want. I'm going on," he said. "I'll take this side and you can take that. We'll meet here in thirty minutes and see how it looks." He gave Irene's cheek a perfunctory kiss before he headed off. She stared after him anxiously. I thought she was going to say something, but she let the moment pass.

"Would you like to tell someone at the nursing home where we'll be?"

"Never mind," I said. "Dietz will figure it out."

13

We started with the house diagonally across from the nursing home. Like many others in the neighborhood, it was substantially constructed, probably built in the early years of the century. The façade was wide, the two-story exterior shingled in cedar tinted with a pale green wash. A prominent gabled porch sat squarely in the center, matching large bay windows reflecting blankly the sprawling branches of an overhanging oak. I thought I saw movement in an upstairs window as we came up the walk. Irene was clinging to my arm for support. Already, I could tell she was going to slow me down, but I didn't have the heart to mention it. I was hoping her anxiety would ease if she could help in the search.

I pressed the bell, which jangled harshly. Moments later, the front door opened a crack and a face appeared, an older woman. The burglar chain was still judiciously in evidence. Had I been a thug, I could have kicked the door open with a well-placed boot.

"Yes?"

I said, "Sorry to bother you, but we're talking to everybody in the neighborhood. An elderly woman's disappeared from the nursing home across the street and we're wondering if you might have seen her. About seven this morning. We think that's when she left."

"I don't get up until eight o'clock these days. Doctor's orders. I used to get up at five, but he says that's ridiculous. I'm seventy-six. He says there's nothing going on at that hour that I need to know about."

"What about your neighbors? Have you heard anybody mention . . ."

She waved an impatient hand, knuckles speckled and thick. "I don't talk to them. They haven't cut that hedge in the last fifteen years. I pay the paperboy to come in once a month and trim it up. Otherwise, it'd grow clear up through the telephone wires. They have a dog comes over in my yard, too. Does his business everywhere. I can't step a foot out without getting dog doodie on my shoe. My husband's always saying, 'Pee-you, Ethel. There's dog doodie on your shoe again.' "

I took out one of my business cards, jotting the number of the nursing home on the back. "Could I leave you my card? That way if you hear anything, you can give me a call. We'd appreciate your help."

The woman took it reluctantly. It was clear she didn't have much interest in geriatric runaways. "What's this woman's name?"

"Agnes Grey."

"What's she look like? I can't very well identify someone I've never laid eyes on before."

I described Agnes briefly. With Irene standing there, I couldn't very well suggest that Agnes looked like an ostrich.

"I'll keep an eye out," she said. And then the door closed.

We tried the next house, and the next, with about the same results. By the time we reached the corner, forty-five minutes had gone by. It was slow work and so far, unproductive. No one had seen Agnes. We headed east on Concorde. A UPS truck approached and we waited on the curb until we'd seen it pass. I put a hand under Irene's arm as we crossed the street, supervising her safety as Dietz supervised mine.

A fine tremor seemed to be vibrating through the dark green silk of her dress. I studied her uneasily. Years of bleaching had left her hair a harsh white-blond, very thin, as if she'd succeeded finally in eliminating any whisper of color from the wispy strands. She had no brows to speak of, just two brown lines she'd penciled in by hand, wide arcs like a child might have drawn on a happy face. I could see that she might have been considered a beauty once upon a time. Her features were fine, the blue eyes unusual in their clarity. One of her false lashes had come loose, sticking out like a tiny feather. Her complexion was too pale to seem healthy, but the texture of her skin was remarkable. She reminded me of an obscure one-role movie actress of the forties—someone you're surprised to find alive after all these years. She put a trembling hand on mine, her fingers so icy that I drew back in alarm. Her breathing was rapid and shallow.

"Irene, my God. Your hands are like ice. Are you all right?"

"This happens now and then. I'll be fine in a minute."

"Let's find you a place to sit down," I said. We were approaching a three-story clapboard house, tall and narrow with a porch on three sides. The yard was sunny, with the grass newly mown and not much attention to the flower beds. I knew it was a board-and-care because Rosie and I had been given the address. I'd never actually seen the inside of the house. Once Rosie realized there was no wheelchair access, we had crossed it off our list. I remembered the owner as an energetic fellow in his seventies, pleasant enough, but apparently not equipped to handle anyone who wasn't ambulatory. I'd already opened the shrieking iron gate and I could see the front curtain move as someone peered out. This seemed to be a neighborhood where people were on the watch. I couldn't believe Agnes had managed to get even half a block without someone spotting her.

We reached the front porch and Irene sank down on the bottom step. She put her head between her knees. I put a hand on the back of her neck, peering closely at her face. I could hear the wheezing in her throat.

"You want to lie down?"

"No, please. I'll be fine. It's my asthma acting up. I don't want a fuss made. Just let me sit here for a bit."

"Just slow your breathing down, okay? You're starting to hyperventilate. I don't want you passing out."

I checked the street for Clyde, but he was nowhere to be seen. I climbed the steps and crossed to the front door. The owner of the board-and-care emerged just as I was preparing to ring the bell.

He was a man who might have been hefty in his youth. Once-muscular shoulders had softened with age, sloping beneath his shirt. He was clean-shaven and balding, his extended forehead giving him a look of babyhood. He had pouches under his eyes and a mole stuck to his left cheek, like a raisin. "Something I can help you with?" His eyes strayed to Irene and I found my gaze following his. If she fainted, I was going to have a real problem on my hands.

"She'll be all right. She's feeling light-headed and just needs to sit down for a bit," I said. "A woman's disappeared from the nursing home down the block and we're checking with the neighbors, hoping someone's seen her."

He had focused on my face, surveying me quizzically. "You look familiar. Do I know you?"

"Kinsey Millhone," I said. "I was here a couple of weeks ago with a friend of mine—"

"Right, right, right. I remember now. Spunky little redhead with a sister in a wheelchair. I was sorry we couldn't accommodate her. She the one who's missing?"

"No. This is someone else," I said. I held a hand up above my own head, describing her again. "Tall, very thin. She's been gone since early this morning and we can't seem to get a line on her. I can't believe she got far."

"Some of those old folk move fast," he said. "They can fool you if you don't keep an eye out. Wish I could help you, but I've been working in the back. Have you called the police?"

"They were notified first thing. I understand they've searched this whole area. We thought we'd try again."

"Happens occasionally, especially in this neighborhood. Usually they turn up."

"Let's hope. Thanks, anyway."

His gaze strayed back to Irene still sitting on the bottom step. "How about a glass of water for your friend?"

"She'll be okay, but thanks," I said. I closed the conversation with my usual request for assistance. "Here. Let me leave you my card. If you see the woman or talk to anyone who might have noticed her, could you let me know? If I'm not available, you can always call the nursing home."

He took my card. "Certainly," he said. Someone spoke to him from inside, a feeble voice, faintly petulant. He excused himself and went in.

I helped Irene up. We made our way down the walk and out the gate. She was shaky on her feet, her face drawn and tense.

"I really think I ought to take you back," I said.

She shook her head emphatically. "Not yet. I'm feeling better." She straightened her back as if to illustrate the point.

I could see a fine mist of sweat beading on her forehead, but she seemed determined to go on. I had my doubts, but there wasn't much I could do. "One more, then," I said, "and then we'll check back with Clyde."

The house next door was a blocky bungalow with a low-pitched roof, a story and a half sheathed in fawn-brown clapboard. The porch was open and wide, the overhang supported on squat brick stanchions with wooden railings between. We were heading up the walk when I saw one of the wooden porch rails split, raw wood opening up like a flower blossoming. I heard a popping sound and glass broke. I jumped, thinking that some shift in the earth was causing the structure to snap apart. I heard Dietz's Porsche roar around the corner to our left. I turned to look for him and registered peripherally the UPS delivery truck still idling at the curb. The UPS man was coming up the walk behind us. He was smiling at me and I felt myself smile automatically in response. He was a big man, muscular, clean-shaven, with blond curly hair, stark blue eyes in a tan face, full mouth curving into dimpled cheeks. I thought I must know him because he seemed glad to see me, his eyes soft, the look on his face both sensual and warm. He moved nearer, bending toward me, almost as if he meant to kiss me. He was so close I registered the heady bouquet of his personal scent: gunpowder, Aqua Velva aftershave, and a whiff of Juicy Fruit chewing gum. I felt myself drawing back, perplexed. Behind me, wood snapped like a tree being cracked by lightning. I could see his face suffuse with heat, like a lover at the moment of his climax. He said something. I glanced down at his hands. He seemed to be holding the nozzle of a hose, but why would a UPS man wear gardening gloves? Light spurted from the hose. I blinked uncomprehendingly and then I understood. I grabbed Irene by the arm, nearly lifting her off her feet. I hauled her up the two low stairs and toward the front door. The occupant of the house, a middle-aged man, was opening the front screen, puzzled by the noise. I could tell from his expression he wasn't expecting company. I snagged him by his shirtfront and shoved him aside, pushing him out of the line of fire as I shouldered us through the door. A front window shattered, spraying glass across the floor. Irene and I went down in a heap. She was too surprised to shriek, but I could hear the wind being knocked out of her as she hit the bare hardwood floor. The door banged back on its hinges, exposing the hallway and the stairs. The owner of the house had taken refuge in the living room, crouched beside the sofa, his arms folded across his head. He reminded me of a little kid who believes he's invisible just because his eyes are squeezed shut. A bullet ripped a hole through the back wall. Plaster dust blew inward like a bomb going off, with a fine cloud rising in its wake.

There was silence. I heard someone running, pounding steps receding in the grass, and I knew instinctively that Dietz would give chase. Crouching, I duck-waddled my way into the dining room and peered cautiously out the side window, eyes barely above the sill. I saw Dietz round the corner of the house and disappear. Behind me, Irene was beginning to wail, from fear, from injury, from shock and bewilderment. Belatedly, I felt a rush of adrenaline that made my heart thunder in my throat. My mouth went dry. I clung to the windowsill and laid my cheek against the cold wall, which was papered in cabbage roses, maroon and pink on a field of gray. I closed my eyes. In my mind, the moment was being played out all over again. First the man . . . that warm light in his eyes, mouth curving up in a familiar smile. The sense that he meant to kiss me, husky voice saying something, then the muzzle flash. From the sound, I knew he'd had a suppressor on the gun, but I'd seen light spurt out. Didn't seem likely in daylight unless my mind had somehow supplied the image out of past experience. How many shots had he fired? Five? Six?

Dietz came into the house, striding across the room. He was winded, tightly controlled, sweating, his manner grim. He pulled me to my feet, his face stony. I could feel his hands digging into my upper arms, but I couldn't voice a protest.

"Are you okay?"

He gave me a shake and I nodded, feeling mute. He set me aside like a rag doll and moved away, crossing to Irene who was weeping as piteously as a three-year-old. She sat on the floor with her legs spread, skirt askew, arms limp in her lap, her palms turned up. Dietz put an arm around her, pulling her close. He kept his voice low, reassuring her, bending down so she could hear. He asked her a question. I saw her shake her head. She was gasping, unable to say more than a few words before she was forced to stop for breath.

The owner of the house was standing in the hallway, his fear having given way to outrage. "What's going on here? What is this, a drug bust? I open my door and I nearly get myself killed! Look at the damages. Who's going to pay for this?"

Dietz said, "Shut up and call the cops."

"Who are you? You can't talk to me that way! This is a private residence."

I sank down on a dining room chair. Through the front window, I could see that neighbors had begun to congregate, murmuring anxiously among themselves—little groups of two and three, some standing in the yard.

What had the man said to me? I ran it back again: I'd heard Dietz's car rumbling in the street and that's when I'd turned, smiling at the man who was smiling at me. I could hear his words now, understood at last what he'd said to me as he approached—"You're mine, babe"—his tone possessive, secretive, and then the incredible sexual heat in his face. I felt tears rise, blurring my vision. The window shimmered. My hands began to shake.

Dietz patted Irene's arm and returned to me. He hunkered at my side, his face level with mine. "You did great. You were fine. There was no way you could have known that would happen, okay?"

I had to squeeze my hands between my knees so the shaking wouldn't travel up my arms. I looked at Dietz's face, gray eyes, the blunt nose. "He tried to kill me."

"No, he didn't. He tried to scare you. He could have killed you the first time, in Brawley on the road. He could have nailed you just now with the first shot he fired. If he kills you, the game is over. That isn't what he wants. He's not a pro. He's sick. We can use that to get him. Can you understand what I'm saying? Now we know his weakness."

"Yeah, it's me," I said, forever flip. Actually, I didn't understand much of anything. I'd looked into the face of Death. I'd mistaken him for a friend. Other people had tried to kill me—out of vengeance, out of hate. It had never really seemed personal until the man on the walk. No one had ever connected to me as intimately as he had.

I glanced over at Irene. Her respiratory distress, instead of subsiding, seemed to be getting worse. Her breathing was rapid, shallow, and ineffectual, the wheezing in her throat like two high-pitched notes on a bagpipe. Her fingertips were turning a shadowy blue. She was suffocating where she sat. "She needs help," I said.

Dietz turned to look at her. "Oh hell . . ."

He was on his feet instantly, striding across the room. The owner of the house was standing at the telephone, repeating his address to the police dispatcher.

Dietz said, "We need an ambulance, too," and then to Irene, "Take it easy. You'll be fine. We'll have help for you soon. Don't panic . . ."

I saw Irene nod, which was as much as she could manage.

In the midst of the confusion, Clyde Gersh appeared, drawn by the scattering of neighbors who were standing out in front. He told me later that when he saw the damages to the house his first thought was that Agnes had been discovered and had put up some kind of fight. The last thing he expected was to see Irene on the floor in the midst of a stage III asthma attack. Within minutes, the cops arrived, along with the paramedics, who administered oxygen and first aid, loaded Irene on a gurney, and hustled her away. In the meantime, I felt strangely removed. I knew what was expected and I did as I was told. I rendered a detailed account of events in a monotone, letting Dietz fill in the background. I'm not sure how much time passed before Dietz was allowed to take me home. Time had turned sluggish and it seemed like hours. I never even heard the name of the guy who owned the house. The last glimpse I saw of him, he was standing on the porch, looking like the sole survivor of an 8.8 earthquake.

14

➡ ➡ ➡ When we got home, I fumbled my way up to the loft. I pulled my shoes off. I stretched out on the bed, propping the pillows up behind me while I took stock of myself. All the niggling aches and pains in my body were gone, washed away by the wave of adrenaline that had tumbled over me during the attack. I was feeling drained, lethargic, my brain still crackling while my body was immobilized. Downstairs, I heard the murmur of Dietz talking on the phone.

I must have dozed, sitting upright. Dietz appeared. I opened my eyes to find him perched on the bed beside me. He was holding some papers in one hand and a mug of tea in the other. "Drink this," he said.

I took the mug and held it, focusing on the heat. Tea has always smelled better than it tastes. I can still remember how startled I was as a kid when I was first allowed to have a sip. I glanced up at the skylight, which showed a circle of lavender and smoke. "What time is it?"

"Ten after seven."

"Have we heard from Clyde?"

136

"He called a little while ago. She's fine. They treated her and sent her home. No sign of Agnes yet. How are you?"

"Better."

"That's good. We'll have some supper in a bit. Henry's bringing something over."

"I hate being taken care of."

"Me, too, but that's bullshit. Henry likes to feel useful, I'm starving, and neither of us cook. You want to talk?"

I shook my head. "My soul's not back in my body yet."

"It'll come. I got a line on the guy from the L.A. police. You want to take a look?"

"All right."

There was a sheaf of LAPD bulletins, maybe six. I studied the first. WANTED FELONY TRAFFIC SUSPECTS. There were ten mug shots—like class photos—one circled in ballpoint pen. It was him. He looked younger. He looked pale. He looked glum—one of life's chronic offenders at the outset of his career. His name was Mark Darian Messinger, alias: Mark Darian; alias: Darian Marker; alias: Buddy Messer; alias: Darian Davidson. Male, Caucasian, thirty-eight years old, blond hair, blue eyes, tattoo of a butterfly on the web of his right hand (I'd missed that). His date of birth was July 7, Cancer, a real family man at heart. His California driver's license number was listed, his Social Security number, his NCIC file number, FBI number, his department report number, his warrant number. The arrest, apparently in the summer of 1981, was for violation of Vehicle Code Section 20001 (hit-and-run resulting in death) and Penal Code Section 192(3)(a) (vehicular manslaughter while driving under the influence). The photograph was an inch and a half wide square, taken straight on. It helped to see him shrunk down to Lilliputian proportions, the size of a postage stamp. He looked like a low-life punk, the black-and-white mug shot not nearly as sinister as the flesh-and-blood reality.

The second police bulletin read: ARREST FOR MURDER OF A POLICE OFFICER, Felony Warrant LACA, with a string of numbers, charging Penal Code Section 187(a) (murder) and Section 664/187 (attempted murder) with a six-line narrative attached. "On October 9, 1981, two Los Angeles police officers responded to a domestic disturbance during which the above suspect fired an unknown type semiautomatic at his common-law wife. When the police officers attempted to subdue him, suspect shot one of the officers in the face, resulting in his death. The suspect then fled on foot."

The names of two detectives, assigned to the case, were listed below that, along with several telephone numbers if information came to light. At the bottom of the page was a line in bold print. KINDLY NOTIFY CHIEF OF POLICE, LOS ANGELES, CALIFORNIA, it said. KINDLY KILL THIS MAN ON SIGHT, I thought.

The third bulletin was dated less than two months back. ONE MILLION DOLLAR ROBBERY INFORMATION WANTED. And there he was again, in a police composite drawing, this time with a mustache, which he must have shaved off in the interim. According to the victim's account, the suspect had followed a wholesale gold dealer into a gold exchange business in the Jewelry Mart section of downtown Los Angeles on March 25, where he relieved the victim of the gold he was transporting, valued in excess of $625,000. The suspect had produced a gun and robbed the victim and another employee of an additional $346,000 in gold "granules" and $46,000 in cash. Mark Messinger had been identified from fingerprints at the scene.

I leafed through the remaining bulletins. There was apparently no crime Mark Messinger was incapable of committing—the well-rounded felon with a major in murder and minors in armed robbery and assault with a deadly weapon. He seemed to operate with equal parts impulse and brute force. He didn't go in for the intellectual stuff, nothing with finesse. The million-dollar robbery was probably the most sophisticated thing he'd ever done.

"Now we know how he can afford to take on a cut-rate hit," I said.

Dietz tapped the paper, pointing to one of the last lines of print. A brief note indicated that the suspect was reported to have relatives in Santa Teresa. "That's how he knew Tyrone Patty. From here. They were cellmates in the county jail four years ago. I guess they kept in touch."

"Have the cops here talked to his family?"

Dietz nodded. "No luck. His father claims he hasn't talked to Messinger in years. He's probably lying, but you can't do much about that. Dolan says they delivered a stern lecture about aiding and abetting. The old man swore a Boy Scout oath he'd notify the cops if the guy showed up."

I could feel a knot of dread begin to form in my gut. "Let's talk about something else."

"Let's talk about fighting back."

"Tomorrow," I said. "Right now, I'm not in the mood."

"Drink your tea and get cleaned up. I'll see you downstairs."

Henry had put together a meal of comfort foods: succulent meatloaf with mushroom gravy, mashed potatoes, fresh green beans, homemade rolls, fresh lemon meringue pie, and coffee. He ate with us, saying little, watching me with worried eyes. Dietz must have cautioned him not to chide me for leaving the premises. It was clear Henry wanted to fuss, but he had the presence of mind to keep his mouth shut. I felt guilty anyway, as if the attempt on my life was something I had done. Henry studied the police bulletins, memorizing Mark Messinger's face and the details of his (alleged) crimes. "A nasty piece of work. You mentioned a little boy. How does he figure into this?" he said to Dietz.

"He kidnapped the kid from his common-law wife. Her name is Rochelle. She works in a massage parlor down in Hollywood. I talked to her a little while ago and the woman's a mess. The kid's name is Eric. He's five. He was enrolled in a day-care center in Rochelle's neighborhood. Messinger picked him up about eight months ago and that's the last she's seen of him. I got boys of my own. I'd kill anyone came after them." Dietz ate like he did everything else, with intense concentration. When he finished the last scrap of food, he sat back, patting automatically at the shirt pocket where he'd kept his cigarettes. I saw a quick head shake, as if he were amused at himself.

They moved on to other subjects: sports, the stock market, political events. While they talked, I gathered the empty plates and utensils and took them to the kitchenette. I ran a sinkful of soapy water and slid the dishes in. There's nothing so restful as washing dishes when you need to separate yourself from other folk. It looks dutiful and industrious and it's soothing as a bubble bath. For the moment, I felt safe. I didn't care if I ever left the apartment again. What was wrong with staying right here? I could learn to cook and clean house. I could iron clothes (if I had any). Maybe I could learn to sew and make craft items out of Popsicle sticks. I just didn't want to go out again. I was beginning to feel about the real world as I did about swimming in the ocean. Off the Santa Teresa coast, the waters of the Pacific are murky and cold, filled with USTs (unidentified scary things) that can hurt you real bad: organisms made of jelly and slime, crust-covered creatures with stingers and horny pincers that can rip your throat out. Mark Messinger was like that: vicious, implacable, dead at heart.

Henry left at ten o'clock. Dietz turned the TV on, waiting up for the news while I went back to bed. I stirred twice during the night, glancing at the clock; once at 1:15 A.M., and again at 2:35. The light was still on downstairs and I knew Dietz was awake. He seemed to thrive on very little sleep while I never got quite enough. The light coming over the loft rail was a cheery yellow. Anyone coming after me would be forced to contend with him. Reassured, I drifted off again.

Given my anxiety level, I slept well and woke with some of my old energy, which lasted almost until I got downstairs. Dietz was still in the shower. I made sure the front door was locked. I considered loitering outside the bathroom, listening to him sing, but I was afraid he'd catch me at it and perhaps take offense. I made a pot of coffee, set out the milk, the cereal boxes, and the bowls. I peered out one of the windows, opening the wooden shutter just a crack. All I could see was a slit of the flower bed. I pictured Messinger across the street with a bolt-action sniper rifle with a 10x scope trained so he could blow my head off the minute I stirred. I retreated to the kitchenette and poured some orange juice. I hadn't felt this threatened since my first day in elementary school.

Coming out of the bathroom, Dietz seemed surprised to find me up. He was wearing chinos and a form-fitting white T-shirt. He looked solid and muscular, without an ounce of extra fat. He disarmed the portable alarm system, opened the door, and brought the paper in. I noticed I was careful to hang back out of the line of fire. Some forms of mental illness probably feel just like this. I pulled a stool out and sat down.

He tossed the paper on the counter and then did a brief detour into the living room. He came back with the Davis, which he'd apparently taken from my purse. He placed it on the counter in front of me. He poured himself some coffee and sat down on the stool across from mine.

I murmured, "Good morning."

He nodded at the Davis. "I want you to dump that."

"What for?"

"It's a pocket pistol. Useless under the circumstances."

I resisted the temptation to say something flip. "I just got that!"

"Get another one."

"But why?"

"It's cheap and unreliable. It's not safe to carry with a round in the chamber, which means you have to keep the magazine full, the chamber empty, and the safety off. If you're in trouble, I don't want you having to rack the slide to chamber a round in order to put it into action. You can get a new holster while you're at it."

I stared at him. He didn't seem that impressed with the look I was giving him.

He said, "Where's the closest gun shop?"

"I don't have the money. You're talkin' five or six hundred bucks."

141

"More like eleven hundred for the gun you should have."

"Which is what?"

"Heckler & Koch P7 in nine-millimeter. You can get it used somewhere. It's the latest yuppie firearm. It looks good in the glove compartment of a BMW, but it's still right for you."

"Forget it!" I said.

This time he stared at *me*.

I felt myself faltering. "Even if I bought a gun today, I'd have to wait two weeks to pick it up."

"You can use the Davis until then, but not with those cartridges. You should be using a high-velocity hollow-point like the Winchester Silvertip or a prefragmented round like the Glaser Safety Slug. I suggest the Winchester Silvertip."

"Why those?" Actually it didn't matter. I was just feeling stubborn and argumentative.

He ticked his reasons off, using his fingers for emphasis. "It's less expensive for one thing and it's fairly widely used by law enforcement. With the underpowered thirty-two round, penetration is the most important—"

"All right. I got it," I said irritably. "Is that all you did last night? Sit around thinking up this stuff?"

"That's all I did," he said. He opened the paper and checked the front page. "Actually I have a Colt .45 out in the car. You can practice with both guns when we go up to the firing range."

"When are we doing that?"

"After the gun shop opens at ten."

"I don't want to go out."

"We're not going to let the guy affect your life this way." His gray eyes came up to mine. "Okay?"

"I'm scared," I said.

"Why do you think we're doing this?"

"What about the banquet?"

"I think we should go. He won't make another move for days. He wants you to think about your mortality. He wants your anxiety to mount until you jump every time the phone rings."

"I already do that."

"Have some breakfast. You'll feel better."

I poured my cereal and some milk, still brooding while I ate.

Dietz broke the silence, looking across the paper at me. "I want to say one thing again so listen carefully," he said. "A truly professional assassin kills either at close range or very long range. Up close, the weapon of choice would probably be a suppressed .22 long rifle with subsonic ammunition. From a distance, a bolt-action .308. Messinger is a bad-ass, but he's also an amateur. I'm going to nail him."

"What if he gets you first?"

"He won't." He went back to the sports section.

I felt better, I swear to God.

15

▄▄ ▄▄ ▄▄ Dietz and I went to the office first. I checked
my answering machine (no messages) while he glanced at the
mail from the day before (no letter bombs). I locked up again
and we went next door to the California Fidelity offices,
where Vera was just getting in. She was wearing a two-piece
outfit of red parachute material, long flowing skirt, blousy
top with long sleeves and a red belt at the waist. Since I'd seen
her yesterday, her hair had turned very blond, with streaks,
and her glasses had changed to aviator shades with blue
lenses. As usual she looked like the kind of woman any guy
would love to jump out of an airplane with, an effect that
wasn't lost on Dietz. She was carrying a garment on a hanger,
covered by a cleaning bag. "Oh hi. You guys going tonight?"

"That's what we stopped by to tell you," I said. "Should I
call the hotel?"

"I already did that," she said. "I figured you'd be there.
This is for you." She indicated the cleaning bag. "Come on
back to my office and you can take a look. This is girl stuff,"
she said to Dietz. "You still off cigarettes?"

"Day three," he said.

I hadn't realized he was counting.

144

"This is day seven for me," she said.

"How are you doing?"

"Not too bad. I've got all this manic energy. I feel amped. I must have counted on the nicotine to mellow me out. What about you?"

"I'm okay," he said mildly. "I like to do things to test myself."

"I'll bet you do," she said and laughed down in her throat. "We'll be back in a sec." She breezed on toward the back.

"Was that nasty, what you said to him? It sounded nasty," I asked, scurrying to keep up.

She glanced over her shoulder. "Listen, babycakes, when I get around to nasty you won't have any doubts."

She anchored the hanger over the edge of her cubicle and stuck an unlit Virginia Slim in her mouth, dragging on it cold. She closed her eyes, as if praying. "Oh God, for a light . . . for smoke . . . for the first heady hit of a cigarette . . ." She opened her eyes and shook her head. "I hate doing things that are good for me. Why did I decide to do this?"

"You were coughing up blood."

"Oh yeah. I forgot that part. Ah well. Take a look." She eased the plastic bag off the hanger. Under it was a black silk jumpsuit with spaghetti straps and a tiny belt. The matching jacket had a Mandarin collar and long sleeves. "What do you think?"

"It looks perfect."

"Good. Make sure it fits. Otherwise give me a call and I'll scare up something else. You can bring it with you at six and get dressed in my room. I'm staying at the Edgewater so I won't have to drive myself home afterward. I hate having to monitor my alcohol intake."

"Don't you have a date? I thought you'd be coming with Neil."

"I'm meeting him there. That way he's free to do anything he wants. I'll bring the jewelry tonight and maybe help you do something with your hair. I can tell I'm going to have to dress you."

"Vera, I'm not helpless."

145

"Of course you're not *helpless*. You're completely ignorant when it comes to clothes. I'll bet you've never even had your colors done."

I gave a little noncommittal shrug, trying to look like I had my colors done sometimes twice a week.

"Don't bother. You're a Summer. I can save you the fifty bucks. You shouldn't wear black, but to hell with it. You'll look great." She paused to study my face. "Very becoming, those bruises . . . especially the one turning green." She began to ease the plastic bag back over the outfit, unlit cigarette bobbing from the corner of her mouth. "How's it feel to spend twenty-four hours a day with a hunk?"

"You mean Dietz?"

Vera sighed and rolled her eyes. "No, I'm talking about Don Knotts. Never mind. You probably like him because he's competent, right?"

"Well, yeah. Isn't that the point?" I said. "You know what puzzles me? How come I'm surrounded by bossy people? Rosie, Dietz, Henry . . . now you."

"You're cute, you know that? You think you're such a hard-ass."

"I *am* a hard-ass," I said defensively.

"Neil's going to love you. Have you called him yet?"

"I haven't had a chance. We just got back."

"He's only coming tonight to meet you. Just remember. Don't eat."

I squinted at her. "How come? This is a retirement dinner, isn't it?"

"Suppose you want to go to bed with him."

"I don't," I said.

"But suppose you did."

"What's that got to do with eating dinner?"

She was losing patience with me, but stopped to spell it out. "Never go to bed with a guy after a big meal. Your stomach will pooch out."

"Why would I go to bed with a guy I can't have a big meal with first?"

146

"You can eat later, when you're married."

I had to laugh. "I'm not getting married later, but thanks for the tip."

"You're welcome. See you tonight."

I found Dietz sitting out by Darcy's desk, leafing through a pamphlet on uninsured losses. I took the outfit downstairs with us, tucking it carefully in his trunk when we reached the parking lot. "There's no way I'm wearing any body armor under this," I said.

Dietz made no comment and I took that for assent.

On our way to the firing range, we stopped by the gun shop and spent an hour bickering about guns. He knew far more than I did and I had to yield to his expertise. I left a deposit on an H&K P7 in 9-millimeter, filling out all the necessary paperwork. I ended up paying twenty-five bucks for fifty rounds of the Winchester Silvertips Dietz had insisted on. In exchange for my compliance, he had the good taste not to mention that all of this was his idea. I'd expected to find it galling to take his advice, but in reality, it felt fine. What did I have to prove? He'd been at it a lot longer than I had and he seemed to know what he was talking about.

Dietz drove up the pass in his little red Porsche like a man pursued. Maybe we were practicing for a car chase later on. The Porsche was not equipped with passenger brakes, but I kept my foot jammed to the floorboards in hopes. From where I sat, it looked like one of those camera's-eye views of the Indy 500, only speeding straight uphill. I was wishing I believed in an afterlife, as I was about to enjoy mine. Dietz didn't seem to notice my discomfiture. Since he was totally focused on the road, I didn't want to spoil his concentration with the piercing screams I was having to suppress.

The gun club was deserted except for the rangemaster, to whom we paid our fees. The May sun was hot, the breezes dry, scented with bay laurel and sage. The rains wouldn't come again until Christmastime. By August, the mountains would be parched, the vegetation desiccated, the timber primed for burning. Even now, looking down toward the valley, I could see a haze in the air, ghostly portent of the fires to come.

Dietz set up a B-27 human silhouette target at a distance of seven yards. I'd been practicing with the Davis at twenty-five yards, but Dietz just shook his head. "A .32's designed for self-defense inside fifteen yards, preferably inside ten. The round has to penetrate deeply enough to get to the vital organs and blood vessels, eight to ten inches in. The Silvertip has a better chance of getting far enough to make a difference."

"Nice business we're in," I said.

"Why do you think I'm getting out?"

I loaded the magazine on my little Davis while he detailed an exercise he referred to as a Mozambique drill. He had me start from the guard position: pistol loaded, round chambered, safety on, finger off the trigger, pointing at a forty-five-degree angle downward. "Bring the pistol up to shooting position and fire two quick shots into the upper chest, level with the sternum. Do a quick visual check to see where you've hit and then fire a third more careful shot into the head right around here," he said, indicating his eye sockets.

I put on my ear protectors and did as I was told, feeling self-conscious at first under his scrutiny. It was clear that in the years since the police academy, my skills had deteriorated. I'd come up here often, on an average of once a month, but I'd begun to think of it almost as a meditation instead of schooling in self-defense. Left to my own devices, I'd been neither rigorous nor exact. Dietz was a good teacher, patient, methodical, suggesting corrections in a way that never made me feel criticized.

"Now let's try it with your gun in your purse," he said when he was satisfied.

"How do you know all this stuff?"

He smiled faintly. "Weapons are a passion of mine. My first formal training in defensive pistolcraft was a class designed for certifying security guards to carry weapons on the job. The practical shooting part was minimal, but it did give me a fair grounding in the laws related to firearms. I went to the American Pistol Institute after that." He paused. "Are we up here to work or chat?"

"I get to choose?" I said.

Apparently not. He had me try the .45, but it was too much gun for me coming off the .32. He relented on that point and let me continue with the Davis. We went back to work, the smell of gunpowder perfuming the air as I concentrated on the process. I'd ceased to think about Mark Messinger as a person. He'd become an abstract—no more than a flat, black silhouette seven yards away—with a paper heart, paper brain. It was therapeutic firing at him, watching his midriff shred. My fearfulness began to fall away and my confidence returned. I fired at his paper neck and hit an inky artery. I pretended to tattoo my initials on his trunk. By the time we packed up and left the range at noon, I was feeling like my old self again.

We had lunch at the Stage Coach Tavern, tucked up against the mountain with a stream trickling down through the rocks close by. Live oak and bay laurel kept the tavern shrouded in chill shade. The quiet was undercut by the gossiping of the birds. Only an occasional car climbed the grade out in front, heading for the main road. Dietz was still vigilant—scanning the premises—but he seemed more at ease somehow, sipping beer, one foot propped up on the crude wooden bench where he sat. I was seated on his left with my back to the wall, watching as he did, though there wasn't much to see. There were only three other customers, bikers sitting at one of the rough plank tables outside.

We'd ordered the chili verde, which the waitress brought: two wide bowls of fragrant pork and green chili stew with a dollop of cilantro pesto on top and two folded flour tortillas submerged in the depths. This might be as close to heaven as a sinner could get without repenting first.

"What's your deal with California Fidelity?" he asked, between bites.

"They provide me office space and I provide them services

maybe two or three times a month. It varies. Usually I investigate fire and wrongful death claims, but it could be anything."

"Nice arrangement. How'd you set that up?"

"My aunt worked for them for years so I knew a lot of those guys. She used to get me occasional summer jobs when I was still in high school. I went through the academy when I was nineteen and since I couldn't actually join the PD till I was twenty-one, I worked as the CF receptionist. Later, after I finally left the police force, I joined a private agency until I could get licensed, and then I went out on my own. One of the first big investigations I did was for CF."

"A lot more women getting into it," he said.

"Why not? It's fun, in some sick sense. You end up feeling pretty hard-bitten sometimes, but at least you can be your own boss. It's in my nature. I'm curious at heart and I like sticking my nose in where it doesn't belong," I said. "What about you? What will you do if you leave the field?"

"Hard to say. I'm talking to a guy out in Colgate who sets up antiterrorist training exercises for military bases overseas."

"Simulated attacks?"

"That's right. Dead of night, he takes a crew in, breaches perimeter fences, infiltrates the compound, and puts the whole maneuver on film to show 'em where they need to beef up their defenses."

"Cops and robbers without the firepower."

"Exactly. All the hype and none of the jeopardy." He paused, mopping the bottom of his bowl with a folded tortilla. "You look like you've got all your ducks in a row."

"I feel that way," I said. "Vera would disagree. She thinks I'm hopeless. Too independent, unsophisticated . . ."

"What's the story on her?"

"I've never figured it out, to tell you the truth. She's the closest thing to a friend I've got and even then, I can't claim we know each other very well. I'm gone a lot so I don't socialize much. She tends to circulate in the singles scene, which I've never been good at. I do admire her. She's smart. She's got style. She doesn't take any guff . . ."

"What is this, a sales pitch?"

I laughed, shrugging. "You asked."

"Yeah, well she's one of those women I've never figured out."

"In what way?"

"Don't know. I never figured that out either. Just something about her puzzles me," he said.

"She's a good soul."

"No doubt." He finished cleaning his bowl without another word on the subject. It was hard to tell sometimes what he was really thinking and I didn't know him well enough to press.

16

We left for the hotel at six. Dietz had already cleaned up and was dressed for the occasion in casual pants, a dress shirt, patterned tie, and dark sport coat, cut western-style: broad across the shoulders, tapered at the waist. He was wearing black boots, visible where his cuffs broke, the toes polished to a hard shine. Under his sport coat, of course, he was wearing a Kevlar vest that would stop a .357 Magnum at ten feet. I'd also watched him strap on a holster that he wore behind the hip on his right-hand side, and into which he'd tucked his .45.

I'd showered and hopped right back in my jeans, turtle-neck, and tennis shoes, intending to slip into the silk jump-suit once I reached Vera's room. I'd tried it on quickly just before we left the house. The pants were slightly too long, but I'd bunched 'em up at the waist and that took care of it. I'd packed black pumps, panty hose, black underpants, and some odds and ends in a little overnight case. Dietz had excused me from the bulletproof vest, which would have looked absurd with spaghetti straps. The Davis was tucked in an outside pouch of my big leather handbag, which looked more like a diplomatic pouch than an evening purse. The normally bulky bag was further plumped up by the inclusion of a nightscope Dietz had asked me to carry. The scope only weighed about a pound, but it was the size of a zoom lens for a 35-millimeter camera and made me list to one side. "Why're we taking this thing?" I asked.

"That's my latest toy. I usually keep it in the car, but I don't want to leave it in the hotel parking lot. Cost me over three thousand bucks."

"Oh."

Dietz took a roundabout route, saying little. Despite his assurances that Mark Messinger would be laying off me for a day or two, he seemed on edge, which made my stomach churn in response. He was focused, intense, already vigilant. He pushed the car lighter in and then reached reflexively toward his cigarettes. "Shit!" he said. He shook his head, annoyed with himself.

He rounded a corner, downshifting. "Times like this I envy the guys who do government work," he remarked. "You'd have a squad of bodyguards. They've got unlimited manpower, access to intelligence sources, and the legal authority to kick butt. . . ."

I couldn't think what to say to that so I kept my mouth shut.

We pulled into the wide brick drive in front of the hotel and Dietz got out, slipping the usual folded bill to the parking attendant with instructions to keep the car within sight. It was still light outside and the landscape was saturated with late afternoon sun. The grass was close-cropped, a dense green, the lawn bordered with pink and white impatiens and clumps of lobelia, which glowed an intense, electric blue. On the far side of the road, the surf battered at the seawall, clouding the air with the briny smell of the thundering Pacific.

In addition to the Edgewater's sprawling main building, there were a line of bungalows at the rear of the property, each the size of the average single-family dwelling in my neighborhood. The architecture was Spanish-style, white stucco exterior, heavy beams, age-faded red tile roofs, interior courtyards. Under an archway that led to the formal gardens, a wedding party was beginning to assemble: five bridesmaids in dusty pink and a manic flower girl skipping back and forth with a basket of rose petals. Two young men in tuxedos, probably ushers, looked on, contemplating the efficacies of birth control.

As usual, Dietz took me by the elbow, keeping himself slightly in front of me as he walked us toward the entrance. I found myself scanning, as he did, the smattering of guests in the immediate vicinity. He was keyed up, eyes watchful as we entered the spacious lobby, which was flanked by two oversize imported rose marble desks. We approached the concierge and had a brief chat. Dietz had apparently had a second conversation with the management up front because shortly afterward, Charles Abbott, the director of security, appeared. Introductions went around. Abbott was in his late sixties and looked like a retired Fortune 500 executive in a three-piece suit, complete with manicured nails and a Rolex watch. This was not a man you'd ever refer to as Charlie or Chuck. His silver hair was the same tone as the pale gray of his suit and a diamond stickpin winked from the center of his tie. I had the feeling what he did now was lots more fun than whatever he did then. He led us over to a corner of the lobby where three big leather wing chairs were grouped together in the shelter of a ten-foot rubber plant.

Dietz had brought photocopies of the mug shots of Mark Messinger. "This is the guy we're worried about. I'd like to distribute these among the staff who'll be working the banquet tonight."

Abbott gave a cursory glance to the pictures before he handed them back. He had luminous blue eyes and made lots of eye contact. "Mr. Dietz, I have to remind you that we're not equipped to handle any kind of sophisticated security measures for a private citizen. We cooperate with the Secret Service when the occasion arises, but the hotel can't accept any liability in the event of some kind of unfortunate incident. We're here primarily to protect the safety of our registered guests. As long as I'm kept informed, we'll be happy to do what we can, but beyond that I can't promise much."

Dietz smiled. "I understand that," he said pleasantly. "This is purely precautionary on our part. We don't anticipate any problems, but it's wise to tag a few bases just to ensure that everything goes smoothly."

Abbott said, "Of course."

Dietz was on his best behavior, casual, relaxed. He must have really needed this man's help.

Abbott's expression was bemused. He looked like the kind of man who'd use a cigarette holder and a small gold Dunhill. "How else can I help? I can make one of my security staff available."

"I don't think that'll be necessary, but thanks. We do have a California Fidelity employee, Vera Lipton, registered here for the night. I'd like to have her room number and the names of guests occupying the rooms on either side of her. Is that something you can do?"

Abbott considered the request. Under the smooth and easygoing manner, there was ice and flint. "I don't see why not." He excused himself and moved over to the front desk. After a short conversation with the desk clerk, he jotted a note in a small leather notebook he'd taken from his right pocket. He returned, tore the leaf off, and handed it to Dietz.

"You know either of these couples?" Dietz asked.

"I know both. The Clarks have stayed here many times. Mr. and Mrs. Thiederman happen to be my aunt and uncle."

Dietz tucked the paper away and shook Abbott's hand. "Thanks. We appreciate this."

"Happy to be of help," the man said.

We moved down a carpeted hallway to the right, following the room numbers in descending order. Dietz kept an eye on the corridor behind us, the ever-present hand on my elbow for leverage. At any unexpected occurrence, he had a modicum of control.

Vera's room was located in the same wing as the banquet room. "Did you set this up?" I asked him when I saw how close it was.

"I didn't want you hiking the length of the hotel, getting there and back." He knocked once. There was a pause. My guess was that Vera was peering through the tiny fish-eye porthole in the door. We heard a bolt turn, and there she was, squinting at us from behind the burglar chain. She was in a green silk kimono with a lot of cleavage visible where the fabric gaped in front. She glanced down and pulled the yawning lapels together with one hand. "I kept the chain on. Wasn't that smart?"

Dietz said, "You're a peach, Vera. Now let us in."

She tilted her head, gaze angling down the hall. "How do I know somebody's not holding you at gunpoint?"

Dietz laughed. I looked at him quizzically. I'd only heard him laugh once. "Good point," he said.

I personally didn't think the point was that good, but nobody was asking me, right?

Vera closed the door so she could slide the chain off and then let us in. The room was enormous: king-size bed, king-size antique armoire housing a king-size television set. The dominant color was pale yellow: thick pale yellow carpet, wallpaper strewn with delicate white Japanese irises. The pattern of the wallpaper had been repeated in the polished cotton bedspread and matching polished cotton drapes, pulled back on brass rods. The sheers were closed, lights outside indicating that the room faced the entrance drive. The two upholstered chairs were done in pale green with white latticework cut on the diagonal. Through a doorway, I spied a bathroom that continued the color scheme: a vase of white silk flowers, fat yellow hand towels rolled up in a willow basket on the sink.

Vera had her personal effects on every conceivable surface: discarded clothing tossed on the bed, hanging clothes hooked on the closet door, which stood open to the room. There were cosmetics on the chest of drawers, hot rollers and a curling iron on the bathroom counter, a damp towel on the toilet seat. A suitcase open on the luggage rack revealed a frothy tumble of soft chiffon lingerie. A pair of panty hose had been flung on one of the upholstered chairs, sprawling there with the legs spread and the diamond-shaped cotton crotch looking like an arrow, pointing up. Dietz headed straight for the door to the adjoining room, making sure it was locked. Then he closed the drapes.

Vera crossed to the coffee table. She'd had a bottle of champagne delivered, resting in a frosted silver ice bucket with four champagne flutes on a tray. She picked the bottle up by the neck and began to loosen the foil. "Grab a seat. We can have a drink."

"Not for me, thanks. I have to work," he said. And then to me, "Keep the door locked. If the phone rings, you can answer it, but don't identify yourself. If it's someone you know, keep the conversation brief. Don't give out information of any sort to anyone. If you get a wrong number, let me know. It's probably someone checking to see if the room is still occupied." He glanced at his watch. "I'll be back at seven, straight up, to walk you over to the banquet room."

Once Dietz left the room, she held her arms up and shimmied. "Let's get down!" she said and then did a little bump and grind, accompanied by a whoop. She twisted the wire off the champagne bottle and draped a towel across the top, working the cork back and forth with both thumbs until it popped. She filled two flutes and handed me one. "I've already done my makeup," she said. "Why don't you hop in the shower while I get dressed. Then we'll do your hair."

"I've already showered. All I have to do is put on the jumpsuit and I'm done."

She gave me a look to let me know how wrong I was.

Under her critical gaze, I slipped out of my jeans and into the jumpsuit. She only winced a little bit at the sight of my bruises. Meanwhile, my facial expression was probably the equivalent of an ailing dog on its way to the vet's. Ugh. Makeup. I pulled the suit on and started tucking the pants up at the waist.

She smacked my hand. "Don't do that," she said. She knelt and turned my pant legs under to a length that suited her and then secured them with fabric tape she'd brought in her purse.

157

"You think of everything," I said.

" 'Prepared' is my middle name, honeybun."

Then she went to work on the rest of me.

I sat on the closed toilet lid with a towel around my neck, Vera's body inserted between me and the wall-to-wall mirror that ran along the countertop. "What are you going to do about the bruises on my face?"

"Trust me, kid."

She had bottles and powders, lotions, creams, goo in jars, brushes, applicators, sponges, Q-tips. She worked with her face very close to mine, issuing instructions. "Close your eyes. Now look up . . . God, quit blinking! You're making a mess." She painted on lipstick with a brush, her own lips forming the shape she wanted me to form with mine.

Forty minutes later, she stepped back, scrutinizing her handiwork. She twisted the lipstick back down in the tube. "Yeah. I like it," she said. "What do you think?" She moved aside so I could see my reflection in the mirror.

I looked at myself. Suddenly, I had these dramatic eyes, all the color of a maiden in the first blush of youth, dewy mouth, hair standing out in a dark windblown tumble. I cracked up.

"Go ahead and laugh," she said acidly. "You look damn good."

Dietz returned to the room at seven, glancing at us both without remark. Vera had done herself up in six minutes flat, her personal best she said. She was wearing a black dress with a low-cut top filled to the brim with bulging breasts, black hose with a seam up the back, black spike heels. She stopped dead in her tracks and put her hands on her hips. "What do you say, Dietz? Come on. Cough it out."

"You look great. No shit. Both of you look swell."

" 'Swell' doesn't even come close." And then to me, "I'll bet he still calls women 'gals.' "

"Not so far," I said.

Dietz smiled to himself, but refused to engage. He pro-pelled us across the hall and down three doors into the safety of the banquet room, which was small and elegant: chandelier, white woodwork, walls padded in cream-colored silk. Six tables for six had been laid out with a spray of orchids as the centerpiece. Each table was numbered and I could see that place cards were set out, names in script.

Many of the CF employees were already there, standing together in groups of three and four, drinks in hand. I spotted Mac Voorhies and his wife Marie, Jewel and her husband (whom I'd only met once), Darcy Pascoe and her boyfriend, the (allegedly) dope-peddling mailman. Vera slipped her hand through Dietz's arm and the three of us circled the room while everyone was introduced to everyone else and we all promptly forgot who was who. I could see Vera doing an eyeball cruise, checking across the heads to see if Neil Hess had arrived yet. I was just hoping he'd be tall enough for her to spot.

Dietz bought us each a drink. His was a plain soda water with lime, mine a white wine, and Vera's a tequila sunrise. She sucked that one down and bought herself another. I watched her with interest. I'd never seen Vera so tense. She turned to Dietz. "God, how can you drink without smoking a cigarette?"

"This isn't alcohol."

She rolled her eyes. "That's even worse. I'm going to bum one," she said. "No, I'm not. Well, maybe one. A puff."

"Is that Neil?" I asked. A doctorish type was poised in the doorway, searching for a familiar face. Without a reference point, of course, it wasn't possible to tell just how short he was, but he looked okay to me. Pleasant face, dark hair cut stylishly. He wore a navy suit, pale blue shirt I could have bet would have monogrammed cuffs. The bow tie was unexpected—I hadn't seen one in years. Vera raised a hand. His face brightened when he spotted her. He made his way across the room while she moved to join him, tucking her arm in his when they connected at the midpoint. She had to bend a bit to talk to him, but the disparity in their heights didn't seem remarkable to me. I tried to picture him with his head on my pillow, but it really didn't wash.

17

▰▰ ▰▰ ▰▰ Vera, in charge of the seating, had of course
set it up so that Neil Hess and I were together. She and Dietz
were at the table to our left. Dietz had apparently interceded
to some extent, arranging it so that I was secured in one
corner of the room, facing the entrance. Dietz was seated
with his back to me, facing the entrance as well so he could
keep an eye on the door. Vera was on his left, fully visible to
me while all I could see of him was the back of his head. Both
tables flanked an emergency exit that the security director
had assured Dietz would remain unlocked for us during the
course of the banquet.

By eight, everyone had arrived and the assembled group
settled at the tables like a flock of birds. The noise level had
risen several decibels as a result of the alcohol consumed.
These were company relationships and there was a sense of
giddiness and unease at the sudden shift from business to
social behaviors. The three-course dinner was served at a
leisurely pace: a salad of baby lettuces, boneless chicken
breasts sautéed with lemon and capers, miniature vegetables,
hot breads, and finally a dense chocolate cake in a puddle of
vanilla sauce. I ate like a forest animal, head coming up to

check the door at any sign of movement, worried that Mark Messinger would show up with an Uzi and mow us down like weeds. Judging from the set of Dietz's shoulders, he was more relaxed than I, but then he was staring down the front of Vera's dress, a titillating distraction for any man.

I tuned into the conversation at the table. Neil and I had been seated with two underwriters and their wives, a foursome talking bridge with an intensity I envied. I gathered they'd just returned from some kind of bridge-oriented cruise in which baby slams and gourmet foods were served up in equal measure. Much talk of no-trump, double finesses, and Sheinwold, whose strategies they were debating. Since neither Neil nor I played, we were left to our own devices, a possibility Vera had probably calculated well in advance.

At close range, the man was attractive enough, though I saw no particular evidence of all the virtues Vera had ascribed to him. Nice hands. Nice mouth. Seemed a bit self-satisfied, but that might have been discomfort masquerading as arrogance. I noticed that when we talked about professional matters (his work, in other words) he exuded confidence. When it came to his personal life, he was unsure of himself and usually shifted the subject to safer ground. By the time the dessert came, we were still groping our way through various conversational gambits, casting about for common interests without much success.

"Where'd you go to school, Kinsey?"

"Santa Teresa High."

"I meant college."

"I didn't go to college."

"Oh really? That surprises me. You seem smart enough."

"People don't hire me for 'smart.' They hire me because I'm too dumb to know when to quit. Also, I'm a woman, so they think I'll work cheap."

He laughed. I wasn't being funny so I gave a little shrug.

He pushed his dessert plate aside and took a sip of coffee. "If you got a degree, you could write your own ticket, couldn't you?"

I looked at him. "A degree in what?"

"Criminalistics, I would guess."

"Then I'd have to go to work for the government or the local cops. I already did that and hated it. I'm better off where I am. Besides, I hated school, too. All I did was smoke dope." I leaned toward him. "Now can I ask you one?"

"Sure."

"How did you and Vera meet?"

He was almost imperceptibly disconcerted, shifting slightly in his seat. "A mutual friend introduced us a couple of months ago. We've been seeing each other ever since . . . just as friends, of course. Nothing serious."

"Oh yeah, right," I said. "So what do you think?"

"About Vera? She's terrific."

"How come you're sitting here with me, then?"

He laughed again, a false, hearty roar that avoided a reply.

"I'm serious," I said. His smile cooled down by degrees. He still wasn't addressing the issue so I tried it myself. "You know what I think it is? I got the impression she had the hots for you herself and didn't know how to handle it."

He gave me a look like I was speaking in tongues. "I have a hard time believing *that,*" he said. He thought about it for a moment. "Anyway, she's a bit tall for me, don't you think?"

"Not at all. You look great together. I was watching when you came in."

He gave his head a slight shake. "I know it bothers her. She's never actually come out and said so, but—"

"She'll get over it."

"You think so?"

"Does it bother you?"

"Not a bit."

"Then what's the problem?"

He looked at me. His face was beginning to appeal to me. His eyes held a nice light, conveying qualities of sincerity and competence. He was probably the kind of doctor you could call at 2:00 A.M., a man who'd sit up with your kid until the fever broke. I was about to hike up my pant leg and show him my bruise, but it seemed kind of gross.

"You should hear the way she talks about you," I went on.

" 'Eight and a half on a scale of ten.' That's how she describes you. I swear to God."

"Are you kidding?"

"Neil, come on. I wouldn't kid about that. She's completely smitten with you. She just hasn't figured it out yet."

Now he laughed the kind of laugh that made his whole face light up. A boyish pleasure showed through and I could swear he blushed. He was really kind of cute. I glanced up in time to see Vera shoot me a stark look. I gave her a little finger wave and turned my attention back to him.

"I mean, what the hell are relationships about?" I asked.

"But she's never given any indication . . ."

"Well, I'm telling you for a fact. I've known her for ages and I've never heard her talk about a guy the way she talks about you."

He was taking it in, but I could tell he wasn't buying it.

"How tall are you?" I said. "You don't look short to me."

"Five seven."

"She's only five nine. What's the big deal?"

Mac Voorhies tapped on his glass with a spoon about then, saying, "Ladies and gentlemen, if I may have your attention . . ." He and Marie had been placed at table two, near the center of the room. Jewel and her husband were at the same table and I could see Jewel begin to squirm, anticipating the speech to come. Maclin Voorhies is one of the California Fidelity vice presidents, lean and humorless, with sparse, fly-away white hair and a perpetual cigar clamped between his teeth. He's smart and fair-minded, honorable, conservative, ill-tempered sometimes, but a very capable executive. The notion of being publicly praised by this man had already brought the color to Jewel's face.

The room gradually quieted.

Mac took a moment to survey the crowd. "We're here to-night to pay homage to one of the finest women I've ever been privileged to work with. As you all know, Jewel Cavaletto is retiring from the company after twenty-five years of service . . ."

There's something hypnotic about the tone and tenor of

an after-dinner speech, maybe because everyone's full of food and wine and the room's too warm by then. I was sitting there feeling grateful that Mac had bypassed the canned humor and was getting straight to the point. I don't know what made me look at the door. Everyone else was looking at Mac. I caught something out of the corner of my eye and turned my head.

It was the kid. I blinked uncomprehendingly at first, as if confronted with a mirage. Then I felt a rush of fear.

The only clear glimpse I'd ever had of him was that first encounter at the rest stop. Mark Messinger had been feigning sleep that day, stretched out on a bench with a magazine across his face while Eric knelt on the pavement with his Matchbox car, making mouth noises, shifting gears with his voice. I'd seen him again one night in the motel parking lot, his features indistinguishable in the poorly lighted alcove where his father had taken him to buy a soft drink. I'd heard his laughter echo through the darkness, an impish peal that reminded me of the shadowy underworld of elves and fairies. The last time I'd seen him, his face had been partially obscured behind the paper sticker on the passenger side of the truck in which his father tried to run me down.

He was small for five. The light in the corridor glinted on his blond head. His hair was getting long. His eyes were pinned on me and a half-smile played on his mouth. He turned to look at someone standing in the corridor just out of sight. He was being prompted, like a kid acting an unfamiliar part in the grade-school play. I could see him say, "What?" I didn't wait to see what the next line would be.

I grabbed my handbag and came up out of my seat, nearly knocking my chair over in the process. Dietz turned to look at me and caught the direction of my startled gaze. By the time he checked the entrance, it was empty. I bolted around Neil's chair, heading toward the hall, tagging Dietz's arm. "It's the kid," I hissed. His gun came out and he grabbed my arm, jerking me along behind him as he moved toward the door. Mac caught the commotion and stopped midsentence, looking up at us in astonishment. Other people turned to see what was going on. Some woman emitted a startled cry at the sight of Dietz's .45, but by then he'd reached the entrance and had flattened himself against the wall. He peered around the doorway to the right, glanced left, and drew back. "Come on," he said.

Still propelling me by the arm, he walk-raced us down the corridor to the left, our footsteps thudding on the tiled surface. I half-expected him to stash me in Vera's room while he ran reconnaissance, but instead he steered us toward the exit at the end of the hall. At the door, we stopped again abruptly while he made sure there was no one out there. The night air hit us like icy water after the warmth of the banquet room. We eased away from the light, hugging the shrubs as we rounded the corner, moving toward the parking lot.

"You're sure it was him?" he asked, his tone low.

"Of course I'm sure."

We were on a darkened walkway that bordered one of the interior courtyards. Crickets were chirring and I could smell the slightly skunky scent of marigolds. Voices up ahead. Dietz drew us into the shelter of some hibiscus bushes bunched against the building. I was clutching the Davis, my hand shoved down in the outside pocket of my shoulderbag. Dietz's fingers dug painfully into the flesh of my right arm, but that was the only indication I had of how tense he was. A couple passed, two of the bridesmaids I'd seen earlier. I could hear their long taffeta skirts rustle as they hurried by.

"Just what I need . . . a guy equipped with a Fourex," one was saying.

"Hey, come on. He's buff . . . ," the other said, voices fading as they turned through the archway to our left.

Dietz moved out onto the walkway, keeping me close. "We'll check the parking lot," he murmured. "I want to make sure the guy's not out there waiting for us."

There was a scattering of guests at the hotel entrance, waiting for their cars to be brought around by three white-jacketed valets who had spread out, at a trot, across the parking lot. The immediate area was washed by a wide spill of light. The windows along the wing to our left formed tall rectangles of yellow, casting soft oblongs of illumination on the grass below. Banana palms intersected the light source at intervals. To our right, against the darkness, a thick cluster of birds-of-paradise was highlighted in blue and green outdoor spots that made them look like a flock of beaky fowl staring intently into the middle distance. A car eased out of the driveway and turned right, headlights flashing across the upright supports of the seawall. The ocean beyond was a pounding presence limned in moonlight.

The back end of Dietz's red Porsche was in plain view, parked close to the line of shrubs that bordered the circular driveway.

Dietz motioned for the nightscope, which I dug out of my handbag. He held the scope to his eye, scanning the grounds. "Here. You look," he murmured and handed me the device. I peered through the scope, startled by the sudden eerie green clarity of the landscape. Where the black had seemed dense and impenetrable, there was now a fine haze of green, with objects outlined in neon. The kid was crouching in a thicket of ferns beside a palm tree. He was sitting on his heels, arms wrapped around his bony knees, which were bared in shorts. While I was watching, he lifted his head, peering toward the entrance, perhaps in hopes of catching sight of us. His young body conveyed all the tension of a game of hide-and-seek. I didn't see Messinger, but he had to be somewhere close. I touched Dietz's arm and pointed. He took the scope and scanned again.

"Got him," he murmured. He checked with his naked eye and then again with the scope. Without a word, we retreated, retracing our steps. We circled the main building, slipping into the hotel through a service entrance at the rear. Dietz used one of a bank of wall phones near the kitchen to call a cab, which picked us up on a side street behind the hotel minutes later.

18

By the time we got home it was nearly eleven o'clock and Dietz was in a foul mood. He'd been silent in the cab, silent as he unlocked the door and let us in. Impatiently, he stripped off his jacket. The right sleeve got hung up on his cuff link. He jerked it free, wadded the jacket up and flung it across the room, ignoring the fact that it didn't go that far. He went into the kitchenette, opened the bottle of Jack Daniel's, and poured himself a jelly glass of whiskey, which he tossed down.

I picked up the jacket from the floor and folded it across my arm. "It's not your fault," I said.

"The fuck it's not," he snapped. "I was the one who insisted we go tonight. It was stupid . . . way too risky . . . and for what? Messinger could have walked in there with an Uzi and mowed us all down."

Actually it was hard to argue that one, as the same thing had occurred to me. "What happened? Nothing happened."

He reached for a cigarette, but caught himself abruptly. "I'm going out," he said.

"And leave me here by myself?" I yelped.

He flashed a dark look at me, his fingers tightened on the glass until I half-expected him to crush it in his grip. Something about the gesture made my temper climb.

"Oh, for God's sake. Just cut it out, okay? The guy's showing off again. Big deal. He wants me nervous and he wants you kicking your own butt. Well, so far, so good. You storm out to buy a pack of cigarettes and he can step in and finish me off without any interference. Thanks a lot."

He was silent for a moment. He set the glass aside and leaned, stiff-armed, against the counter, head down. "You're right."

"Damn right I'm right," I said peevishly. "Lighten up and let's figure out some way to kill his ass. I hate chickenshit guys trying to shoot me. Let's get him first."

That gave his mood a lift. "How?"

"I don't know how."

There was a knock at the door and both of us jumped. Dietz whipped his gun out and motioned me into the kitchenette. He crossed to the front door and flattened himself against the wall to the right. "Who is it?"

The voice was muffled. "Clyde Gersh."

I moved toward the door, but Dietz waved me back with a scowl. He tilted his head against the doorframe. "What do you want?"

"Agnes was picked up. She's in the emergency room at St. Terry's and she's asking for Kinsey. We left a couple of messages on the answering machine, but when we didn't hear back, we thought we'd stop by. We're on our way to the hospital. Is she home yet?"

Dietz said, "Hang on." He pointed to the answering machine, which rested on the bookshelf behind the sofa. I eased across the room and checked the message light, which indicated that two calls had been recorded. I turned the volume down, pushed the auto playback button, and listened to the tape. The first message was from Irene, the second from Clyde, both saying much the same thing. Agnes had been found and was asking for me. Dietz and I exchanged a look.

He lifted his brows in a facial shrug. He flipped the porch light on, peered through the spyhole, and opened the door with caution. Clyde was standing by himself on the doorstep in a circle of wan light. Beyond him, all was darkness. The fog was rolling in and I could see faint wisps of it curling around the light. "Sorry for the inconvenience," he said. "I don't like to disturb people this late, but Irene insisted."

"Come on in," Dietz said, stepping back so Clyde could enter. Dietz closed the door behind him and motioned Clyde to have a seat, an offer Clyde declined with a brief shake of his head. "Irene's waiting in the car. I don't want to leave her too long. She's anxious to get over there."

He was looking weary, his baggy face weighted with anxiety. He wore a tan gabardine topcoat, hands shoved down in his pockets. His gaze flickered across Dietz's holster but he refrained from comment, as if mentioning the gun might be a breach of etiquette.

"How's Agnes doing? Has anybody said?" I asked.

"We're not really sure. The doc says minor cuts and bruises . . . nothing serious . . . but her heartbeat's irregular and I guess they put her on some kind of monitor. She'll be admitted as soon as we sign the paperwork. I gather it's nothing life-threatening, but the woman is eighty-some-odd years old."

"The cops picked her up?"

Clyde nodded. "Some woman spotted her, wandering in the street. She was the one who called the police. The officer who called said Agnes is disoriented, has no idea where she is or where she's been all this time. The doc says she's been talking about you since they brought her in. We'd appreciate your coming with us if it's not too much trouble."

I said, "Sure. Let me change my clothes. I don't want to go like this."

"I'll let Irene know you're coming," he said to me. And then to Dietz, "Will you follow in your car or ride with us?"

"We'll come in your car and grab a cab back," Dietz said.

I was on my way up to the loft, stripping off the black silk jacket as I went, kicking off my shoes. I leaned my head out over the railing. "Where'd they find her?"

Clyde turned his face up to mine with a shrug. "Same neighborhood as the nursing home . . . somewhere close by . . . so she didn't get far. I can't figure out how we missed her unless she saw us and hid."

"I wouldn't put it past her." I ducked back, peeling off the jumpsuit, hopping on one foot as I tugged my jeans on over the black panty hose. I put a bra on, grabbed a polo shirt out of the chest of drawers, pulled it on, and shook my hair out. I stepped into my high-top Reeboks and left the laces for later. I was clopping down the narrow staircase two seconds later, reaching for my shoulderbag.

"Let's hit it," I said, as Dietz opened the door.

Clyde's white Mercedes sedan was parked at the curb. Irene, in the front, turned a worried face toward us as we approached.

The fifteen-minute drive to St. Terry's was strained. Dietz and I sat in the backseat with Dietz angled sideways so he could check out the back window for any cars following. I was perched, leaning forward, arms resting on the front seat close to Irene, who clutched my hand as if it were a lifeline. Her fingers were icy and I found myself listening unconsciously for the wheezing that might signal another asthma attack. No one said much. The information about Agnes was limited and there didn't seem to be any point in repeating it.

The small parking lot in front of the emergency room was full. A black-and-white occupied the end slot. Clyde pulled up to the entrance and let us out, then went off to find parking on the street. Irene hung back, evidently reluctant to go in without him. She wore a lightweight spring coat, double-breasted, bright red, which she pulled around her now as if for warmth. I could see her peering off toward the streetlights, hoping to catch sight of him.

"He'll be with us shortly," I said.

She clung to my arm while Dietz brought up the rear. The double doors slid open automatically as we approached. We passed into the reception area, which was deserted as far as I could tell. I was struck by the silence. Somehow I'd expected activity, urgency, some sense of the medical drama that plays out in every ER: patients with broken bones, puncture wounds, cuts, insect bites, allergic reactions, and superficial burns. Here, the rooms felt empty and there was no indication of acute care of any sort. Perhaps it was the hour, perhaps an unpredictable lull in the ordinary course of events.

Irene and I waited at the curved front counter, a C-shape enclosing a desk papered with forms. To our immediate right were two patient registration windows, shuttered at this hour. On our left, there was a room divider with two pay phones on the near side and a waiting area beyond. I could see a color television set, tuned to a news show, the sound too low to register. Everything was done in muted blues and grays. All was in order, tidy and quiet. Through an open doorway, I caught a glimpse of the nurses' station, ringed by examining rooms. There was no sign of the police officer or hospital personnel.

Dietz was restless, snapping his fingers against the palm of his hand. He ambled over to the interior door and peered in, checking the layout, automatically eyeballing avenues of escape in case Messinger showed up again. The receptionist must have spotted him because she emerged from the rear moments later, smiling at us politely. "Sorry to keep you waiting. How may I help you?"

"We're here to see Agnes Grey," I said.

She was a woman in her forties, wearing ordinary street clothes: polyester pants, cotton sweater, rubber-soled shoes. A stethoscope, like a pendant, dangled from her neck. Her eyes were a rich chocolate brown, lending warmth to her face. She checked some papers on her desk and then looked up at Irene. "Are you Mrs. Gersh?"

"That's right," Irene said.

The woman's tone was pleasant, but I could see her smile falter. Her attitude suggested the carefully controlled neutrality you'd merit if the actual test results were not what you'd been led to expect. "Why don't you come on back and have a seat in the office," she said. "The doctor will be right with you."

Irene blinked at her fearfully, her voice close to a whisper. "I'd like to see Mother. Is she all right?"

"Dr. Stackhouse would prefer to talk to you first," she said. "Would you like to follow me, please?"

I didn't like it. Her manner was entirely too kindly and benign. She could have made any one of a number of responses. Maybe she'd been advised not to discuss medical matters. Maybe she'd been chastised for offering her opinion before the doctor could offer his. Maybe hospital policy forbade her to editorialize about the patient's condition for complicated reasons of liability. Or maybe Agnes Grey was dead. The woman glanced at me. "Your daughter's welcome to come with you . . ."

"You want me to come?" I asked.

"Yes, please," Irene said to me. Then to the receptionist, "My husband's parking the car. Will you tell him where we are?"

Dietz spoke up. "I'll let him know. You two go on back. We'll be right there."

Irene murmured a thank-you. Dietz and I exchanged a look.

The receptionist stood by the open door while we passed through. She led the way while we followed along a corridor with high-gloss white flooring. She showed us into an office evidently used by any doctor on duty. "It won't be long. Can I get you anything? Coffee? A cup of tea?"

Irene shook her head. "This is fine."

We sat down in blue tweed chairs with upholstered seats. There were no exterior windows. The Formica shelf-desk was bare. There was a gray leather couch showing doctor-size indentations in the cushions. As an impromptu daybed, it was slightly too short and I could see where his shoes had scraped against the arm at one end. A white Formica bookcase was filled with standard medical texts. The potted plant was fake, a Swedish ivy made of paper with curling vines as stiff as florist's wire. The only pictures on the wall looked like reproductions from *Gray's Anatomy*. Personally, I can do without all the skinless arms and legs. The saphenous vein and its branches looked like an overview of the Los Angeles freeway system.

Irene shrugged her coat off and smoothed the lap of her skirt. "I can't believe there weren't any papers to fill out. They must have admitted her."

"You know hospitals. They have their own way of doing things."

"Clyde has the insurance information in his wallet. Blue Cross, I think, though I'm not sure she's covered."

"Bill the nursing home," I said. "It's their responsibility."

We sat for a moment saying nothing. I wondered if this was what it felt like to have family. Geriatric crises, accompanied by homely discussions about what should be done with Granny. We heard footsteps in the hall and the doctor came into the room. I was half-expecting the receptionist with Clyde and Dietz in tow, so it took me a second to compute the expression on this guy's face. He was in his early thirties, with carrot-colored curly hair and a ruddy complexion. He was wearing an unstructured cotton shirt in a hospital green, V-neck, short sleeves, matching cotton pants, soft-soled baggy shoes. He had a stethoscope around his neck and a white plastic name tag that read, "Warren Stackhouse, MD." With his red hair and freckles, the surgical greens gave him a certain Technicolor vibrancy, like a cartoon character. He smelled like adhesive tape and breath mints and his hands looked freshly scrubbed. He was holding a manila folder, which contained only one sheet. He placed that on the desk, lining up the edges.

"Mrs. Gersh? I'm Dr. Stackhouse." He and Irene shook hands and then he leaned against the desk. "I'm afraid we lost her."

"Oh, for God's sake," Irene snapped. "Can't anybody keep track of her?"

Uh-oh, I thought, Irene wasn't getting it. "I don't think he means it that way," I murmured.

"Mrs. Grey went into cardiac arrest," he said. "I'm sorry. We did everything we could, but we weren't able to revive her."

Irene grew still, her face blank, her tone of voice nearly petulant. "Are you saying she's dead? But that's impossible. She couldn't be. You've made some mistake. Clyde said her injuries were minor. Cuts and bruises. I thought he talked to you."

I was watching the doctor and I could see him pick his words with care. "When she was first brought in, she was already showing symptoms of cardiac arrhythmia. She was confused and disoriented, suffering from exposure and stress. In a woman her age, given her fragile state of health . . ."

Irene let out a sigh, finally taking it in. "Oh, the poor thing." Her eyes filled with sudden tears, which spilled down her cheeks. Blotches of color had come up in her face and neck. She began to tremble uncontrollably, quivering like a wet dog in the midst of a bath. I grabbed her hand.

Clyde appeared in the doorway. From the look in his eyes, he'd been told what was going on. The receptionist had probably informed him as soon as he came in.

Irene turned beseechingly. "Clyde . . . Mother's *gone*," she said. She reached for him, coming out of the chair and into his arms. He seemed to fold her in against him. For the first time, I realized how tiny she was. I looked away, not wanting to intrude on their intimacy.

I saw Dietz through the open doorway, leaning against the wall. His posture was identical to my first sight of him. Cowboy boots, his tweed coat. The hospital down in Brawley. All he needed was the toothbrush in his pocket, sticking up like a fountain pen. His gaze moved casually to mine, moved to Irene, came back to mine and held. The look in his eyes was quizzical, perplexed. His expression shifted from self-assurance to uncertainty. I felt an unexpected flash of heat.

I broke off eye contact, feeling flushed. My gaze drifted back. He was still looking at me, with a wistfulness I hadn't seen before.

We all waited uncomfortably for Irene's tears to pass. Finally, Dr. Stackhouse moved toward the door and I followed. The two of us withdrew, moving out into the corridor. As we walked back to the emergency room, Dietz fell into step with us, placing his hand on the back of my neck in a way that made me feel curious and alert. It was a gesture of possession and the physical connection was charged with a sudden current that made the air between us hum.

Dr. Stackhouse shook his head. "God, I'm sorry. It was a lousy break. Are you her granddaughter? Someone's going to have to talk to the police officer."

I focused on the situation as if coming up for air. "I'm a friend of Mrs. Gersh's. Kinsey Millhone," I said.

He glanced at me. "The one she was asking for."

"So I'm told," I said. "Do you have any idea what it was?"

"Well, I can tell you what she said, but I don't think it means much. She kept saying it was summer. 'Tell her it used to be summer . . .' Is that significant?"

"Not to me," I said. In her mind, it was probably connected to the long rambling tale she'd told me down at the desert. Emily and the earthquake, the Harpster girls and Arthur James. "That's all she said?"

"That's the only thing I heard."

"Will there be an autopsy?"

"Probably. We put a call through to the coroner's office and a deputy's on the way. He'll talk to the pathologist and decide if it's warranted."

"Which pathologist? Dr. Yee or Dr. Palchak?"

"Dr. Palchak," he said. "Of course, the deputy may just go ahead and authorize us to sign the death certificate."

"What about Agnes? Can we see her?"

He nodded. "Of course. She's just down the hall here. Whenever Mrs. Gersh is ready, the nurse will take you in."

Agnes had been moved temporarily to a little-used examining room at the end of the hall. Once we were gone, she'd be wheeled down to the basement and left in the refrigerated darkness of the morgue. Dietz waited in the hall with Clyde while Irene and I stood silently beside the gurney on which her mother lay. Death had smoothed many of the lines from her face. Under the white sheeting, she seemed small and frail, her beaky nose protruding prominently from the peaceful folds of her face.

There was a discreet knock at the door. A young uniformed police officer came into the room and introduced himself. He'd brought Agnes in and he talked to Irene briefly about his encounter with her mother. "She seemed like a very nice person, ma'am. I just thought you might like to know she didn't give me any trouble . . ."

Irene's eyes brimmed. "Thank you. I appreciate that. Was she in pain? I can't stand to think about what she must have gone through."

"No, ma'am. I wouldn't say so. She might have been confused, but she didn't seem to be in pain or anything like that."

"Thank God for that. Did she ask for me?"

Color tinted his cheeks. "I couldn't say for sure. I know she mentioned somebody named Sheila."

"Sheila?" Irene said blankly.

"I'm pretty sure that was it. She did cry some. She said she was sorry to be a bother. I kept talking to her, telling her everything was fine. She quieted down after that and seemed all right till we got here. I know the staff did everything possible to save her. I guess sometimes they just go like that."

Irene's chin began to quiver. She pressed a handkerchief to her mouth while she shook her head, whispering. "I had no idea she was dying. My God, if we'd only hurried we might have been here in time . . ."

The officer shifted uneasily. "I'll step out in the waiting room and finish filling out my report. I believe the sheriff's deputy's out there now. He'll need some information as soon as you're up to it." He moved out into the hall, leaving the door ajar.

176

After a moment, Clyde came in. He put his arm around Irene's shoulder and walked her out toward the reception area. Before the door closed again, I caught a glimpse of the sheriff's deputy in the corridor, conferring with his STPD counterpart. I gathered the city police had reported the death to the county coroner's office since Agnes was listed as missing and the last hours of her life were still unaccounted for. The coroner would make a determination as to the circumstances, manner, and cause of death. If she should be classified as a homicide victim, the city police would assume responsibility for the criminal investigation. I was guessing the death would be considered "nonreportable" in coroner's terms, but that remained to be seen. An autopsy might be done in any event.

Alone with the body, I lifted one corner of the sheet, reaching for the cool, unyielding flesh of Agnes's left hand. Her knuckles were scraped. Two nails were broken. On her ring finger and her pinkie there was soil impacted under the nails. The receptionist came into the room behind me. I slipped her hand under the sheet again and turned. "Yes?"

"Mr. Gersh said to tell you he's taking his wife out to the car. The other gentleman is waiting."

"What happened to her personal effects?"

"There wasn't much. Dr. Stackhouse set aside the articles of clothing for disposition by the coroner. She didn't have anything else with her when she was brought in."

I scribbled a note to Dr. Palchak, asking her to call me. I left the message with the ER nurse as I passed the desk. Dietz wanted to call a cab, but Clyde insisted on dropping us back at my place. Irene cried inconsolably all the way home. I was grateful when Dietz finally unlocked the door and let us in. In the backseat of the Mercedes, he'd placed his hand beside mine, our little fingers touching in a way that made me feel my whole left side had been magnetized.

19

▶▶ ▶▶ ▶▶ The minute I was inside, I headed for the loft, too exhausted to bother with social niceties.

"You want a glass of wine?" he asked.

I hesitated. I looked back at him, caught in midflight. I had one foot on the bottom step, my hand on the curved railing of the spiral staircase. "I don't think so. Thanks."

There was a pause. He said, "Are you all right?"

We were suddenly talking in ways that felt unfamiliar, as if each exchange had a hidden meaning. His face seemed the same, but there was something new in his eyes. Where before his gaze had been opaque, there was now an appeal, some request he couldn't quite bring himself to voice. Sexuality stirred the air like the blades of a fan. Exhaustion fell away. All the danger, all the tension had been converted into this, mute longing. I could feel the lick of it along my legs, seeping through my clothes: something ancient, something dark, humankind's only antidote to death. The heat seemed to arc through the space between us like a primitive experiment, born of night. This is what I understood: this man was like me, my twin, and suddenly, I knew that what I saw in him was a strange reflection of myself—my bravery, my competence, my fear of dependency. I'd been with him three days, separated by externals, neutered by survival instincts. Only desire could render us brave enough to cross that distance, but which of us would risk it?

I watched him lock the door. I watched him flick the lights out and cross the room. I started up the spiral staircase, turning at the third step. I held the railing, sank into a sitting position as he approached. Dietz was before me, his face level with mine. The room behind him was dark. Light spilled down from the loft, illuminating his solemn face. He leaned into the kiss, his mouth cold at first, his lips soft. My craving for him was as tangible as a finger of heat driven up through my core. I was lying on the stairs, metal risers cutting into my back until pain and desire had blended into a single sensation. I stroked his cheek, touched the silky strands of his hair while he buried his face against me, nuzzling my breasts through my cotton T-shirt. We moved together in mock intercourse, clothes on, bodies arching. I could hear the sound of fabric on fabric, his breathing, mine. I reached down and touched him. He made an inhuman sound, lifting away from me, pulling me after him as he moved up the spiral staircase. The bed was better and we undressed by degrees as we kissed. The first shock of heat when he laid his naked flesh along mine made him say, "Oh . . . sweet Jesus," very softly. After that, there were no words until the moment of oblivion. Making love with this man was like no other lovemaking I've experienced . . . some external chord resolved at its peak, ageless music resonating through our bones, the spilling of secrets, flesh on flesh, moment after moment until we were fused. I fell into a deep sleep, my limbs wound into his, and never knew a waking until daylight came. At six o'clock, I stirred, vaguely aware that I was alone in bed. I could hear Dietz moving around downstairs. He had the radio on and I caught strains of a Tammy Wynette tune poignant enough to rip your heart out. For once, I didn't care.

At some point, the doorbell rang . . . the UPS man (a real

one) with the box I'd shipped up from Brawley. Dietz took delivery, as I was still dead to the world. Soon after that, the smell of perking coffee wafted up the stairs. I roused myself, made my bed, fumbled my way into the bathroom and brushed my teeth. I showered, washed my hair, and then got dressed, slipping into the jeans and shirt I'd worn the night before. No point in contributing either to the laundry pile just yet. I went downstairs.

Dietz was perched on a bar stool at the counter, the paper open in front of him, empty juice glass and cereal bowl pushed to one side so he could read. He reached a hand back. I put my arms around him from behind. He kissed me with a mouth so fresh, I could taste the cereal. "You okay?" he asked.

"Yes. You?"

"Mmm. Your package arrived."

The box was sitting just inside the door, addressed to me in my own writing. "Have you inspected this for incendiary devices?"

His tone was dry. "It's clear. Go ahead."

I got a paring knife from the kitchen drawer and slit the strapping tape. The articles were packed as I remembered them, my all-purpose dress close to the surface. I pulled it out and inspected it, relieved to find it in better shape than I'd hoped. It was only moderately encrusted with mold, though it did smell of swamp gas, a scent that hovered somewhere between spoiled eggs and old toilet bowls.

Dietz caught one whiff and turned to me, his face twisted with distaste. "What *is* that? Good God . . ."

"This is my best dress," I said. "I just need to throw it in the wash and it'll be fine."

I set it aside and worked my way through the remaining contents, removing tools and other odds and ends. In the bottom was the child's tea set, still packed in the carton I'd pulled from under Agnes Grey's trailer. "I should drop this off at Irene's," I remarked, placing the carton near the door. There were few, if any, personal items left to commemorate

Agnes Grey's eighty-three years on earth and I thought Irene might appreciate the articles.

Dietz looked up from his paper. "Which reminds me. Dr. Palchak called at seven thirty this morning with the autopsy results. She wanted you to call her whenever you got up."

"That was fast."

"That's what I thought. She says she likes to get in at five when she's got a post."

I dialed the number for St. Terry's and asked for pathology. I'd dealt with Laura Palchak maybe twice before. She's short, plain, heavyset, competent, hardworking, thorough, and very smart, one of several pathologists under contract to the county, handling postmortem examinations for the coroner's office.

"Palchak," she said when she came on the line.

"Hi, Laura. Kinsey Millhone. Thanks for responding to my note. What's the story on Agnes Grey?"

There was a brief pause. "The coroner's office will be contacting Mrs. Gersh a little later this morning so this is just between us, okay?"

"Absolutely."

"The autopsy was negative. We won't have the toxi results back for weeks, but the gross came up blank."

"So what's the cause of death?"

"Essentially, it was cardiac arrest, but hell ... everybody dies of cardiac or respiratory arrest if you want to get right down to it. The point is there was no demonstrable organic heart disease and no other natural findings that contributed to death. Technically, we have to list cause of death as undetermined."

"What's that mean, 'technically'? I don't like the way you said that."

She laughed. "Good question. You're right. I have a hunch about this one, but I need to do some research. I've talked to the hospital librarian about tracking down an article I read a few years back. I don't know what made me think of it, but something about this situation rang a little bell."

"Like what? Can you fill me in?"

"Not yet. I'm having my assistant set up some tissue slides that I can probably take a look at by this afternoon. I have sixteen cases lined up before this one, but I'm curious."

"Do you need anything from me?"

"I do have a suggestion if you're open to this. I'm very interested in what happened to this woman during the hours she was missing. It would be a big help if you can find out where she was all that time."

"Well, I can try," I said, "but it may turn out to be a trick. Am I looking for anything in particular?"

"She had what looked like rope burns on her right wrist, torn and broken nails on her left—"

"Oh yeah, I saw that," I said with sudden recollection. "The knuckles on her left hand were scraped, too."

"Right. It's possible she was held someplace against her will. You might see if anybody has a potting shed or a greenhouse. I took some soil traces from her fingernails and we might find a match. She also had superficial abrasions and contusions across her back. I saw a kid just last week with similar marks on his thighs and buttocks. He'd been beaten with a coat hanger . . . among other things."

"Are you saying *she* was beaten?"

"Probably."

"Does Lieutenant Dolan know about this?"

"He and the police photographer were both present for the post, so he saw the same things I did. The truth is, there was no internal trauma and the injuries were too minor to be considered the cause of death."

"What's your theory then?"

"Unh-unh. Not till I do a bit of checking first. Call me this afternoon, or better yet, let me call you when I've seen what we've got here. By then you may have something to report yourself."

She hung up. I settled the receiver in the cradle and sat there, perplexed.

Dietz was watching me. From my end of the conversation, he could tell there'd been a shift. "What's wrong?"

"Let's pick up your car and go by Irene's. I'd like to talk to Clyde." I made a quick call to let them know we'd be stopping by and then called a cab.

I detailed the situation on the way over to the hotel, Irene's carton in my lap. When we reached the Edgewater, Dietz took his time with the Porsche, inspecting the engine and the electrical system. This wasn't the same car-park attendant we'd dealt with the night before and while the kid swore no one had been near the car, Dietz didn't want to trust him.

"I doubt Messinger knows his ass from his elbow when it comes to bombs, but this is no time to be surprised," he said. I waited while he stretched out on the driveway, inching partway under the car so he could scrutinize the underside. Evidently, there were no unidentified wires, no visible blasting caps, and no tidy bundles of dynamite. Satisfied, he got up and brushed himself off, then ushered me into the passenger seat. Dietz started the car and pulled out of the lot.

For once he drove slowly, his expression preoccupied.

"What are you chewing on?" I asked.

"I've been thinking about Messinger and I wonder if it wouldn't be smart to talk to his ex-wife."

"Down in Los Angeles?"

"Or get her up here. We know he's got Eric with him, at least as of last night. She'd probably jump at the chance to get the kid back. Maybe we could help her and she could turn around and help us."

"How?"

Dietz shrugged. "I don't know yet, but it's better than doing nothing."

"You know how to get in touch with her?"

"I thought I'd drop you off and go talk to Dolan."

"Sounds good. Let's do that."

We parked in front of the Gershes'. Dietz held the carton for me while I extricated myself from the low-slung seat. When we reached the front porch, he left the carton by the door while I rang the bell. Our agreement was that I would wait here until he came back to pick me up. "Make it fast,"

I murmured. "I don't want to be stuck with Irene all day."

"Forty-five minutes max. Any longer, I'll call. Be careful." He backed me against the house with a kiss that made my toes curl, then gave a careless wave and moved off down the walk.

Jermaine opened the front door, stepping back to admit me as the Porsche ignition turned over and the car pulled away from the curb. I was still collecting myself, trying to look like a sober private investigator when, in truth, my drawers were wet. Jermaine and I made the proper mouth noises at one another. I could hear the telephone ring somewhere in the house. She heard it too and raised her voice, as if projecting to the rear of an auditorium. "I'll get it!" She excused herself, waddling toward the kitchen with surprising grace.

The house was otherwise silent, the living room veiled in shadow from the junipers along the property line. I crossed to one of the end tables and snapped on a lamp. I leaned sideways, peering through an archway to my left. Irene was sitting at a little desk in the solarium just off the living room. A small portable radio was playing classical music and I assumed that's why she hadn't heard the front doorbell. She wore a bathrobe and slippers, looking worse than she had the night before. Her complexion, always pale, had taken on the tone of skin bleached by adhesive tape. It was clear she'd wept a good deal and my guess was that she hadn't slept much. The false lashes were gone and her eyes seemed puffy and remote.

"Irene?"

Startled, she looked up, her gaze searching the room for the source of the sound. When she caught sight of me, she pushed herself to her feet, using the desk for leverage. She came into the living room on shaky feet, hands held toward me like a toddler on a maiden voyage, making little mewing sounds as if every step hurt. She clung to me as she had before, but with an added note of desperation.

"Oh, Kinsey. Thank goodness. I'm so glad you're here.

Clyde had a meeting at the bank, but he said he'd be back as soon as he could make it."

"Good. I was hoping to talk to him. How are you?"

"Awful. I can't seem to get organized and I can't bear to be alone."

I guided her toward the couch, struck by the sheer force of her neediness. "You don't look like you've slept much."

She sank onto the couch, refusing to let go of my hands. She clutched at me like a drunk, sloppy with excess, grief perfuming her breath like alcohol. "I sat down here most of the night so I wouldn't disturb Clyde. I don't know what to do. I've been trying to fill out Mother's death certificate and I discover I don't know the first thing about her. I can't remember anything. It's inconceivable to me. So shameful somehow. My own mother . . ." She was beginning to weep again.

"Hey, it's okay. This is something I can help you with." I held a hand up, palm toward her. "Just sit. Relax. Is the form in there?"

She seemed to collect herself. She nodded mutely, eyes fixed on me with gratitude as I moved into the adjacent room. I gathered up a pen and the eight-by-eight-inch square form from the desk and returned to the couch, wondering how Clyde endured her dependency. Whatever compassion I felt was being overshadowed by the sense that I was shouldering a nearly impossible burden.

20

▸▸ ▸▸ ▸▸ "Treat this like a final exam," I said. "We'll do the easy questions first and then tackle the tough ones. Let's start with 'Name of Decedent.' Did she have a middle name?"

Irene shook her head. "Not that I ever heard."

I wrote in "Agnes . . . NMI . . . Grey."

Irene and I sat with our heads bent together, meticulously filling in the meager information she had. This took a little over one minute and covered race (Caucasian), sex (female), military service (none), Social Security number (none), marital status (widowed), occupation (retired), and several subheadings under "Usual Residence." What distressed Irene was that she didn't know the year of her mother's birth and she didn't have a clue about where Agnes was born or the names of her parents, facts she felt anyone with an ounce of caring should have at her fingertips.

"Quit beating yourself, for God's sake," I said. "Let's work backward and see how far we get. Maybe you know more than you think. For instance, everybody's been saying she was eighty-three, right?"

Irene nodded with uncertainty, probably wishing the form

186

had a few multiple-choice questions. I could tell she was still agitated at the notion of her own ignorance.

"Irene, you cannot flunk this test," I said. "I mean, what are they going to do, refuse to bury her?" I hated to be flip, but I thought it might snap her out of the self-pity.

She said, "I just don't want to get it wrong. It's important to do it right. It's the least I can do."

"I can understand that, but the world will not end if you leave one slot blank. We know she was a U.S. citizen so let's put that down. . . . The rest of the information we can pick up from your birth certificate. That would tell us your parents' place of birth and their ages the year you were born. Can you lay your hands on it?"

She nodded, blowing her nose on a handkerchief, which she then tucked in her robe pocket. "I'm almost sure it's in the file cabinet in there," she said. She indicated the solarium, which she'd set up as a home office. "There's a folder in the top drawer labeled 'Vital Documents.'"

"Don't get up. You stay here. I'll find it."

I went into the next room and pulled open one of the file drawers. "Vital Documents" was a thick manila folder right in the front. I brought the entire file back and let Irene sort through the contents. She extracted a birth certificate, which she handed to me. I glanced at it briefly, then squinted more closely. "This is a photocopy. What happened to the original?"

"I have no idea. That's the only one I ever had."

"What about when you applied for a passport? You must have had a certified copy then."

"I don't have a passport. I never needed one."

I stared at her, amazed. "I thought I was the only person without a passport," I remarked.

She seemed faintly defensive. "I don't like to travel. I was always afraid of getting ill and not having proper medical help available. If Clyde had to travel overseas on business, he went by himself. Is that a problem?" My guess was that she and Clyde had argued about her position more than once.

"No, no. This will do, but it strikes me as odd. How'd you come by this one?"

She closed her mouth and her cheeks flooded with pink, like a sudden restoration to good health. At first, I thought she wouldn't answer me, but finally she pursed her lips. "Mother gave it to me when I was in high school. One of the more humiliating moments in my life with her. We were writing our autobiographies for an honors English class and the teacher made us start with our birth certificates. I remember Mother had trouble finding mine and I had to turn my report in without it. The teacher gave me an 'incomplete' ... the only one I ever got ... which just made Mother furious. It was awful. She brought it to school the next day and flung it in the teacher's face. She was drunk, of course. All my classmates looking on. It was one of the most embarrassing things I've ever been through."

I studied her with curiosity. "What about your father? Where was he in all this?"

"I don't remember him. He and Mother separated when I was three or four. He was killed in the war a few years later. Nineteen forty-three, I think."

I glanced down at the birth certificate, getting back to the task at hand. We'd really hit pay dirt. Irene was born in Brawley, March 12, 1936, at 2:30 A.M. Her father was Herbert Grey, birthplace, Arizona, white, age thirty-two, who worked as a welder for an aircraft company. Agnes's maiden name was Branwell, birthplace California, occupation housewife.

"This is great," I said and then I read the next line. "Oh wait, this is weird. This says she was twenty-three when you were born, but that would make her ... what, seventy now? That doesn't seem right."

"That has to be a typo," she said, leaning closer. She reached for the document and peered at the line of print as I had. "This is off by years. If Mother's eighty-three now, she would have been thirty-six when I was born, not twenty-three."

"Maybe she's much younger than we thought."

"Not *that* much. She was nowhere near seventy. You saw her yourself."

I thought about it briefly. "Well, it doesn't make any difference as far as I can see."

"Of course it does! One way or the other, we'd be off by thirteen years!"

I disconnected my temper. There was no point in being irritated. "We don't have any way to verify the information," I said. "At least that I can think of. Leave it blank."

"I don't want to do that," she said stubbornly.

I'd seen her in this mood before and I knew how unyielding she could be. "Do whatever suits. It's your business."

I heard a key in the lock. The front door opened and Clyde came in, dressed in his usual three-piece suit. He was toting the cardboard carton I'd brought. He crossed to the couch, murmured a hello to me, and placed the box on the coffee table. Then he leaned over to kiss Irene's cheek, a ritualistic gesture without visible warmth. "This was on the front porch—"

"That's Irene's," I said. "I found it under Agnes's trailer and had it shipped up. It arrived this morning." I pulled the box closer and opened the top flaps, reaching down among the nesting cups, which were still swaddled in newspaper. "I wasn't sure if this was a good time or not, but these were just about the only things the squatters hadn't ripped off."

I unwrapped one of the teacups and passed it over to Irene. The porcelain handle had a hairline crack near the base, but otherwise it was perfect: pale pink roses, hand-painted, on a field of white, scaled down to child-size. Irene glanced at it without comprehension and then something flickered in her face. A sound seemed to rumble up from the depths of her being. With a sudden cry of revulsion, she flung it away from her. Fear shot through me in reaction to hers. Clyde and I both jumped and I uttered an automatic chirp of astonishment. Her scream tore through the air in a spiraling melody of terror. As if in slow motion, the cup bounced once against the edge of the coffee table and cracked as neatly in two as if it'd been cut with a knife.

Irene rose to her feet, her eyes enormous. She was hyperventilating: rapid, shallow breathing that couldn't possibly be delivering enough oxygen to her system. I could see her begin to topple, eyes focused on my face. She clawed at me as she fell, pitching forward in a convulsion that rocked her from head to toe. Clyde grabbed her as she went down, moving faster than I thought possible. He eased her back onto the couch and elevated her feet.

Jermaine thundered into the living room, a dish towel in her hand. Her eyes were wide with alarm. "What's the matter? What's happening? Oh my God . . ."

Irene's eyes had rolled back in her head and she jerked repeatedly, wracked by some personal earthquake that sent shock waves through her small frame. The acrid scent of urine permeated the air. Clyde peeled his jacket off and went down on his knees beside her, trying to restrain her so she wouldn't hurt herself. Jermaine stood by spellbound, twisting the dish towel in her big dark hands, making anxious sounds at the back of her throat.

Gradually, the spasm passed. Irene began to cough, a tight unproductive sound that made me ache in response. The cough was followed by a high-pitched wheeze that helped to mobilize me again. I put a supporting hand under Irene's right arm and shot Clyde a look. "Let's sit her upright. It'll make her breathing easier."

We hefted her into a sitting position, a surprisingly awkward maneuver given how light she was. She couldn't have weighed more than a hundred pounds, but she was limp and dazed, her eyes moving from face to face without comprehension. It was clear she had no idea where she was or what was going on.

"You want I should call emergency, Mr. Clyde?" Jermaine asked.

"Not yet. Let's hold off on that. She seems to be coming around," he said.

A fine layer of perspiration broke out on Irene's face. She reached for me blindly. Her hands had that clammy feel to them, like a still-animated fish in the bottom of a boat.

Jermaine disappeared and returned moments later with a cold, damp rag that she passed wordlessly to Clyde. He wiped Irene's face. She'd begun to make small sounds, a weeping, hopeless and childlike, as if she were waking from a nightmare of devastating impact. "There were spiders. I could smell the dust . . ."

Clyde looked at me. "She's always been phobic about spiders . . ."

I picked up the two halves of the teacup automatically, wondering if she'd seen something in the bottom. I half-expected one of those old dead spiders lying on its back, legs curled in against its belly like a blossom closing up at twilight. There was nothing. Meanwhile, Irene was inconsolable. "The paint ran down the wall in horrible streaks. The violets were ruined and I was so scared . . . I didn't mean to be bad . . ."

Clyde made soothing noises while he patted her hand. "Irene, you're okay. It's fine now. I'm right here."

The look in her eyes was pleading, her voice reduced to a plaintive whisper. "It was Mother's tea set from when she was little . . . I wasn't supposed to play with it. I hid so I wouldn't get spanked and spanked. Why did she keep it?"

"I'm putting her to bed," he said. He eased one arm under her bent knees, put the other behind her, and lifted, not without some effort. He inched away from the coffee table, walking sideways till he was clear, and then he headed toward the stairs. Jermaine accompanied him, hovering close by to help steady the load.

I sank down on the couch and put my head in my hands. My heart rate was beginning to return to normal, no mean feat given the rush of adrenaline I'd experienced. Other people's fear is contagious, a phenomenon magnified by proximity, which is why horror movies are so potent in a crowded theater. I smelled death, some terrifying experience neither Irene nor Agnes could deal with all these years afterward. I could only guess at the dimensions of the event. Now that Agnes was dead, I doubted the reality would ever be resurrected.

I stirred restlessly, glancing at my watch. I'd been here only thirty minutes. Surely Dietz would return soon and get me the hell out of here. I leafed through a magazine that was sitting on the coffee table. At the back of the issue there was a whole month's worth of dinner menus laid out, totally nutritious, well-balanced meals for mere pennies a serving. The recipes sounded awful: lots of Tuna Surprise and Tofu Stir-Fry with Sweet 'n' Sour Sauce. I set the magazine aside. Idly, I picked up the halves of the teacup, rewrapped them in newspaper, and tucked them back in the box. I got up and crossed the room, setting the box by the door. No point in having Irene face that again. Later, if she was interested, I could always bring it back. I looked up to find Clyde coming wearily down the stairs.

21

■▶ ■▶ ■▶ He looked like a zombie. I followed as he crossed to one of two matching wing chairs and took a seat. He rubbed his eyes, then pinched the bridge of his nose. His dress shirt was wrinkled, the tiny blue pinstripe stained with sweat at the armpits. "I gave her a Valium. Jermaine said she'd stay with her until she goes to sleep."

I stayed on my feet, clinging to whatever psychological advantage I had in towering over him. "What's going on, Clyde? I've never seen anyone react like that."

"Irene's a sick cookie. She has been ever since we met." He snorted to himself. "God . . . I used to think there was something charming about her helplessness . . ."

"This goes way beyond helpless. That woman's terrified. So was Agnes."

"It's always been like that. She's phobic about everything—closed spaces, spiders, dust. You know what she's afraid of? The hook and eye on a door. She's afraid of African violets. Jesus, *violets*. And it just gets worse. She suffers from allergies, depression, hypochondria. She's half dead from fear and probably hooked on all the prescription drugs she takes.

I've taken her to every kind of doctor you can name and they all throw up their hands. The shrinks love to see her coming, but then they lose interest when the old voodoo doesn't work. She doesn't want to get better. Trust me. She's hanging on to her symptoms for dear life. I try to have compassion, but all I feel is despair. My life is a nightmare, but what am I supposed to do? Divorce her? I can't do it. I couldn't live with myself if I did that. She's like a little kid. I thought when her mother died . . . I thought once Agnes was gone, she'd . . . improve. Like a curse being lifted. But it won't happen that way."

"Do you have any idea what it is?"

He shook his head. He had the hopeless air of a rat being badgered by a cat.

"What about her father? Could this be connected to him? She says he died in the war . . ."

"Your guess is as good as mine," he said, smiling wistfully. "Irene probably married me because of him . . ."

"Wanting a father?"

"Oh sure. Wanting everything—comfort, protection, security. You know what I want? I want to live one week without drama . . . seven days without tears and uproar and dependency and neediness, without all the juice being drained right out of me." He shook his head again. "Not going to happen in my lifetime. It's not going to happen in hers either. I might as well blow my brains out and be done with it."

"She must have suffered some kind of childhood trauma—"

"Oh, who gives a damn? Forty years ago? You're never going to get to the bottom of it and if you did, what difference would it make? She is who she is and I'm stuck."

"Why don't you bail out?"

"Leave Irene? How am I supposed to do that? Every time I think of leaving, she ends up flat on her back. I can't kick her when she's down . . ."

I heard a tap at the front window. Dietz was peering in. I let out a deep breath. I was never so relieved to see anyone.

"I'll get that," I said and moved to the front door. Dietz came in, his gaze straying to Clyde, who had leaned his head

194

against the back of the chair, eyes closed, playing dead. Dietz's mere presence caused the tension in the air to dissipate, but he could tell at a glance that all was not well. I lifted my brows slightly, conveying with a look that I'd fill him in once we were alone. "How'd it go?" I asked.

"Tell you about it in a minute. Let's get out of here."

I said, "Clyde . . ."

"I heard. Go ahead. We can talk later. Irene will sleep for hours. Maybe I'd be smart to get a little shut-eye myself."

I hesitated. "One question. Yesterday, when we were scouring the neighborhood for Agnes . . . do you remember anyone with a toolshed or a greenhouse on the property?"

He opened his eyes and looked at me. "No. Why?"

"The pathologist mentioned it. I said I'd get back to her."

He shook his head. "I was bumping front doors. There might have been a shed in somebody's backyard."

"If you remember something of the sort, will you let me know?"

He gestured a yes both dismissive and resigned.

I picked up the box and we walked out to the car. Dietz tucked me in the passenger seat.

"What's the matter, she didn't like the tea set?" he said. He shut the door on the passenger side and I was forced to hold my reply until he'd rounded the car and gotten in himself. He fired up the engine and pulled out. I gave him a quick rendition of Irene's collapse.

"What do you think she's sitting on?" he asked when I was done.

"Beats me. I can think of a few possibilities. Abuse of some kind, for one," I said. "She might have been a witness to an act of violence, or maybe *she* did something she feels guilty about."

"A little kid?"

"Hey, kids sometimes do things without meaning to. You never know. Whatever it is, if she has any conscious recollection, she's never mentioned it. And Clyde doesn't seem to have a clue."

"You think Agnes knew about it?"

"Oh sure. I think Agnes even tried to tell me, but she couldn't bring herself to do it. I sat with her late one night down in a Brawley convalescent home and she told me this long, garbled tale that I'm almost sure now had the truth embedded in it someplace. I'll tell you one thing. I'm not interested in driving back down to the desert to investigate. Forget that."

"Be pointless anyway after all these years."

"That's what Clyde says. What's the deal on Rochelle Messinger?"

Dietz pulled a slip of paper from his shirt pocket. "I got her number in North Hollywood. Dolan didn't want to give it to me, but I finally talked him into it. He says if we get a line on the guy, we're to stay strictly the hell away."

"Of course," I said. "What now?"

He looked over at me with his lopsided smile. "How about a Quarter Pounder with Cheese?"

I laughed. "Done."

We got back to the apartment at one o'clock, fully carbed up, our fat tanks on overload. I could feel my arteries hardening, plaques piling up in my veins like a logjam in a river, blood pressure going up from all the sodium.

Dietz tried calling Rochelle Messinger. When he got no answer after fifteen rings, he turned the phone over to me. I was aching for a nap, but I thought I'd better find out if Dr. Palchak had seen the slides yet. I didn't like the idea of cruising the neighborhood around the nursing home, bumping all those doors again. With luck, I wouldn't have to.

I put a call through to the pathology department at St. Terry's and had Laura Palchak paged. I had Irene's cardboard box on my lap, using it as an armrest. For ten cents, I would have put my head down and gone to sleep right there. Sometimes I long for the simplicity of kindergarten, which is where I learned to nap on command.

She picked up the phone on her end.

"Hi, Laura. Kinsey Millhone," I said. "I was wondering if you'd had a chance to examine the tissue slides."

"You bet," she said. There was a grim satisfaction in her voice.

"I take it your hunch turned out to be right on the money."

"Sure did. This is one I've never run across myself, but I remembered an abstract on the subject from a few years back. The hospital librarian tracked down the journal, which is on my desk somewhere. Hang on."

"What subject?"

"I'm getting to that. This is an article on 'Human stress cardiomyopathy' written by a couple of doctors in Ohio. Here we go. Catch this," she said. "Mrs. Grey suffered a characteristic damage to her heart—a cell death called myofibrillar degeneration brought on by fear-generated stress."

"Can you translate?"

"Sure, it's simple. When the body gets flooded with intolerable levels of adrenaline, heart cells are killed. The pockets of dead cells interfere with the normal electrical network that regulates the heart. When the nerve fibers are disrupted, the heart starts beating erratically and, in this case, that led to cardiac failure."

"Okay," I said cautiously. I had the feeling there was more. "So what's the punch line here?"

"This little old lady was quite literally scared to death."

"What?"

"It's just what it sounds like. Whatever happened to her in those hours she was gone, she was so badly frightened it killed her."

"Are you talking about her being lost or something more than that?"

"I suspect something more. The theory is that, under certain circumstances, the cumulative burden of psychological stress and pain can generate lethal charges in cardiac tissue."

"Like what?"

"Well, take a little kid. Her father beats her with a belt, ties her up, and leaves her bound in a vacant room overnight. Next morning, she's dead. The actual physical injuries aren't sufficient to cause death. I'm not talking about the stress levels most of us experience in the ordinary course of events. Without getting graphic about it, it's analogous to certain animal experiments relating focal myocardial necrosis to stress."

"You're telling me this is a homicide."

"In essence, yes. I don't think Dolan would consider it such, but that's my guess."

I sat for a moment while the information sank in. "I don't like this."

"I didn't think you would," she replied. "In the meantime, if you haven't figured out yet where she was, you might want to try again."

"Yes." I felt a heaviness in my chest, some ancient dread activated by the proximity to murder. I'd done my job efficiently. I'd tracked the woman down. I'd helped facilitate the plan to move her to Santa Teresa, despite her fears, despite her pleadings. Now she was dead. Was I inadvertently responsible for that, too?

After I hung up, I sat there so long I found Dietz staring at me with puzzlement. I was picking at the flaps of the cardboard box, peeling the first layer of paper away from the corrugation. I tried to imagine Agnes Grey's last day. Had she been abducted? If so, to what end? There'd been no demand for money. As far as I knew, there hadn't been contact of any kind. Who had reason to kill her? The only people she knew in this town were Irene and Clyde. Not beyond the possible, I thought to myself. Most homicides are personal crimes—victims killed by close relatives, friends, and acquaintances . . . which is why I limit mine.

Blindly, I looked down. The paper was coming loose from around the cup I'd rewrapped. The broken halves lay in a torn half-sheet of newsprint that was yellow with age. I blinked, focusing on the banner partially visible across the top. I tilted my head so I could read the newsprint. It was the business section of the *Santa Teresa Morning Press*, a precursor of the current *Santa Teresa Dispatch*. Puzzled, I removed the paper from the box and smoothed it across my lap. January 8, 1940. I checked the exterior of the box, but there were no postmarks and no shipping labels. Curious. Had Agnes been in Santa Teresa? I could have sworn Irene told me her mother had never been here.

I looked up. Dietz was standing right in front of me, hands on his knees, face level with mine. "Are you all right?"

"Look at this." I handed him the paper.

He turned it over in his hands, checking both sides. He noted the date as I had and his mouth pulled down in speculation. He wagged his head back and forth.

"What do you make of it?" I asked.

"Probably the same thing you do. It looks like the box was packed in Santa Teresa in January of nineteen forty."

"January eighth," I said, correcting him.

"Not necessarily. A lot of people save newspapers for a time at any rate. This might have been sitting in a stack somewhere. You know how it is. You need to wrap up some dishes and you grab a section from the pile."

"Well, that's true," I said. "Do you think Agnes did it? Was she actually *in* this town at that point?" It was a question we couldn't answer of course, but I needed to ask it anyway.

"You're sure the box was hers? She might have been holding it for someone else."

"Irene recognized the teacup. I could see it in her face for the half second before she started screaming."

"Let's see what else we've got here," Dietz said. "Maybe there's more."

We spent a few minutes carefully unpacking the box. Every piece of china—cups, saucers, creamer, sugar bowl, teapot with its rose-sprigged lid, some fifteen pieces in all—was wrapped in the same edition of the paper. There was nothing else of significance in the carton and the news itself didn't reveal anything of note.

I said, "I think we ought to get Irene out of bed and find out what's going on."

Dietz picked up his car keys and we were out the door.

• • •

We rang the Gershes' bell, waiting impatiently while Jermaine came to the door and admitted us. I had pictured her tidying things in our absence, but the living room looked exactly as it had when we'd left it, a little more than an hour ago. The couch cushions were still askew where Irene's thrashing had displaced them, the birth certificate, death certificate, and the "Vital Documents" file still strewn haphazardly across the coffee table. I caught a whiff of drying urine. The characteristic silence had descended again, as if life itself here were muffled and indistinct.

When I asked to see Clyde or Irene, Jermaine's dark face became stony. She crossed her arms, body language echoing her manner, which was clearly uncooperative. She said Mrs. Gersh was sleeping and she refused to wake her. Mr. Gersh was having "a little lay-down" and she refused to disturb him, too.

"This is really important," I said. "All I need is five minutes."

I could see her face set with stubbornness. "No, ma'am. I'm not about to bother them poor peoples. You leave them lay."

I glanced at Dietz. The shrug was written in his face. I looked back at Jermaine and indicated the coffee table with a nod. "Can I pick up the papers I left here earlier?"

"What papers? I don't know nothin' about that."

"For now all I need are the forms Irene and I were working on," I said. "I can come back later for a chat with her."

Her gaze was pinned on me with suspicion. I kept my expression bland. "Go on, then," she said. "If that's all you want."

"Thanks." Casually, I crossed to the coffee table and picked up the birth certificate and the entire document file. Thirty seconds later, we were out on the porch.

"What'd you do that for?" Dietz said as we headed down the steps.

"It just seemed like a good idea," I said.

22

I asked him to pull around the corner and park in an alleyway. We sat there in the dappled shade of an overhanging oak while I sorted through the contents of the Gershes' "Vital Documents" file. Nothing looked that vital to me. There was a copy of the will, which I handed to Dietz. "See if this tells us anything astonishing."

He took the stapled pages, reaching automatically toward his shirt pocket. I thought he was looking for a cigarette, but it turned out to be a pair of reading glasses with half-rims that he'd tucked there instead. He put them on and then looked over at me.

"What?" he said.

I nodded judiciously. "The glasses are good. Make you look like a serious adult."

"You think so?" He craned so he could see himself in the rearview mirror. He crossed his eyes and stuck his tongue out, just to show how adult he could look.

He began leafing through the will while I glanced at insurance policies, the title to the house, a copy of the emission inspection information for a vehicle they owned, an American Express flight insurance policy. "God, this is boring," I said.

"So's this."

I looked over at him. I could see his gaze skimming down the lines of print. I returned to my pile of papers. I picked up Irene's birth certificate and squinted at it in the light.

"What's that?"

"Irene's birth certificate." I told him the story she'd told me about the autobiography for her senior English class. "Something about it bothers me, but I can't figure out what it is."

"It's a photocopy," he said.

"Yeah, but what's the big whoopee-do about that?"

"Let me take a look." He placed it up against the windshield, letting the light shine through. The heading read: STATE OF CALIFORNIA DEPARTMENT OF HEALTH VITAL STATISTICS, STANDARD CERTIFICATE OF BIRTH. The form thereafter was comprised of a series of two-line boxes into which the data had been typed. He held it close to his face, like a man whose eyesight is failing rapidly. "Lot of these lines are broken and the type itself isn't very crisp. We ought to check with Sacramento and track down the original."

"You think it's been tampered with?"

"It's possible. Dab some kind of correction fluid on the original. Type over the blanks and then make a copy. It couldn't be used for much, but it'd be sufficient for a school project. Maybe that's why it took Agnes a day to produce the damn thing. The point of certified copies is that they're certified, right?" He gave me that crooked smile, gray eyes clear.

"Wow, what a concept," I said. "Wonder what she had to hide?"

Dietz shrugged. "Maybe Irene was illegitimate."

"Right," I said. "Can you think of anyone we can contact in Sacramento?"

"Department of Health? Not right offhand. Why not check with the county recorder here and have them call?"

"You think they'd do that?"

"Sure, why not?"

"Well, it's worth a try," I said. "Besides, if we do the research now, Irene will pay for it. Wait two weeks and she'll forget she ever gave a damn."

"Let's give it a shot, then," he said. "You want me to look at any other documents?"

"Nope. That's it."

"Great." He handed me the will and the birth certificate, both of which I tucked back into the file. He started the car and headed out to the street.

"Where to?" I asked.

"Let's hit the office first and call Rochelle Messinger."

We parked in the back lot and went up the exterior stairs. Dietz was, as usual, paranoid about everyone within range. He kept a hand on my elbow, his gaze scanning the area, until we were safely in the building. The second-floor corridor was empty. As we passed the rest rooms, I said, "I need to pop into the ladies' room. You want the office keys?"

"Sure. I'll see you in a few minutes." Dietz started to check out the ladies' room and was greeted by a shriek of outrage. He moved on down the corridor while I went into the john.

Darcy was standing at one of the sinks, splashing water on her face. From her pasty complexion and the eyes pinched with pain, I gathered she was still hung over from the banquet the night before. She stared at herself in the mirror, hair mashed flat in two places. "You know you're really in trouble when your hair goes out on you," she remarked, more to herself than to me.

"What time did you get in?" I asked.

"It wasn't that late, but I'd been drinking anisette and I was wrecked. I started upchucking about midnight and haven't stopped yet," she said. She rubbed her face and then pulled her lower lids down so she could inspect the conjunctivas. "Nothing like a hangover to make you long for death . . ."

A toilet flushed and Vera emerged from one of the four stalls. She was buttoning up an olive and khaki camouflage outfit, a jumpsuit with big shoulder pads and epaulettes, looking like she was moments away from a landing on Anzio Beach. The glance she gave me was not friendly. "What happened to you last night?" she said waspishly. I was exhausted and my nerves were on edge, so her tone didn't sit well and neither did her attitude.

I said, "Well, jump right in, Vera. Agnes Grey died, among other things. I didn't get to bed till after three A.M. How about you?"

Vera crossed to the sinks, her high heels snapping against the ceramic tiles. She turned the water on way too hard and splashed herself. She jumped back. "*Shit!*" she said.

"Agnes Grey?" Darcy said. She was watching our reflections in the mirror, her expression wary.

"My client's mother," I said. "She dropped dead of a heart attack."

Darcy frowned. "That's weird."

"Actually it was weird, but how did you know?"

"Do you *mind*?" Vera said to Darcy pointedly. Apparently, she wanted to talk to me alone. It occurred to me belatedly that she and Vera had been discussing me just before I came in. Oh boy.

Darcy shot me an apologetic look. She dried her hands hastily under the wall-mounted blower, blotting the residual water on the back of her skirt. "See you later, gang," she said. She took her purse and departed with a decided air of relief.

The door hadn't closed behind her when Vera turned and looked at me. "I don't appreciate the crap you told Neil last night," she said. Her face was tense, her gaze fiery.

I felt a rush of heat go through me. I needed to pee, but it seemed inappropriate. "Really," I said. "Like what?"

"I am not *smitten* with him. We're strictly friends and that's all it is. Get it?"

"What are you in such a snit about?"

She leaned against the sink, a hand on her hip. "I introduced you to the man because I thought you'd get along with him, not to have you turn around and ... *manipulate* the circumstances."

"How did I do that?"

"You know how! You told him I had a crush on him and now he's behaving like an idiot."

"What'd he do, break it off?"

"Of course he didn't break it off! He *proposed* to me last night!"

"He did? Well, that's great! Congratulations. I hope you said yes."

Vera's mouth turned down at the corners and she burst into tears. I was taken aback. For a sophisticated woman, she was bawling like a little kid. I found myself with my arms around her, patting her awkwardly. It's not easy to comfort someone twice your size. She had to hunch down slightly while I raised up on tiptoe. It was not the full California body hug of longtime friends. Contact was limited to the upper portions of our torsos where we were linked like the two bowed wings of a wishbone.

"What am I gonna doooo?" she wailed into my right ear.

"You might think about getting married," I suggested helpfully.

"I caaaan't."

"Of course you can, Vera. People do it every day."

"I'm too old and too tall and he says he wants kids."

I could feel a laugh bubble up, but I resisted the urge to make a flip remark. I said mothering-type things, "There, there" and "It's all right." Remarkably, it seemed to work. Within a minute, she calmed down to a series of hiccups and sniffs. She let out a big sigh and then blew her nose noisily on a piece of shriveled Kleenex she found in her jumpsuit. She pressed the tissue to her eyes and then she did a quick burbling laugh while she checked her makeup. "When I saw you and Neil with your heads bent together last night I wanted to kill you."

"Yeah, I caught the look. I just wasn't sure what it meant," I said.

"And right about then, Mac started making his speech and next thing I knew you were gone. What was that about?"

I filled her in on (some, but not all of) my night's activities and then quizzed her on hers.

She spent the next few minutes detailing the portion of the banquet I'd missed. Neil had slipped over into Dietz's chair while Mac finished his speech. After-dinner drinks arrived. She was so upset with Neil because of his apparent interest in me, she started tossing down brandies and the next thing she knew, the two of them were back in her room making love. She started laughing again. "We didn't even make it to the bed. The maid came in to turn the sheets down and there we were *grappling* on the floor. We never even heard her knock. It turned out she was a patient of his at the clinic where he works. You know how you do when the phone rings and you're on the pot? He sort of scrambled to his feet and hobbled off to the bathroom with his trousers down around his knees."

"Vera, if I laugh now, I'll end up peeing in my pants." I gave her a quick pat and headed straight to the nearest stall, relieving myself while I talked to her across the top of the cubicle. "What happened to the maid? She must have been mortified," I said. "Her own doctor with his bum hanging out of his pants? My God."

"She was out of there like a shot and that's when he proposed. He started screaming it was my fault. He said if I'd marry him we could grapple on our own floor without all the interruptions—"

"The man's got a point."

"You really think so?"

I flushed the toilet and emerged. "Vera, do me a favor. Just marry the guy. He's a doll. You'll be deliriously happy for eternity. I promise." I washed my hands and dried them, grabbing up my shoulder bag. "Dietz is waiting for me. I gotta go or he'll think I've been kidnapped. I get dibs on maid of honor, but I won't wear dusty rose. Let me know when you set the date." When I left, she was staring after me with a dazed look on her face.

As I passed California Fidelity, I caught sight of Darcy at

the file cabinet behind the receptionist's desk. She was barely moving, apparently intent on cooling her fevered brow against the cold metal of the cabinet top where she'd laid her head. I detoured into the office. She managed to raise her eyes without moving her head. "Vera chew your ass out?"

"We're fine. She's getting married. You can be the flower girl," I said. "I need to know what you were talking about when I mentioned that Agnes died. You said it was weird. What was weird?"

"Oh, I wasn't referring to her death," Darcy said. "That's the name of a book."

"A *book*?"

"*Agnes Grey*. It's a novel by Anne Brontë, written in eighteen forty-seven. I know because it was the subject of my senior thesis at UNLV."

"You went to college in Las Vegas?"

"What's wrong with that? I grew up there. Anyway, I was a lit major and it was the only paper I ever wrote that netted me an A-plus."

"I thought the name was Charlotte Brontë."

"This is a sister. The youngest. Most people only know about the two older ones, Charlotte and Emily."

A chill tiptoed over me like a daddy longlegs. "Emily . . ."

"She wrote *Wuthering Heights*."

"Right," I said faintly. Darcy went on talking, waxing eloquent about the Brontës. I was sifting back through Agnes's account of Emily's death, the hapless "Lottie" who was simpleminded and couldn't remember how to get in and out the back door. Was her real name Charlotte? Could Agnes Grey's real name be Anne something, or was that strictly a coincidence? I moved back toward the corridor.

"Kinsey?" Darcy was startled, but I didn't want to stop and explain what was going on. I didn't get it myself.

When I got to my office, Dietz was just hanging up the phone. "Did you talk to Rochelle?" I asked, distracted.

"It's all taken care of. She's hopping in her car and heading straight up. She has a friend who runs a motel on Cabana called the Ocean View. I said we'd meet her there at four. You know the place?"

"As a matter of fact, I do," I said. The Ocean View had been the setting of my last and most enlightening encounter with an ex-husband named Daniel Wade. Not my best day, but liberating after a fashion. What had Agnes told me about Emily? She was killed in an earthquake. Down in Brawley or somewhere else? Lottie was the first to go. Then the chimney fell on Emily. There was more, but I couldn't remember what it was.

Dietz glanced at his watch. "What shall we do till she gets here? You want to pop by your place?"

"Give me a minute to think." I sat down in my client chair and ran my hand through my hair. Dietz had the good sense to hold his tongue and let me ruminate. At this point, I didn't even want to have to stop and bring him up to speed. Could Emily's death have been the event that precipitated Agnes Grey's departure from Santa Teresa? Had she actually been here? If the name Agnes Grey was a phony, then what was her real name? And why the subterfuge?

"Let me try this on you," I said to Dietz. I took a few minutes then to fill him in on Darcy's remark. "Suppose her name really wasn't Agnes Grey. Suppose she used that as a cover name . . . a kind of code. . . ."

"To what end?" he asked.

"I don't know," I said. "I think she wanted to tell the truth. I think she wanted someone to know, but she couldn't bring herself to say it. She was terrified about coming up to Santa Teresa, I do know that. At the time, I figured she was nervous about the trip—unhappy about the nursing home. I just assumed her anxiety was related to the present, but maybe not. She might have lived here once upon a time. I gather she and Emily were sisters and there was a third one named Lottie. She might have known some critical fact about the way Emily died. . . ."

"But now what? At this point, we don't even know what her real name was."

I held a finger up. "But we do know about the earth-quake."

"Kinsey, in California, you're talking eight or ten a *year*."

"I know, but most of those are minor. This one was big enough that someone died."

"So?"

"So let's go to the public library and look up the Santa Teresa earthquakes and see if we can find out who she was."

"You're going to research every local earthquake with fatalities," he said, his voice flat with disbelief.

"Not quite. I'm going to start with January six or seven, nineteen forty . . . the day before that box was packed."

Dietz laughed. "I love it."

23

The periodicals room at the Santa Teresa Public Library is down a flight of stairs, a spacious expanse of burnt-orange carpeting and royal blue upholstered chairs, with slanted shelves holding row after row of magazines and newspapers. A border of windows admits ample sunshine and recessed lighting heightens the overall illumination. We traversed the length of the room, approaching an L-shaped desk on the left.

The librarian was a man in his fifties in a dress shirt and tie, no coat. His gray hair was curly and he wore glasses with tortoiseshell frames, a little half-moon of bifocal in the lower portion of each lens. "May I help you?"

"We're trying to track down the identity of a woman who might have died in one of the Santa Teresa earthquakes. Do you have any suggestions about where we might start to look?"

"Just a moment," he said. He consulted with another of the staff, an older woman, and then crossed to his desk and sorted through a pile of pamphlets, selecting one. When he returned he had a local publication, called *A Field Guide to the*

Earthquake History of Santa Teresa. "Let's see. I can give you the dates for earthquakes that occurred in nineteen sixty-eight, nineteen fifty-two, nineteen forty-one—"

"That's a possibility," I said to Dietz.

He shook his head. "Too late. It would have been before nineteen forty if that newspaper has any bearing. What other dates do you show?"

The librarian flipped the booklet open to a chart that listed the important quakes offshore in the Santa Teresa channel. "November four, nineteen twenty-seven, there was a seven point five quake, but that was west of Point Arguello and the damage here was slight."

"No casualties?" Dietz asked.

"Evidently not. There was an earthquake in eighteen twelve that destroyed the mission at La Purisima. Several more from July to December nineteen oh-two . . ."

"I think we want something after that," I said.

"Well then, your best bet would probably be to start with the big quake in nineteen twenty-five."

"All right. Let's try that."

The man nodded and moved to a row of wide gray file cabinets, returning moments later with a box of microfilm. "This is April first through June thirtieth. The quake actually occurred on the twenty-ninth of June, but I don't believe you'll find a newspaper reference until the day after." He pointed to the left. "The machines are over there. Use the schematic diagram to thread the film."

"If I find something I need, can I get a copy?"

"Certainly. Simply position that portion of the page between the two red dots on the screen and press the white button in the front."

We sat down at one of four machines, placing the spool on the spindle to the left, slipping the film across the viewer and attaching it so that it would wind onto the spool on the right side of the machine. I turned the automatic-forward knob from off to the slow speed position. The first page of the paper came into view against a background of black. The edges of the pages were ragged in places, but for the most part the picture was clear. Dietz stood behind me, looking over my shoulder as I turned the knob to fast forward.

Days whipped across the screen in a blur, like a cinematic device. Now and then, I'd halt the process, checking to see how far we'd gone. April 22. May 14. June 3. I slowed the machine. Finally, June 30 crept into view. The big earthquake had occurred at 6:42 A.M. on June 29. According to the paper, the severity of the quake was such that the concrete pavement buckled and street signs were snapped as if they were threads. The reservoir broke and sent a flood of mud and water into Montebello. Gas and electric power were shut off immediately and in consequence, there was only one fire, easily contained. Many buildings downtown were badly damaged, the streetcar track was snapped, the asphalt pavement sank six inches in places. Residents slept outside that night and many cars were reported on the highway heading south. In all, there were thirteen fatalities. Both the dead and injured were listed. Sometimes ages and occupations were specified, along with home addresses if they were known. None among the dead seemed remotely related to the tale Agnes Grey had told me.

I was hand-cranking the machine by then, stopping the film at intervals so that we could scan each column. A prominent widow had been crushed to death when the walls of a hotel toppled in on her. The body of a dentist was removed from the ruins of his office building. There was no mention of anyone named Emily. "What do you think?" I said to Dietz.

He made a thumbs-down gesture. I rewound the microfilm and took it off the spindle. We returned the box of film to the main counter, consulting in low tones, trying to figure out what to try next, if anything. Dietz said, "What year was Agnes born?"

"Nineteen hundred, as nearly as we can tell . . . though there's some question. It might have been nineteen thirteen."

"So she would have been somewhere between twelve and

twenty-five in nineteen twenty-five. If you figure her sister was in a five- or six-year age range of her, she could have been any age from six to thirty."

"We didn't see a female earthquake victim even close to that," I said.

Dietz lifted his brow. "For all we know, Emily was the family dog."

The librarian approached, smiling politely. "Find what you were looking for?"

"Not really," I said. "Would you have anything else?"

He took up his field guide with patient interest in our plight. "Let's see here. Well ... it looks like there was an aftershock to that nineteen twenty-five earthquake. Here ... June twenty-nine, nineteen twenty-six ... exactly one year later to the day. One fatality. The only other earthquake of note would have been November four, nineteen twenty-seven, but there were no fatalities recorded in that one. Would you like to take a look at the one in 'twenty-six?"

"Sure."

We went back to the same machine, repeating the process of threading the film. Again, we flew through the calendar, time flashing by in a whir of gray. As we reached the end of the reel, I slowed the machine, hand-cranking my way from day to day, scanning one column at a time. Dietz was leaning over my shoulder, making sure I didn't miss anything. I was losing hope. I thought it was a good theory—hell, it was my *only* theory. If this didn't pay off, we were out of luck.

I read about Babe Ruth, who'd just hit his twenty-sixth homer of the season back in Philadelphia. I read about some woman whose six-year marriage was annulled when she found out her former spouse was still alive. I read about Aimee Semple McPherson's stout defense of her alleged kidnapping at the hands of strangers ...

"There it is," Dietz said. He put a finger on the screen.

I let out a yelp and laughed. Six library patrons turned around and looked at me. I put a hand across my mouth sheepishly. I peered at the machine. It was like a gift—such an unexpected pleasure—lines leaping off the page. The article was brief and the style faintly antique, but the facts were clear and it all seemed to fit.

WOMAN KILLED AS BRICKS FALL
Chimney Crushes Out the Life of Local Resident

Emily Bronfen, 29-year-old bookkeeper employed by Brookfield, McClintock and Gaskell, met death yesterday afternoon when bricks fell from a chimney at the family home, 1107 Sumner Street, and crushed her during an earth tremor at 3:20 P.M. The body was taken to the Donovan Brothers funeral parlor and will be cremated today at 4:00.

The Associated Press reported that the shock, which swung doors at Pasadena and swayed hanging electric light drops at Santa Monica, was also felt in Los Angeles, where occupants of office buildings noticed their swivel chairs doing a wild shimmy along the floor.

Ventura reported two separate shocks lasting about four or five seconds each. Santa Monica reported a second shock shortly after 7:00 last night.

L. L. Pope, Santa Teresa City Building Inspector, made the rounds of the city yesterday afternoon and reported that he found no damage to any building erected under provisions of the new building code. "There was very little structural damage of any kind," he declared. "It was virtually all confined to old fire walls, some of which were fractured in the earthquake of one year ago . . ."

I turned and looked up at Dietz. We locked eyes for a moment and his mouth came down on mine. I'd reached a hand up, closing my fist in his hair. He reached a hand down my shirt and rubbed his fingertips across my left breast.

"Print it," he said hoarsely.

"Oh God," I breathed.

At the counter, the librarian pulled his glasses down and peered at us over the rims.

Blushing, I straightened my collar and adjusted my shirt. I pressed the button. We picked up an invoice for the photocopy at the desk when we turned in the microfilm. We left the periodicals room without further reference to the two librarians, who seemed to be conversing together about some terribly amusing subject.

"Bronfen. I like that. It's close enough to Brontë," I said as I followed him up the stairs. "The parents must have been big on Victorian literature."

"Possibly," Dietz said. "I don't know what it proves at this point."

On the main floor, we checked back through various city directories. The 1926 edition showed a Maude Bronfen (occupation, widow) at the address listed in the paper. "Shoot," I said. "I was hoping we'd find Anne."

Dietz said, "Maude was probably their mother. What now?"

"Let's try the Hall of Records. It's just across the street. Maybe we can track down Irene's birth certificate."

We paid for the photocopy, left the library, and headed over to the courthouse, crossing the one-way street. Dietz had taken me by the elbow, his gaze divided equally among cars approaching from the left, pedestrians in the general vicinity, and possible vantage points in the event Mark Messinger had chosen this location to pick me off. "So what's the operating theory here?" I asked.

He considered that for a moment. "Well, if I were altering a document like that, I'd try to keep the changes to a minimum. There's less chance of screwing up."

"You think Irene's first name is real then?"

"Probably. I'd guess the attending physician, date, and time of birth are okay, too, along with the filing date and the name of the registrar or deputy."

"Why would Agnes change her age? That seems peculiar."

"Who knows? Maybe she was older than the guy and too vain to have it part of the public record. As long as you're altering reality, you might as well eliminate anything that doesn't suit."

The recorder division of the county clerk's office is in an annex to the Santa Teresa Courthouse, a ground-floor office in the northwest corner of the building. We cut across the big square of side lawn to the entrance, pushing through the fifteen-foot wood-and-glass door. The interior was comprised of an outer office with a counter running along our left, a glossy red tile floor, a table and chairs available for those filling out forms, and on the right, glass display cases mounted on the wall, filled with samples of foreign currency. Behind the counter was a large, open office space broken up by the ubiquitous "action stations" that seem to characterize every other office I've seen of late.

There was one couple at the counter ahead of us, apparently picking up a marriage license. The husband-to-be was one of those skinny guys with a narrow butt and tattoos all up and down his arms. The bride was twice his size and so pregnant she was already into her Lamaze. She clung to the counter, her face damp with perspiration, panting heavily while the clerk completed all the papers in haste.

"You sure you're okay? We can probably get a wheelchair from someplace," she said. The clerk was in her sixties and didn't seem anxious so much as intent on efficiency. Visions of lawsuits were probably dancing in her head. Also, she might not have been certified in midwifery. I wondered if Dietz had any experience in delivery.

The bride, at the pinnacle of a contraction, shook her head mutely. "I'm ... fine ... unh ... I'm fine ..." She had a gardenia pinned in her hair. I tried to picture the wedding announcement in the papers. "The bride, in a peau-de-soie maternity smock, was accompanied by her obstetrician ..."

"Judge Hopper's waiting for us upstairs," the husband said. He smelled of Brylcreem and cigarettes, his blue jeans pleated up around his waist with a length of rope.

The clerk handed over the certificate. "Why don't I have June get the judge on the phone and have him come down here?"

A second clerk, her eyes rolling, picked up the telephone

and made a quick call while the bride crept haltingly toward the door. She seemed to be singing to herself. "Uh . . . uh . . . unh . . ."

The groom didn't seem that distressed. He simply matched his pace to hers, his gaze pinned on her shuffling feet. "You're not breathing right," he said crossly.

The clerk turned to us. "What can I do for you folks?"

Dietz was still staring off at the departing couple with a look of uneasiness.

I held out the copy of the birth certificate. "I wonder if you can help us," I said. "We suspect maybe this birth certificate's been tampered with and we'd like to check for the original in Sacramento. Is there any way you can do that? I notice there are some file numbers."

The clerk held the paper at arm's length, her thumbnail moving from point to point across the document. "Well, here's your first problem right here. You see that district number? That's incorrect. This says Brawley on the face of it, but the district number's off. Imperial County would be thirteen something. This fifty-nine fifty indicates Santa Teresa County."

"It does? That's great," I said. "You mean you'll have a copy of it here?"

"Oh sure. That little two in the margin tells you the book number and this number here is the page. Just a minute and I'll have someone pull the microfilm. Machines are right through there. You just have a seat and someone will be with you directly."

We waited maybe five minutes and then the second clerk, June, appeared with a microfilm cartridge, which she loaded into the machine.

Once we located the page, it didn't take us long to find Irene's name. Dietz was right. The date and time of birth and the physician's name were the same on both documents. Irene's name, the ages of both parents, and her mother's occupation were also the same. Everything else had been altered.

Her father's name was Patrick Bronfen, his occupation car salesman. Her mother's first name was Sheila, maiden name Farfell.

"Who the hell is this?" I said with disbelief. "I thought her mother's name would be Anne."

"Isn't Sheila the name Agnes mentioned to the cop who brought her into emergency?"

I turned around and stared at him. "That's right. I'd forgotten."

"If it's true, it might imply that Agnes and Sheila are the same person."

I made a face. "Sure shoots our Brontë theory. But hey, check this." I pointed to the screen. The address listed was the same one given for Emily Bronfen, whose death had occurred ten years before Irene's birth—fourteen years before the tea set had been packed away in the box. I found myself squinting, trying to make sense of it. Dietz seemed equally mystified. What the hell *was* this?

24

We paid eleven dollars and waited another ten minutes for a certified copy of Irene's birth certificate. I didn't think she'd believe us unless she saw it for herself. As we left the Hall of Records, I paused briefly at the counter, where the clerk who had helped us was sorting through a pile of computer forms.

"Do you have a city map?" I asked.

She shook her head. "The docent might have one at the information booth around the corner on the first floor," she said. "What street are you looking for? Maybe I can help."

I showed her the address on the birth certificate. "This says Eleven Oh-seven Sumner, but I've never heard of it. Is there such a street?"

"Well, yes, but the name was changed years ago. Now it's Concorde."

"Concorde used to be Sumner?" I said, repeating the information blankly. News to me, I thought. And then I got it. I lowered my head for a moment. "Dietz, *that's* what Agnes was talking about in the emergency room. She didn't say 'it used to be summer.' She was saying 'Sum*ner*.' That's where the nursing home is. She knew the street."

"Sounds good," Dietz said. He took me by the elbow and we pushed through the double doors, heading back to the public garage where his car was parked.

We were getting close to the answer and I was beginning to fly. I could feel my brain cells doing a little tap dance of delight. I was half-skipping, excitement bubbling out of me as we crossed the street. "I love information. I love information. Isn't this great? God, it's fun . . ."

Dietz was frowning in concentration as he scanned the walkway between the library and the parking structure, unwilling to be distracted from his assessment of the situation. We reached the three-story garage and started climbing the outside stairs.

"What do you think the story is?" he finally asked as we passed the second landing. I was straggling behind him, working hard to keep up. For a man who'd only quit smoking four days before, he was in remarkable shape.

"I don't know yet," I said. "Patrick could have been a brother. They lived at the same address. The point is, Emily did die in the earthquake just like Agnes said. Or at least that's how it looked. . . ."

"But what's it got to do with Irene Gersh? She wasn't even born then."

"I haven't figured that part out yet, but it has to fit. I think she witnessed an act of violence. It just wasn't Emily. Let's go to Eleven Oh-seven Concorde and see who lives there. Maybe we can get a line on this Bronfen guy."

"Don't you want to go talk to Irene about it first?"

"No way. She's too stressed out. We can fill her in afterwards."

I arrived at the top level of the structure, heart pounding, out of breath. One of these days, I was going to have to start jogging again. Amazing how quickly the body tends to backslide. When we reached the car, I shifted impatiently from foot to foot while Dietz went through his inspection routine with the Porsche, checking the doors first for any signs of a booby trap, peering at the engine, the underside of the chassis, and up along the wheel mounts. Finally, he unlocked the door on my side and ushered me in. I leaned across the driver's seat and unlocked his door for him.

He got in and started up the engine. "Lay you dollars to doughnuts, there's nobody left. If this traumatic event took place in January nineteen forty, you're talking more than forty years ago. Whatever happened, all the principal players would be a hundred and ten . . . if any were alive."

I held my hand out. "Five bucks says you're wrong."

He looked at me with surprise and then we shook hands on the bet. He glanced at his watch. "Whatever we do, let's be quick about it. Rochelle Messinger's due up here in an hour."

Pulling out of the parking structure, he cut over one block and headed left on Santa Teresa Street. Concorde was only nine blocks north of the courthouse, the same quiet tree-lined avenue Clyde Gersh and I had walked yesterday in our search for Agnes. Unless I was completely off, this had to be an area she recognized. Certainly, it was the address given for Emily Bronfen at the time of her death. It was also the house where Irene's parents resided at the time of her birth ten years later.

Dietz turned right onto Concorde. The nursing home was visible above the treetops, half a block away. I was watching house numbers march upward toward the eleven-hundred mark, my gut churning with a mixture of anticipation and dread. Please let it be there, I thought. Please let us get to the bottom of this . . .

Dietz slowed and pulled into the curb. He turned the engine off while I stared at the house. It was right next door to the place where Mark Messinger had caught up with me and sprayed the porch with gunfire.

I held a hand out to Dietz without even looking at him. "Pay up," I said, gaze still pinned on the three-story clapboard house. "I met Bronfen yesterday. I just figured out how I know him. He turned the place into a board-and-care. I met him once before when a friend of mine was looking for a facility for her sister in a wheelchair." I saw a face appear briefly at a second-floor window. I opened the car door and grabbed my handbag. "Come on. I don't want the guy to scurry out the back way."

Dietz was right behind me as we pushed through the shrieking iron gate and went up the front walk, taking the porch steps two at a time. "I'll jump in if you need me," he murmured. "Otherwise, you're the boss."

"You may be the only man I ever met who'd concede that without a fight."

"I can't wait to see how you do this."

"You and me both." I rang the bell. The owner took his sweet time about answering. I really hadn't even formulated what I meant to say to him. I could hardly pretend to be doing a marketing survey.

He opened the door, a heavyset man in his seventies, diffuse light shining softly on his balding pate. It was strange how different he looked to me. Yesterday, his elongated forehead had lent him a babylike air of innocence. Today, the furrowed brow suggested a man who had much to worry him. I had to make a conscious effort not to stare at the mole on his cheek. "Yes?"

"I'm Kinsey Millhone. Do you remember me from yesterday?"

His mouth pulled together sourly. "With all the gun battles going on, it'd be hard to forget." His gaze shifted. "I don't remember this gent."

I tilted a nod at Dietz. "This is my partner, Robert Dietz."

Dietz reached past me and shook hands with Bronfen. "Nice to meet you, sir. Sorry about all the uproar." He put his left hand behind his ear. "I don't believe I caught your name."

"Pat Bronfen. If you're still looking for that old woman, I'm afraid I can't help. I said I'd keep an eye out, but that's the best I can do." He moved as though to close the door.

I held a finger up. "Actually, this is about something else." I took the birth certificate from my handbag and held it out to him. He declined to take it, but he scanned the face of it.

His expression shifted warily when he realized what it was. "How'd you get this?"

The inspiration came to me in a flash. "From Irene Bronfen. She was adopted by a couple in Seattle, but she's instituted a search for her birth parents."

He squinted at me, but said nothing.

"I take it you're the Patrick Bronfen mentioned on her birth certificate?"

He hesitated. "What of it?"

"Can you tell me where I might find Mrs. Bronfen?"

"No, ma'am. That woman left me more than forty years ago, and took Irene with her," he said, with irritation. "I never knew what happened to the child, let alone what became of Sheila. I didn't even know she put the child up for adoption. Nobody told me the first thing about it. That's against the law, isn't it? If I wasn't even notified? You can't sign someone's child away without so much as a by-your-leave."

"I'm not really sure about the legalities," I said. "Irene hired me to see what I could find out about you and your ex-wife."

"She's not my ex-wife. I'm still married to the woman in the eyes of the law. I couldn't divorce her if I didn't know where she was." He gestured impatiently, but he was running out of steam and I could see his mood shift. "That wasn't Irene, sitting on my front porch steps yesterday, was it?"

"Actually, it was."

He shook his head. "I can't believe it. I remember her when she was this high. Now she'd have to be forty-seven years old." He stared down at the porch, brow knitting parallel stitches between his eyes. "My own baby girl and I didn't recognize her. I always thought I'd be able to pick her out of a crowd."

"She wasn't well. You really never got a good look at her," I said.

He looked up at me wistfully. "Did she know who I was?"

"I'm sure she didn't. I didn't realize it myself until a little while ago. The certificate says Sumner. It took us a while to realize the address was still good."

"I'm surprised she didn't recognize the house. She was almost four when Sheila took her. Used to sit right there on the steps, playing with her little dollies." He shoved his hands in his pockets.

It was occurring to me that Irene's asthma attack might well have been generated by an unconscious recognition of the place. "Maybe some of the memories will come back to her once she knows about you," I said.

His eyes had come back to mine with curiosity. "How'd you track me down?"

"Through the adoption agency," I said. "They had her birth certificate on file."

He shook his head. "Well, I hope you'll tell her how much I'd like to see her. I'd given up any expectation of it after all these years. I don't suppose you'd give me her address and telephone number."

"Not without her permission," I said. "In the meantime, I'm still interested in finding Mrs. Bronfen. Do you have any suggestions about where I might start to look?"

"No, ma'am. After she left, I tried everything I could think of—police, private investigators. I put notices in the newspapers all up and down the coast. I never heard a word."

"Do you remember when she left?"

"Not to the day. It would have been the fall of nineteen thirty-nine. September, I believe."

"Do you have any reason to think she might be dead?"

He thought about that briefly. "Well, no. But then I don't have any reason to think she's still alive either."

I took a small spiral-bound notebook from my handbag and leafed through a page or two. I was actually consulting an old grocery list, which Dietz studied with interest, looking over my shoulder. He gave me a bland look. I said, "The adoption agency mentions someone named Anne Bronfen. Would that be your sister? The files weren't clear about the connection. I gathered she was listed as next-of-kin when the adoption forms were filled out."

224

"Well now, I did have a sister named Anne, but she died in nineteen forty . . . three or four months after Sheila left."

I stared at him. "Are you sure of that?"

"She's buried out at Mt. Calvary. Big family plot on the hillside just as you go in the gate. She was only forty years old, a terrible thing."

"What happened to her?"

"Died of childbed fever. You don't see much of that anymore, but it sometimes took women in those days. She married late in life. Some fellow named Chapman from over near Tucson. Had three little boys one right after the other, and died shortly after she was delivered of her third. I paid to bring her back. I couldn't believe she'd want to be buried out in that godforsaken Arizona countryside. It's too ugly and too dry."

"Is there any possibility she might have heard from Sheila in those few months?"

He shook his head. "Not that she ever told me. She was living in Tucson at the time Sheila ran off. I suppose Sheila might have gone to her, but I never heard of it. Now, how about you answer me one. What happened with that old woman who wandered off from the nursing home? You never said if she turned up or not."

"Actually she did, about eleven o'clock last night. The police picked her up right out here in the street. She died in the emergency room shortly afterward."

"Died? Well, I'm sorry to hear that."

We went through our good-bye exercises, making appropriate noises.

Walking back to the car, Dietz and I didn't say a word. He unlocked the door and let me in. Once he eased in on his side, we sat in silence. He looked over at me. "What do you think?"

I stared back at the house. "I don't believe he was telling the truth."

He started the car. "Me neither. Why don't we check out the gravesite he was talking about?"

25

They were all there. It was eerie to see them— Charlotte, Emily, and Anne—their gravestones lined up in date order, first to last. The markers were plain; information limited to the bare bones, as it were. Their parents, the elder Bronfens, were buried side by side: Maude and Herbert, bracketed on the left by two daughters who had apparently died young. Adjoining those plots, there was an empty space I assumed was meant for Patrick when the time came. On the other side were the three I knew of: Charlotte, born 1894, died in 1917; Emily, born 1897, died in 1926; and Anne, who was born in 1900 and died in 1940.

I stared off down the hill. Mt. Calvary was a series of rolling green pastures, bordered by a forest of evergreens and eucalyptus trees. Most of the gravestones were laid flat in the ground, but I could see other sections like this one, where the monuments were upright, most dating back to the late nineteenth century. The heat of the afternoon sun was beginning to wane. It wouldn't be dark for hours yet, but a chill would settle in as it did every day. A bird sang a flat note to me from somewhere in the trees.

I shook my head, trying to make the information compute.

Dietz had the good sense to keep his mouth shut, but his look said "What?" as clearly as if he'd spoken.

"It just makes no sense. If Sheila Bronfen and Agnes Grey are the same person, then why don't their ages line up right? Agnes couldn't have been seventy when she died. She was eighty-plus. I know she was."

"So the two aren't the same. So what? You came up with a theory and it didn't prove out."

"Maybe," I said.

"Maybe, my ass. Give it up, Millhone. You can't manipulate the facts to fit your hypothesis. Start with what you know and give the truth a chance to emerge. Don't force a conclusion just to satisfy your own ego."

"I'm not forcing anything."

"Yes, you are. You hate to be wrong—"

"I do not!"

"Yes, you do. Don't bullshit me—"

"That has nothing to do with it! If the two aren't the same, so be it. But then, who was Agnes Grey and how'd she end up with Irene Bronfen?"

"Agnes might have been a cousin or a family friend. She might have been the *maid* . . ."

"All right, great. Let's say it was the maid who ran off with the little girl. How come he didn't tell us that? Why pretend it was his wife. *He's* convinced Sheila took the child, or else he's lying through his teeth, right?"

"Come on. You're grasping at straws."

I sank down on my heels, pulling idly at the grass. My frustration was mounting. I'd felt so close to unraveling the knot. I let out a puff of air. I'd been secretly convinced Agnes Grey and Anne Bronfen were one and the same. I wanted Bronfen to be lying about Anne's death, but it looked like he was telling the truth—the turd. Out of the corner of my eye, I saw Dietz sneak a look at his watch.

"Goddamn it. Don't do that," I said. "I hate being pushed." I bit back my irritation. "What time is it?" I said, relenting.

"Nearly four. I don't mean to rush you, but we gotta get a move on."

"The Ocean View isn't far."

He clammed up and stared off down the hill, probably stuffing down a little irritation of his own. He was impatient, a man of action, more interested in Mark Messinger than he was in Agnes Grey. He bent down, picked up a dirt clod, and tossed it down the hill. He watched it as if it might skip across the grass like a pebble on water. He shoved his hands in his pockets. "I'll wait for you in the car," he said shortly and started off down the hill.

I watched him for a moment.

"Oh hell," I murmured to myself and followed him. I felt like a teenager, without a car of my own. Dietz insisted on my being with him almost constantly, so I was forced to trail around after him, begging rides, getting stuck where I didn't want to be, unable to pursue the leads that interested me. I doubled my pace, catching up with him at the road. "Hey, Dietz? Could you drop me off at the house? I could borrow Henry's car and let you talk to Rochelle on your own."

He let me in on my side. "No."

I stared after him with outrage. "No?" I had to wait till he came around. "What do you mean, 'No'?"

"I'm not going to have you running around by yourself. It's not safe."

"Would you *quit* that? I've got things to do."

He didn't answer. It was like I hadn't said a word. He drove out of the cemetery and left on Cabana Boulevard, heading toward the row of motels just across from the wharf. I stared out the window, thinking darkly of escape.

"And don't do anything dumb," he said.

I didn't say what flashed through my head, but it was short and to the point.

The Ocean View is one of those nondescript one-story motels a block off the wide boulevard that parallels the beach. It was not yet tourist season and the rates were still down, red neon VACANCY signs alight all up and down the street. The

Ocean View didn't really have a view of anything except the backside of the motel across the alley. The basic cinderblock construction had been wrapped in what resembled aging stucco, but the red tiles on the roof had the uniform shape and coloring that suggested recent manufacture.

Dietz pulled into the temporary space in front of the office, left the engine running, and went in. I sat and stared at the car keys dangling from the ignition. Was this a test of my character, which everyone knows is bad? Was Dietz *inviting* me to steal the Porsche? I was curious about the exact date Anne Bronfen had died and I was itching to check it out. I had to have a car. This was one. Therefore . . .

I glanced at the office door in time to see Dietz emerge. He got in, slammed the door, and put the car in reverse. "Number sixteen, around the back," he said. He smiled at me crookedly as he shifted into first. "I'm surprised you didn't take off. I left you the keys."

I let that one pass. I always come up with witty rejoinders when it's too late to score points.

We parked in the slot meant for room 18, the only space available along the rear. Dietz knocked. Idly, I felt for the gun in my handbag, reassured by its weight. The door opened. He was blocking my view of her and I had too much class to hop up and down on tiptoe for an early peek.

"Rochelle? I'm Robert Dietz. This is Kinsey Millhone."

"Hello. Come on in."

I caught my first glimpse of Rochelle Messinger as we stepped through the door into her motel room.

"Thanks for coming up on such short notice," Dietz was saying.

I don't know what I expected. I confess I'm as given to stereotyping as the next guy. My notion of ladies who work in massage parlors leans toward the tacky, the blowsy, and (face it) the low class. A tattoo wouldn't have surprised me . . . a hefty rear end, decked out in blue jeans and spike heels, tatty dark hair pulled up in a rubber band.

Rochelle Messinger was my height, very slim. She had fly-away blond hair, a carelessly mussed mop that probably cost her $125 to have touched up and snipped every four weeks. Her face was the perfect oval of a Renaissance painting. She had a flawless complexion—very pale, finely textured skin—pale hazel eyes, long fingers with lots of silver rings, expensive ones by the look. She was wearing an ice-blue silk blouse, a matching silk blazer, pale blue slacks that emphasized her tiny waist and narrow hips. She smelled of some delicate blend of jasmine and lily of the valley. In her presence, I felt as dainty and feminine as a side of beef. When I opened my mouth, I was worried I would moo.

"God, how'd you end up with a piece of shit like Mark Messinger?" I blurted out instead.

She didn't react, but Dietz turned and gave me a hard look.

"Well, I really want to know," I said to him defensively.

She cut in. "It's all right. I understand your curiosity. I met him one night at a party in Palm Springs. He was working as a bodyguard for a well-known actor at the time and I thought he had class. I was mistaken, as it turns out, but by then we'd spent a weekend together and I was pregnant—"

"Eric," I said.

She nodded almost imperceptibly. "That was six years ago. I'd been told I could never have children, so for me, it was a miracle. Mark insisted on marriage, but I refused to compound the initial error in judgment. Once Eric was born, I didn't even want him to see the child. I knew by then how twisted he was. He hired a high-powered attorney and took me to court. The judge awarded him visitation rights. After that, it was simply a matter of time. I knew he'd make a try for Eric, but there was nothing I could do."

So far, she'd left more unexplained than she'd managed to clarify, but I thought it was time to back off and give Dietz room to operate. By unspoken agreement, this was his gig in much the same way the Bronfen interview had been mine. Dietz was getting into work mode, his energy intensifying, restlessness on the increase. He'd started snapping the fingers of his right hand against his left palm, a soft popping sound. "When did you last talk to him?" Dietz asked her.

"To Mark? Eight months ago. In October, he picked Eric up at the day-care center and took him to Colorado, ostensibly for a weekend. He called me shortly after that to say he wouldn't be returning him. He does allow the boy to call me from time to time, but it's usually from a pay phone and the contact's too brief to put a trace on. This is the first time I've actually known where he was. I want my child back."

Dietz said, "I can appreciate that. We understand Mark has family in the area. Will they know where he is?"

She smiled contemptuously. "Not bloody likely. Mark's father denounced him years ago and his mother's dead. He does have a sister, but I don't believe they're on speaking terms. She turned him in to the police the last time he got in touch."

"No other relatives? Friends he might have tried to contact?"

She shook her head. "He's strictly solo. He doesn't trust a soul."

"Can you suggest how we can get a line on him?"

"Easy. Call all the big hotels. The cops quizzed me as to his whereabouts after the gold mart robbery. He'll be loaded and, believe me, he's the sort of man who knows how to treat himself well. He'll book himself into first-class accommodations somewhere in town."

Dietz said, "Do you have a telephone book?"

Rochelle crossed to the bed table and opened the drawer. Dietz sat down on the edge of the king-size bed and turned to the yellow pages. I could tell he was dying for a cigarette. Actually, if I were a smoker, I'd have wanted one myself. It was the same bed where I'd caught my ex-husband with a lover during the Christmas holidays. What a jolly season that was . . .

Dietz looked at me. "How many big hotels?"

I thought about it briefly. "There are only three or four that might appeal to him," I said, and then to her, "Will he be registered under his real name?"

"I doubt it. When he's on the road, he tends to use one of his aliases. He favors Mark Darian or Darian Davidson, unless he's got a new one altogether, in which case I wouldn't know."

Dietz had flipped through the yellow pages to the hotel/motel listings.

"Hey, Dietz?"

He looked up at me.

"I'd try the Edgewater first," I said. "Maybe his showing up at the banquet last night was just a piece of dumb luck."

He stared for a moment until the logic sank in. Then he laughed. "That's good. I like that." He found the number and punched it in, his attention focusing as someone picked up on the other end. "May I speak to Charles Abbott in security? Yes, thanks. I'll hold." Dietz put a palm over the mouthpiece of the receiver and used the interval to fill Rochelle in on events to date. He interrupted himself abruptly. "Mr. Abbott? Robert Dietz. We talked to you yesterday about security on the banquet . . . Right. I'm sorry to bother you again, but I need a quick favor. I wonder if you can check to see if you have a guest registered there. The name is Mark Darian or Darian Davidson . . . possibly some variation. Same man. We believe he'll have his little boy with him. Sure . . ."

Apparently, Dietz was on hold again while Charles Abbott checked with the reservations desk. Dietz turned to Rochelle and took up the narrative where he'd left it. She didn't seem to have any trouble following. Watching her, I began to realize how strung-out she was, despite the poised façade. This was a woman who probably didn't eat when she was under stress, who lived on a steady diet of coffee and tranqs. I'd seen mothers like her before—usually pacing back and forth in a cage at the zoo. No appearance of domestication would ever undercut the savagery or the rage. Personally, I was happy I'd never laid a hand on her pup.

By the time Dietz caught her up, her expression was dark. "You have no idea how ruthless he is," she said. "Mark is very, very smart and he has all the uncanny intuitions of a psychopath. Have you ever dealt with one? It's almost like a form of mind reading. . . ."

Dietz was on the verge of replying when Charles Abbott cut back in. Dietz said, "You do. That's right, the boy is five." He listened for a moment. "Thanks very much. Absolutely." He placed the receiver in the cradle with exaggerated care. "He's there with the kid. They're in one of the cottages out in back. Apparently, the two of them have just gone down to the pool to have a swim. I told Mr. Abbott there'd be no trouble."

She said, "Of course not."

"You want to call the police?"

"No, do you?"

From the look that passed between them, they understood each other exactly. She picked up a leather handbag from the bed and took out a little nickel-plated derringer. Two shots. I gave him a smirky look, but his expression was neutral. God, and he'd criticized *my* gun.

"What's your intention if we succeed in getting Eric back? You can't go home," he said to her.

"I have a rental car, which I'm dropping at the airport. My brother's a pilot and he'll pick us up at a charter place called Neptune Air. Mark and I used it once."

Dietz turned to me. "You know it?"

"More or less. It's this side of the airport on Rockpit Road."

He turned back to Rochelle. "What time's he flying in?"

"Nine, which should give us time enough. don't you think?"

"It should. What then?"

"I've got a place we can hole up for as long as we want."

Dietz nodded. "All right. It sounds good. Let's do it."

I held a finger up, snagging Dietz's attention. I tilted my head toward the door. "Could I have a word with you?"

He flicked a look at me, but made no move, so I was forced to charge on.

I said, "I've got something I want to check out and I need some wheels. Why can't I take the rental car while you two take the Porsche? You know where Messinger is and you're on your way over. I don't see why I need to be there."

There was a silence. I had to struggle not to jump in with a lot of pointless dialogue. I'm too old to beg and whine. I just couldn't picture us in a motorcade, driving across town to a kidnapping or a shootout with Mark Messinger. My presence was redundant. I had other fish to fry. Rochelle was loading her gun—both chambers. It was too ludicrous for words, but something about it gave me a leaden feeling in my gut.

I could see Dietz debate my request. In an odd flash of ESP, I knew he'd have felt safer if I were going with him. He held out his car keys, not quite making eye contact. "Take my car. There's a chance Messinger might spot us if we pull into the hotel parking lot in it. We'll take the rental car. What I said before goes. Nothing dumb."

"Same to you," I said, perhaps more sharply than I intended. "I'll meet you out at the charter place."

"Take care."

"You too."

26

It was 4:42 when I turned into the entrance to Mt. Calvary for the second time that day. A long line of eucalyptus trees laid lean shadows across the road. I passed through them as though through a series of gates as I wound my way up the hill. I turned left into a parking area near the office and pulled in beside a splashing stone fountain in a circle of grass. Bright orange goldfish darted among the soft, dark green filaments of algae. I locked the car. The tall carved wooden doors to the nondenominational chapel were standing open. The stone interior was dark.

I passed a double row of flat monuments, displaying various types of granite markers and styles of lettering. Hard to decide which I preferred at such a quick examination. I reached the office and pushed through the glass door. The reception area was empty, the desk bare except for a neat stack of postcards depicting the crematorium. What kind of person would you write to on one of those? I spotted a discreet sign saying PRESS BUZZER FOR SERVICE attached to a device about the size of an electric letter opener. I pressed a lever. Magically, a woman appeared from around the corner.

I wasn't really up on the fine points of cemetery ethics so, of course, I told a lie. "Hello. I wonder if you could help me ..."

From the woman's expression, she was wondering the same thing. She was in her forties, dressed in prim office clothes: a gray wool dress with a touch of white at the neck. I was sporting my usual jeans and tennis shoes. "I certainly hope so," she said. She kept her judgment in reserve just in case I was rich and had a passel of dead relatives in need of lavish burial.

"I believe my aunt is buried here and I need to know the date she died. My mother's in a nursing home and she's worried because she can't remember. Is there some way to check?"

"If you'll give me the name."

"The last name is Bronfen. Her first name was Anne."

"Just a moment." She disappeared. It was hard to picture how she'd find the information. Was all this stuff on a computer somewhere? In some old file cabinet in the back? If the date and place of death didn't coincide with Bronfen's story, I was going to do some digging and see if I could come up with the death certificate. It might mean a few phone calls to Tucson, Arizona, but I'd feel better knowing what had really happened to Anne.

She returned in a remarkably short period of time, holding a white index card which she passed to me. There wasn't much on the face of it, but it was all pertinent. I soaked up the typed information in a flash. Surname, Chapman. Given name, Anne Bronfen. Age, forty. Birthdate, January 5, 1900. Sex, female. Color, white. Place of birth, Santa Teresa, California. Place of death, Tucson, Arizona.

Ah. Date of death, January 8, 1940. That was interesting.

Date of interment, January 12, 1940. The space allotted to the funeral director had been left blank, but the lot number and the plot number were filled in.

"What's this?" I asked. I held the card out, pointing to the bottom line on which the word *cenotaph* had been handwritten in black ink.

"That's a commemorative headstone for someone who's not actually buried in that plot."

"She's not? Where is she?"

The woman took the card. "According to this, she died in Tucson, Arizona. She's probably interred there."

"I don't get it. What's the point?"

"The Bronfens might have wanted her remembered in the family plot. It's a great comfort sometimes to feel that everyone's together."

"But how do you know this woman's really dead?"

She stared at me. "Not dead?"

"Yeah. Don't you require any proof? Can I just come in here and fill out one of these cards and buy somebody a gravestone?"

"It's hardly that simple," she said, "but yes, essentially . . ."

She had launched into an explanation of the particulars, but I was on my way out.

I drove to the board-and-care in a state of suspended animation. All I'd really wanted was corroboration of Bronfen's tale, and here I was with another possibility altogether. Maybe Agnes Grey and Anne Bronfen *were* the same person after all. I thumbed my nose in Dietz's general direction as I turned right on Concorde.

I parked the Porsche at the curb and got out. For once, there was no little twitch of the curtain as I pushed through the gate. I went up the porch steps and rang the bell. I waited. Several minutes passed. I moved over to the porch rail and peered toward the back of the house. At the far end of the driveway, I spotted a single-car garage. Attached to it was a lath house and a dark green potting shed with a big handsome padlock hanging open in the hasp.

Behind me, I heard the front door opening. "Oh, hi. Is that you, Mr. Bronfen?" I said, turning my attention back.

The man in the doorway was someone else—a frail old fellow with an air of shuffling indecision. He was thin and bent, his shoulders narrow, his fingers twisted with arthritis. He wore a much-washed plaid flannel shirt, thin at the elbows, and a pair of pants that came halfway up his chest.

"He's out. You'll have to come again," he said. His voice was a pastel blend of raspiness and tremor.

"Do you have any idea what time he'll be back?"

"About an hour," he said. "You just missed him."

"Oh, gee, that's too bad. I'm the contractor," I said in this totally false warm tone I use. "I guess Mr. Bronfen's thinking about an addition to the shed out back. He asked me to take a look. Why don't I just go on out there and see what's what."

"Suit yourself," he said. He closed the door.

Heart thumping, I made a beeline for the backyard, figuring my time was going to be limited. Patrick Bronfen was not going to appreciate my snooping, but then, if I were quick about it, he'd never know. The shed was perched haphazardly on a concrete foundation that did a sort of zigzag between the single-car garage and the house. This looked like the sort of work that was done without permit and was probably not up to code. Given the slope of the side yard and the retaining wall at the property line, Bronfen probably should have had a team of civil engineers out here before he opened that first sack of Redi-Mix.

I removed the dangling padlock from the hasp and let myself in. The interior was probably eight by ten, smelling of loam, peat moss, and potting soil, overlaid with B1 and fish emulsion. There were no windows and the light level had dropped by more than half. I felt around in the gloom, trying to find a light switch, but apparently the shed wasn't wired for electricity. I groped through my handbag till I came up with a penlight and shone it around. The beam illuminated a large expanse of wall-mounted pegboard, hung with gardening tools. A mower leaned against the wall, its blades flecked with grass clippings. There was a six-foot workbench, its surface littered with clay pots, trowels, spilled potting soil, and discarded seed packs. Damp air clambered over my ankles and feet. Under the bench, I could see a gap in the rotting wood where a board had been pushed out.

To the right was an oblong wooden bin with a hinged lid, knee-high, the sort of unit where tools are stored. A square of newly cut plywood had been nailed across one end. Big plastic bags of bark mulch and Bandini 101 were stacked on top. One of the bags had a rip in the bottom and a trail of bark extended across the cracked cement floor. A pie-shaped wedge of track suggested that the bin had been dragged forward and then pushed back again. I thought about Agnes's torn knuckles and broken nails.

I lifted my head. "Hello," I said, just to check the sound level. The word was muffled, as if absorbed by the shadows. I tried again. "Hello?" No echo at all. I doubted the noise carried five feet beyond the shed. If I'd abducted a half-senile old lady, this would be a neat place to stash her till I decided what to do.

I balanced the penlight on the workbench and removed the twenty-five-pound bags from the top of the bin, stacking them to one side. When I'd cleared the lid, I opened it and peered in. Empty. I retrieved the penlight and checked the rough interior surface. The space was easily the size of a coffin and constructed so poorly that the air flow could probably sustain life, at least for a brief period. I ran the penlight from corner to corner, but there was no evidence of occupancy. I lowered the lid and restored the bags of mulch to their original positions. On my hands and knees, I checked the area around the bin. Nothing. I'd never be able to prove Agnes Grey had been here.

As I backed out of the space, I caught a whiff of foul air, musty and sweet, like a faint wisp of smoke. I felt my skin contract with recognition, hairs standing at attention along the back of my neck. I could feel my lips purse with distaste. This was the odor of dead squirrel trapped in a chimney, rotting gopher parts left on the porch by your cat, some creature guaranteed to perfume your nights until nature had completed the process of decomposition. Jesus. Where was it coming from?

I raised myself up on my knees and fumbled across the workbench until I found the trowel. I ducked under the bench again, running my fingers lightly along the shed's concrete footing. The material was porous, softening with age, the texture mealy. I found a patch of crumbling mortar and began to dig with the trowel, gouging out a pocket. I turned the penlight off and worked by feel, using both hands. Under the hardened outer shell, the stuff felt gritty and wet, as if the groundwater had somehow seeped in, undermining the concrete. The smell seemed stronger. There was something dead down here.

I tried the light again, working my way to the right where I could see two horizontal cracks. I began to chop away at the concrete, doing more damage to the trowel than I was doing to the footing. I pulled myself to my feet again, searching the workbench for a more effective tool. Up on the pegboard, I spotted a short-handled hoe with a pick on the backside of the blade. I crawled back to my little strip mine and began to hack in earnest. I was making so much damn noise, it was a wonder the neighbors didn't complain. A hunk of cement fell away. Tentatively, I scooped some of the debris off, using the pick to excavate. I felt resistance, some sort of root perhaps, or a length of rebar. I turned on the penlight again and peered into the space.

"Oh shit," I whispered. I was looking at the dorsal surface of a little finger bone. I scooted backward across the floor, bumping into the mower. I sucked air through my teeth as my banged elbow sang. The pain was a welcome diversion under the circumstances. I flicked the light off and scrambled to my feet. I shoved a bag of bark mulch in front of the hole and snagged my handbag.

I was making little whimpering sounds as I whipped out of the door again. I placed the padlock where it had been and danced away from the shed with a spasm of revulsion. For a moment, all I could do was shiver, slapping at my arms as if to aid circulation. I paced in a circle, trying to think what to do. I breathed deeply. God, that was vile. From the glimpse I'd had, the bone had been there for years. Whatever the odor, it wasn't emanating from *that*, but what else was down there? In the fading afternoon light, the zigzagging foundation seemed to glow. Someone had been adding outbuildings from time to time. First the lath house had been attached to the garage, then the potting shed had been attached to that. Extending from the side of the potting shed, there was a pad where firewood was stacked. If Anne Bronfen (in the guise of Agnes Grey) was accounted for, then the body had to be Sheila's. Bronfen claimed his wife had run away with Irene, but I didn't believe a word of it. I did one of those all-over body shudders, thinking about the finger. All of the flesh was gone. I gave my head a shake and took two deep breaths, disconnecting my sensibilities. There had to be other answers somewhere on the premises.

I went back to the front door and knocked. I waited, hoping fervently that Bronfen wasn't back. Eventually, the old fellow shuffled his way to the door and opened it a crack. I had to clear my throat, assuming what I hoped was a normal tone of voice.

"Me again," I chirped. "Could I come in and wait for Mr. Bronfen?"

The old gent put a gnarly finger to his lips, giving my request some thought. Finally, he nodded and backed away from the door awkwardly as if controlled by wires. I followed him into the house, quickly checking my watch. I'd been in the shed twenty minutes. I still had plenty of time if I could figure out what I was looking for.

The old man crept toward the living room. "You can have a seat in here. I'm Ernie."

"Nice to meet you, Ernie. Where did Mr. Bronfen go? Did he say anything to you?"

"No. I don't believe so. He'll be home directly I should think. Not long."

"Nice house," I said, peering into the living room. There I was, telling lies again. The house was shabby and smelled of cooked cabbage and peed-in pants. The furniture looked like it had been there since the turn of the century. The once-upon-a-time white curtains hung in limp wisps. The wallpaper in the hallway, with its motif of violets, fanned out in all directions like a bug infestation. Lucky for Klotilde she hadn't qualified for occupancy.

To the left, uncarpeted stairs led up to a second floor. I could see a dining room with a series of decorative plates on the wall. I moved toward the rear of the house, passing a small door that probably opened onto a little storage area under the stairs. Across from that was the basement door. "Is this the kitchen through here? I need to wash my hands." But I was talking to myself—Ernie had shuffled into the living room, forgetting me entirely.

The kitchen was the prototype "before" in any home remodeling magazine. Cracked tile counters, black and white floor tiles, brown woodwork, stained sink, a dripping faucet. Someone, in a jaunty attempt to update the place, had covered the original wallpaper with a modern-day vinyl equivalent: pale green fruits and vegetables intermixed with white and yellow daisies. Along the baseboard, the vinyl strip was curling up like a party favor. I checked the walk-in pantry. The shelves were lined with industrial-size cans of hominy and peas. I went in and stood there, looking out at the kitchen with the door half-shut.

Irene Bronfen had been four when she left. I hunkered down, smelling soot, my eyes level with the doorknob. I returned to the hallway. The door to the storage space beneath the stairs was kept locked. I wondered if she'd used it as a playhouse. I hunkered there, looking left toward the kitchen. Not much visible from that vantage point. Murders are, so often, domestic affairs. Alcohol is a factor in more than sixty percent. Thirty percent of the weapons in these murders are knives, which, after all, antedate gunpowder and don't have to be registered. As a matter of convenience, the kitchen is a favored location for crimes of passion these days. You can sit there with your loved ones, grabbing beers out of the fridge, adding ice to your Scotch. Once your spouse makes a smart remark, the stakes can escalate until you reach for the knife rack and win the argument.

I moved through the kitchen. At the rear of the house,

there was an enclosed wooden porch, uninsulated board and batten, where an antique washer stood. The water heater was out there, looking too small and decrepit to provide much hot water to the residents.

Irene at four had been somewhere in this house. I was willing to bet she'd been playing with the tea set. What had she told me? That the paint ran down the walls and ruined all the violets. I thought about her phobias: dust, spiders, closed spaces. I stood in the doorway, looking through the kitchen toward the hall. The ceilings were high, papered overall with the same repeating pattern of violets as the hall. The kitchen walls had been repapered, but not the ceiling itself. There must have been a time when it was the same throughout. I checked the baseboard near the stretch where the old icebox had once stood. In the wall above it was the square space with the little door to the exterior where the iceman had left his delivery. The next section of wall was a straight shot, floor to ceiling.

I could feel my attention stray to the portion of the vinyl paper that was loose along the bottom. I leaned over and peeled a corner back. Under it was a paper sprigged with roses. Under that layer came the paper with the violets again. I got a grip on the lower edge of the vinyl panel and I pulled straight up. The strip made a sucking sound as it raced up the wall, taking some of the sprigged paper with it. The rust-colored streaks were showing through, drab rivulets coursing through a field of violets, spatters of dull brown that had soaked into the paper, soaked into the plaster underneath. The blood had sprayed in an arc, leaping high along the wall, penetrating everything. Attempts to clean it had failed and the second coat of paper had been layered over the first. Then a third coat over that. I wondered if current technology was sufficiently sophisticated to forge the link between the blood here and the body that was buried in the footing. Lottie was the first to go. Her death must have been passed off as natural since she was buried with the rest. Emily must have come next, her skull "crushed" by falling bricks.

And Sheila after that, with a story to cover her disappearance. That must have been the killing Agnes and Irene witnessed. Bronfen had probably made up the story of Sheila's departure. I doubted there were any neighbors left who could verify the sequence of events. No telling what Bronfen had told them at the time. Some glib cover story to account for the missing.

Agnes had been in exile for years, protecting Irene. I wondered what had tempted her to return to the house. Perhaps, after over forty years, she thought the danger had passed. Whatever her motives, she was dead now, too. And Patrick—dear brother Patrick—was the only one left.

I heard the front door shut.

27

He stood in the kitchen doorway, a brown grocery bag in his arms. He wore a dark green sport shirt and wash pants, belted below his waist. He was wheezing from exertion, sweat beading his face. His gaze was fixed on the length of vinyl wallpaper that now lay on the floor, folded over on itself. His gaze traveled up the wall and then jerked across to mine. "What'd you do that for?"

"Time to take care of old business, my friend."

He crossed to the kitchen table and set the grocery bag down. He removed some items—toilet paper, a dozen eggs, a pound of butter, a loaf of bread—and set them on the table. I could see him try to settle on an attitude, the proper tone. He'd been rehearsing this in his mind for years, probably confident the conversation was one he could handle with a perfect air of innocence. The problem was, he'd forgotten what innocence felt like or how it was supposed to look. "What old business?"

"All the blood on the wall for one."

The pause was of the wrong length. "What blood? That's a redwood stain. I refinished a piece of porch furniture and knocked the can off on the floor. Stuff sprayed all over, went everyplace. You never saw such a mess."

"Arterial blood will do that. You get a pumping effect." I tromped over the crumpled strip of paper, with a scrabbling sound, and washed my hands at the kitchen sink.

He put a half gallon of ice cream in the freezer, taking a moment to rearrange boxes of frozen vegetables. His rhythm was off. An accomplished liar knows how important the timing is in conveying nonchalance.

I dried my hands on a kitchen towel of doubtful origin. It might have been a part of a pillow case, a paint rag, or a diaper. "I drove over to Mt. Calvary and looked for Anne's grave."

"Make your point. I got work to do. She's buried with the family on the side of the hill."

"Not quite," I said. I leaned against the counter, watching him unload canned goods. "I went into the office and asked to see the interment card. You bought her a stone, but there's no body in the grave. Anne left town with Irene in January nineteen forty."

He tried to get huffy, but he couldn't muster any heat. "I paid to bring her all the way from Tucson, Arizona. If she wasn't in the coffin, don't tell me about it. Ask the fellow on the other end who said he put her there."

"Oh, come on," I said. "Let's cut to the chase. There wasn't any husband in Arizona and there weren't any little kids. You made that stuff up. You killed Charlotte and Emily. You killed Sheila, too. Anne was alive until late last night and she told me most of it. She said Emily wanted to sell the house and you refused. She must have pressed the point and you were forced to eliminate her just to end the argument. Once you got Emily out of the way, there was only Anne to worry about. Have her declared dead and you collect the whole estate. . . ."

He began to shake his head. "You're a crazy woman. I got nothing to say to you."

I crossed to the wall-mounted telephone near the hall door.

246

"Fine with me. I don't care. You can talk to Lieutenant Dolan as soon as he gets here."

Now he was willing to argue the point, any means to delay. "I wouldn't kill anyone. Why would I do that?"

"Who knows what your motivation was? Money is my guess. I don't know *why* you did it. I just know you did."

"I did not!"

"Sure you did. Who are you trying to kid?"

"You don't have a shred of proof. You can't prove anything."

"I can't, but somebody can. The cops are really smart, Patrick, and persistent? My God. You have no idea how persistent they are where murder's concerned. The whole of modern technology will be brought to bear. Lab techs, machinery, sophisticated tests. They've got experts out the wazoo and what do you have? Nothing. A lot of hot air. You don't stand a chance. Fifty years ago you might have fooled 'em, but not these days. You're up shit creek, pal. You are totally screwed . . ."

"Now see here. You wait a minute, young lady. I won't have that kind of talk used in my house," he said.

"Oh, sorry. I forgot. You've got standards. You're not going to tolerate a lot of smutty talk from me, right?" I turned back to the telephone. I had picked up the receiver when the window shattered in the back. The two acts came so close together, it looked like cause and effect. I pick up the phone, the window breaks out. Startled, I jumped a foot and dropped the phone in the process, jumping again as the handset thumped against the wall. I saw a hand come through the shattered window and reach around to unlock the door. One savage kick and the door swung back abruptly and banged against the wall. I had grabbed my handbag and was just reaching for my gun when Mark Messinger appeared, his own gun drawn and pointed at me. The suppressor created the illusion of a barrel fourteen inches long.

This time there was no smile, no aura of sexuality. His

blond hair stood out around his head in damp spikes. His blue eyes were as cold and as blank as stone. Patrick had turned, heading toward the front door in haste. Messinger fired at him casually, not even pausing long enough to form an intent, the shooting as simple as pointing a finger. *Spwt!* The sound of the silenced .45 semiautomatic was almost dainty compared to its effect. The force of the bullet drove Patrick into the wall where he bounced once before he fell. Blood and torn flesh bloomed in his chest like a chrysanthemum, shreds of cotton shirting like the calyx of a flower. I was staring at him mesmerized when Messinger grabbed me by the hair, hauling my face up within an inch of his. He shoved the barrel of his gun under my chin, pressing so hard it hurt. I wanted to protest the pain of it, but I didn't dare move. "Don't shoot me!"

"Where's Eric?" he breathed.

"I don't know."

"You're going to help me get him back."

Fear had pierced my chest wall like splinters. All the adrenaline was coursing upward to my brain, driving out thought. I had a brief image of Dietz with Rochelle Messinger. They'd evidently succeeded in plucking the kid from his father's grasp. I could smell chlorine from the swimming pool, mingled with Messinger's breath. He probably couldn't take his gun to the pool without calling attention to himself. I pictured him in the water, Eric on the side just waiting to jump in. If his mother appeared, he'd have run straight to her with a shriek of joy. By now they were probably barreling out to the airport. The plane had been chartered for nine to allow time for the snatch. I willed the thought away. Made my mind blank.

Messinger slapped me across the face hard, setting up a ringing in my head. I was dead. I wouldn't get out of this one alive. He shoved me toward the back door, kicking a chair out of my path. I caught sight of Ernie, the old guy, shuffling toward the kitchen. His expression was perplexed, especially when he spotted Patrick on the floor with the corsage of blood pinned to the center of his chest. Mark Messinger turned and pointed the gun at the old man.

"Oh don't!" I burbled. My voice sounded strange, high-pitched and hoarse. I squeezed my eyes shut and waited for the *spwt!* I looked back. The old fellow had pivoted and was shuffling away in panic. I could hear his howls echo down the hall, as frail and helpless as a child's. Messinger watched him retreat, indecision flickering in his eyes. He lost interest and turned his attention back to me. "Get the car keys."

I saw the bag where I'd dropped it on the floor near the phone. I pointed, temporarily unable to speak. I longed for my gun.

"We'll take my car. You drive."

He grabbed me by the head and buried his grip in my hair again, propelling me with a fury that made me cry out in fear.

"Shut up," he whispered. His face was close to mine as we descended the back stairs. I stumbled, grabbing at the rail with my right hand for balance. My heel slipped off the stair and I nearly went down. I thought he'd pull all my hair out, effectively scalping me with his closed fist, which held me like a vise. I couldn't look down, couldn't move my head to either side. I could feel the gravel driveway underfoot. I proceeded like a blind woman, hands out, using senses other than sight. The car was parked in the drive near the shed. I wondered briefly if a neighbor would spot our clumsy progress. Nearly dark now. In my mind's eye, I could see Rochelle's face. Please be on the plane, I thought. Please be in the air. Take Dietz with you forever and keep him somewhere safe. I pictured his impatience, his intensity. I willed him into a taxi, drove him away from the danger. I couldn't save him, couldn't even save myself this time around. Messinger yanked open the door on the passenger side and pushed me across the front seat. He was driving a yellow Rolls-Royce: walnut dashboard, leather upholstery.

"Start the car," he said. He got in after me, crowding close. He placed the barrel of the gun against my temple. He was breathing hard, his tension concentrated in his grip on the gun. If he shot me, I wouldn't feel it. I'd be dead before the pain could travel along my nerve ends and get the message to my brain. I willed the act, wanted it over with. "Do it," he said. I thought the voice was mine, so nearly did it mimic my thought.

"Start the fuckin' car!" His anger was erratic, sometimes fire, sometimes ice, his command of himself veering inexplicably from unbridled impulse to rigid control.

I felt for the keys in the ignition.

"Where'd they take my son?"

"They didn't tell me."

"You lying *bitch*! I'll tell *you* then." He dropped his voice and I could feel the force of his words against my cheek. The sexuality was back, the same tickle of desire that rises when you dance with a man for the first time—some awareness of the flesh and all the possibilities that wait. He was calm again, confident, his throaty laugh nearly jubilant. "Rochelle's got a twin brother flies a plane," he said. "She knows better than to take Eric back to her place because I'd find him first thing and she'd be dead before she shut the door. She'll try to get him out by air, take him off and hide him somewhere till things cool down." He moved the gun away from my head, gesturing with the barrel. "Back out on the street and take a left. We'll head out to the airport, there's a charter place out there. Drive carefully, okay?"

I nodded dumbly, my mood shifting as abruptly as his. So far, I was alive, not maimed or disabled. I was grateful he hadn't hurt me, thrilled I wasn't dead. I did as I was told. I felt absurdly happy that his manner was pleasant, his tone nearly friendly as I backed out of the drive. He'd reduced my habitual cockiness to humility. There was still hope. There was still a chance. Maybe they'd already left. Maybe they were gone. Maybe I could kill him before he killed me. I had a flash of Rochelle being shot in the chest. He'd kill her as carelessly as he'd killed Patrick Bronfen, with the same matter-of-factness, the same casualness, the same ease. Dietz would die. Messinger would trade me for Eric at the outset and then kill us all. Rochelle, Dietz, and me, in whatever order would maximize the horror. I focused on the road, suddenly conscious of the car. I could smell leather seats, the fresh rose in a crystal vase. The car glided in silence. I turned right on 101 and flew north. There was not a highway patrol car in sight.

My mouth was dry. I cleared my throat. "How did you know where I was?"

"I put a bug on the Porsche the first night it was parked in front of your place. See this? My receiver. I've been following you guys everywhere in a couple of different rental cars."

"Why'd you kill Patrick?"

"Why not. He's a dickface."

I glanced over at him curiously. "Why'd you spare Ernie?"

"That old fart? Who knows? Maybe I'll go back and do him now you mention it," he said. His tone was teasing. A little hit-man humor to show what a devil-may-care kind of guy he was. He'd taken the gun away from my head and it rested now on his knee. "What's the story with this bodyguard? He's a pain in the ass. Two times I nearly had you and he stepped in."

I kept my eyes on the road. "He's good at his job."

He looked over at me. "You makin' it with him?"

"That's none of your business."

"Come on . . ."

"I've only known him four days!" I said, righteously.

"So what?"

"So I don't jump into bed with guys that quick."

"You should have done while you had the chance. Now he's a dead man. I'll make you a deal. How's this? Him or you. Better yet, Rochelle or him. Take your pick. If you don't choose, I kill all three of you."

"You're only getting paid for one."

"True, but I'll tell you, the money doesn't mean that much. When you do what you love, you'd do it for free, am I right?" He leaned toward the tape deck. "Want some music? I got

251

jazz, classical, R&B. No heavy metal or reggae. I hate that shit. You want Sinatra?"

"No thanks." I saw the off-ramp for the university and the airport and eased right. The road curved up and to the left, crossing the freeway, which now passed underneath. It was gone and we hit the straightaway. Two more minutes to the airport and what was I going to do? The digital clock on the instrument panel showed that it was 8:02. A mile farther on, the access ramp to Rockpit Road came into view on the right. I took the turn. I knew the ocean was close by, but all I could smell was the rotten-egg odor of the slough that hugged the road. A fog was rolling in, a dense bank of white against the blackened sky. The university sat up on the bluffs like a walled city, all lights and buff-colored towers. I'd never gone to college. I was strictly blue-collar lineage—like this guy, come to think of it. Like Dietz.

I took Rockpit for half a mile until the hangars and assorted outbuildings of Neptune Air appeared on the left. "Here," he said. I slowed the Rolls and turned in. Messinger sat forward, peering through the windshield, which had been spritzed with fine mist.

There were four miscellaneous vehicles parked in the lot, but there was no sign of Rochelle's rental car. Messinger had me park the Rolls in the lee of a metal-sided hangar. Under the inverted V of the roofline, illuminated by a single bulb, the sign read: FLIGHT INSTRUCTION, FAA REPAIR STATION, 24 HOUR CHARTERS, PIPER DEALER, and AVIONICS SALES & SERVICES. The perimeter fence was made of chain link, wrapped with barbed wire on top, and padlocked. Warnings were posted at intervals. Floodlights on the far side of the hangar glowed blankly on the empty runway.

We left the car. It was cold and a wind whipped along the tarmac, blowing my hair in all directions. As we crossed the parking lot, Messinger took me by the elbow in a gesture so reminiscent of Dietz that the air caught in my throat.

The offices of Neptune Air were closed, the interior darkened, one dim light shining through the plate glass. We circled the building. A broad redwood deck stretched out across the rear. A picnic table and two benches had been set up for those waiting for their charter flights. I pictured the Neptune employees (all three of them) eating lunch out here, watching planes land, drinking canned sodas from the vending machine. To the right, there was a line of small private planes tied down on the tarmac. Beyond them, half a mile away, I could see the Santa Teresa Airport, the upper portion of its tower peeking up above a row of storage sheds. On one of the runways, a United 737 was lumbering across the field in preparation for takeoff. Messinger gestured and we sat down on opposite sides of the picnic table. "It's fuckin' cold out," he said.

I heard voices behind me. I turned and watched as two workmen, probably fuelers, locked the exit door to the hangar and moved off toward the parking lot. Messinger rose to his feet, peering in their direction. He pulled the nose of the .45 up and pointed, making little noises with his mouth . . . *pow, pow.* He blew imaginary smoke away from the barrel and then he smiled. "They don't know how lucky they are, do they?"

"I guess not," I said.

He sat down again.

His hair had dried into ringlets and the wind lifted them playfully. His eyes glinted in the light from a bulb at the upper corner of the building. He was watching me with interest. "Your daddy ever bring you out here to watch planes?"

"He died when I was five."

"Mine didn't either. Cocksucker. No wonder I turned out bad."

"What, he didn't show up to watch you play Little League?"

"He didn't do much of anything except drink, fornicate, and kill folk. That's where I got all my talent. From him."

My fear had receded and in its place, I was beginning to feel a characteristic crankiness settle in. It was one thing to die, and quite another being forced to sit around in a cold wind making small talk with a fatuous ass like Messinger. I'd been thinking I better make nice. Now I wondered what the point was. In the meantime, he was staring at my face. I stared back, just to see what it would feel like.

He nodded judiciously. "Your black eye's looking better."

I ran a finger along my orbital ridge. I kept forgetting what I must look like to the uninitiated observer. The last time I'd assayed my various injuries, I'd noticed the bruises had changed hues dramatically. A lemon-yellow backdrop now blended into lime-green, which was overlaid with plum. "You nearly got me that round."

He waved the compliment away. "That was just a warm-up. I wasn't serious."

"What'd Eric think of it?"

"Didn't bother him. Look at cartoons. Kids see violence all the time and it doesn't count for shit. People don't really die. It's all special effects."

"I doubt he's going to feel that way if you shoot his mom."

"Not *if* I shoot her—when." I saw his gaze shift.

Out on the runway, a tiny plane had landed, sounding like a VW in need of a new fan belt. I lost sight of the aircraft behind some outbuildings and then the plane appeared again, puttering toward us. He got to his feet. "I bet this is him. Come on. And keep your mouth shut or I'll pop you one."

The plane reached the concrete apron beside the hangar and the pilot made a miniature U-turn so that he was now facing out toward the runway. He cut the engine, doused the lights. Messinger had gripped me across the back of the neck, marching me toward the plane in quickstep. I imagined the pilot taking off his headset, writing in his logbook, loosening his seat belt. If this was Rochelle's brother, he was going to recognize Messinger as soon as he caught sight of him.

A column of fear wafted up my spine like smoke. I tried to hang back, resisting, but Messinger's fingers dug into my neck with excruciating pain. We had picked up the pace, almost trotting side by side until we reached the tail unit of the plane. Just in front of us, the door to the cockpit opened and the pilot stepped down. We were less than six feet away.

Messinger said, "Hey, Roy?"

I screamed a warning.

The pilot turned in surprise.

Spwt!

Roy dropped to his knees. He toppled forward on his face. His nose had been shattered by the bullet, which took out a chunk of skull when it exited. I cried out in horror, recoiling from the sight. I felt tears like a stinging blow. A quick cloud of gunpowder perfumed the night air. I put a hand against the plane for support. Messinger had already lifted the dead man by the arms and he was dragging him backward across the tarmac toward the slanted shadows of the hangar.

I pushed away from the plane. I took off, running for dear life. I headed toward the parking lot, hoping to reach the road.

"Hey!"

I could hear Messinger behind me, pounding hard. I didn't dare look. He was faster than I and he was gaining. I felt the shove that sent me tumbling forward on my hands. I tried to roll, but I wasn't quick enough to save myself. I was down and he was on me, winded and raging. He pulled me over on my back. I kept my arms up to ward off the blows he aimed at me.

Something caught his attention and his face jerked up. A car was approaching from the direction of the slough. He pulled me to my feet, half-dragging, half-hauling me across the concrete toward the shelter of the building. He backed up against the stucco, my body clamped against his, half tucked under his armpit. He had his one hand across my mouth, the barrel of the gun at my temple again. I was close to suffocation, both of us breathing hard.

The car pulled into the parking lot. I heard two car doors slam, one right after the other, and then the murmur of voices. I saw Rochelle first, heard her heels tapping on the pavement, saw the pale cheeks, the pale hair above the turned-up collar of her trenchcoat. Eric walked beside her, his face tilted toward hers. The two were holding hands. Dietz was locked up close to her, his attention focused on the surrounding darkness. When he spotted the plane, he hesitated. I could almost see his puzzled squint. He put an arm out to stop Rochelle's progress and Eric halted in his tracks.

Messinger pushed us away from the building. "Hey, pal. Over here. Look what I got."

For a moment, the five of us formed a tableau. I felt like we were part of a pageant, some community theater group acting out a well-known scene from history. No one moved. Messinger had removed his hand from my mouth, but none of us said a word.

Finally, Eric seemed to perk up. "Daddy?"

"Hey, big fella. How're you doin'? I came to pick you up."

Rochelle said, "Mark, let me have him back. I beg you. You've had him eight months. Let him stay with me. Please."

Despite the distance between us, the voices carried easily.

"No way, babe. That's my kid. Tell you what, though. I'll make a deal. I get Eric. You get Kinsey. Fair enough?"

Dietz glanced at Rochelle. "He won't hurt Eric—"

Rochelle lashed out at Dietz. "Shut up! This is between us."

"He'll kill her," Dietz said.

"I don't give a shit!" she snapped.

Messinger cut in. "Excuse me, Dietz? I hate to interrupt, but you're never going to win an argument with her. She's a hardheaded bitch. Believe me, I know."

Dietz was silent, looking at him. Rochelle had put her arms around Eric possessively, holding him against her, much as Messinger held me.

Messinger was concentrating on Dietz for the moment. "I'd appreciate your taking your gun out, pal. Could you do that? I don't want to have to blow this lady's brains out quite yet. I thought you might like to say good-bye to each other first."

"How serious are you about a deal?" Dietz said.

"Let's do the gun first, okay? Then we'll negotiate. I have to tell you I'm feeling tense. I got a .45 with the safety off and the trigger only takes two pounds of pressure. You might want to move kind of slow."

Dietz seemed to proceed in slow motion, removing his gun from the middle-of-the-back holster he was wearing under his tweed sport coat. He held the barrel upright and removed the magazine, which he tossed out on the pavement. I could hear the metal clatter on concrete as he kicked it away. He tossed the gun over his shoulder into the dark. He held his hands up, palm out.

Dietz and I exchanged a look. I could feel Messinger's tension through the bones of my back. I was warmer, laid up against him, and if I didn't move my head, I was hardly aware of the gun barrel. The length of it, with the suppressor attached, prevented him from pointing it, end on, at my head. He was forced to hold it at an angle. I wondered if the sheer weight of it wasn't becoming burdensome.

Messinger was apparently watching Dietz with care. "Very nice. Now why don't you persuade Rochelle to cooperate. See if you can talk her into it because if not, I'm about to collect on this fifteen-hundred-dollar hit."

Rochelle said, "Why don't you ask Eric what he wants to do?"

Messinger's tone was condescending. "Because he's too young to make a decision about his own custody. Jesus Christ, Rochelle. I don't believe some of the shit you come up with. That's just the kind of attitude makes you a terrible parent, you know that? If he stayed with you, you'd turn him into some kind of little fruit. Now let's cut the horseshit and make a little trade here. Just send Eric over and we'll see what we can do."

Dietz looked at Rochelle. "Do what he says."

She said nothing. She stared at Messinger and then her gaze shifted over to me. "I don't believe you. You'll kill her anyway."

"No, I won't," he said, as if falsely accused. "That's why I brought her out here, to trade. I'd never welsh on a deal where my kid is concerned. Are you nuts?"

Dietz said to her, "You'll have another chance to get Eric back. I promise. We'll help you. Just do this for now."

Even at that distance, I could see her face crumple. She gave Eric a little push. "Go on . . ." She was starting to cry, hands shoved down in her coat pockets.

Eric hesitated, looking from her face to his father's.

"It's all right, angel," she said. He began to walk toward us rapidly, head down, his face hidden.

Messinger's grip on me tightened and I could smell the tawny sweat of sex oozing out of his pores. Time seemed to slow as the kid crossed the pavement. All I could hear was the sound of the wind chuffing across the runway.

Eric reached us. I'd never really seen him up close. His face was like a valentine, all pink cheeks, blue eyes, long lashes. So vulnerable. His ears stuck out slightly and his neck seemed too thin. "Don't hurt her, Daddy."

"I wouldn't do that," Messinger said. "The car's parked on the far side of the hangar. You can wait for me over there. Here's the keys."

"Mark?" Rochelle's voice sounded faint against the distant droning of an incoming plane. Tears were streaming down her face. "Can I kiss him good-bye?"

I heard him mutter. "Christ." He raised his voice. "Come ahead then, but make it quick." To Eric, he said, "You wait here for your mommy and then you go get in the car like I said. You eat any supper?"

"We stopped at McDonald's and had a Big Mac."

"I don't believe it. You remember what I told you about junk food?"

Eric nodded, his eyes filling with tears. It was hard to know which parent he was supposed to listen to. In the meantime, Rochelle was walking toward us along a straight line, setting her high heels down one in front of the other as if in modeling school. Over her shoulder, Dietz's gaze locked down on mine. I thought he smiled his encouragement. I didn't want to see Dietz die, didn't think I could bear it, didn't want to live myself if it came down to that.

I looked at Rochelle. She'd stopped a few feet away. Eric walked over and buried his face against her. She leaned forward and laid her cheek against the top of his head. She was weeping openly. "I love you," she whispered. "You be a good boy, okay?"

He nodded mutely and then pulled away, hurrying toward the Rolls without a backward look. His father called after him.

"Hey, Eric? There's some tapes in the glove compartment. Play anything you like."

Rochelle stared at Mark. She pulled the derringer out of her pocket, aimed it straight at his head and pulled the trigger. The blast was remarkably loud for a weapon so petite. I heard his scream. He dropped the .45 and clutched his right eye with both hands, toppling sideways onto the pavement where he lay writhing in pain. Rochelle, with an efficiency she must have learned from him, stepped in close, and fired again. "You son of a bitch. You never honored a deal in your fuckin' life."

Messinger lay still.

Dietz began to cross the tarmac, moving toward me. I went out to meet him.

Epilogue

When the cops finally tore up the area around Bronfen's potting shed, four bodies came to light. The one buried in the footing was tagged as a former resident of the board-and-care, whose pension checks Bronfen had been cashing for a good five months. The pathologists are still working to identify the remaining dead, but one is most assuredly Bronfen's wife, Sheila. Irene is doing better now that she knows the truth. She's found a good therapist who's helping her sort it all out. It may take her years yet, but at least she's on the right path.

A third (and final) hired assassin was apprehended in Carson City shortly after Messinger was killed. Yesterday, I spoke to Lee Galishoff, who told me Tyrone Patty died of a knife wound, the result of a dispute with an inmate half his size.

As for Dietz, he was with me until August 29 when the job he was hoping for materialized. He's in Germany now, filming mock infiltrations of military bases. He swears he's coming back. I'd like to believe him, but I'm not sure I dare. In the meantime, I have work of my own to do and a life that feels richer for his having been a part of it.

Respectfully submitted,
Kinsey Millhone

Sue Grafton
'F' is for Fugitive £5.99

A KINSEY MILLHONE MYSTERY

'I slammed the phone down before the guy got out another word. Sat straight up, heart thudding. Floral Beach. Already I was wishing I'd never come . . .'

It was an old man's dying wish. To clear his son's name and reunite his family. But Bailey Fowler had been missing for sixteen years and there was more than one person in Floral Beach who didn't want him found.

Until the cops turn him up – by accident. And suddenly murder is the hottest game in town all over again. Kinsey Millhone was summoned for the fairy tale ending . . .

And arrived at a tragedy – starring herself . . .

'A woman to identify with . . . a gripping read' PUNCH

'Quiveringly alive' THE DAILY TELEGRAPH

'Private Eye-ette Kinsey Millhone gets more interesting by the book' THE TIMES

Sue Grafton
'E' is for Evidence £5.99

'I could feel my face heat, the icy itch of fear beginning to assert itself. I said. "This isn't the report I saw . . ."'

It was a routine job – and it was Christmas. All things considered, a neutral verdict looked like a good bet.

But when a mystery well wisher weighs in with an unmarked bank deposit for $5,000, Kinsey Millhone's suspicions are finally aroused.

Too late to avoid the set up – and fighting for her life against the oldest trick in the book . . .

'Kinsey Millhone is going to have herself a bright literary future' STANLEY ELLIN

Sue Grafton
'D' is for Deadbeat £5.99

'Dawn was laid out on the eastern skyline like watercolours on a matt board: cobalt blue, violet and rose bleeding together in horizontal stripes . . .'

Kinsey thought the job was cut and dried . . . until the client's cheque bounced. Daggett was about as worthless as his cheque. An ex con, inveterate liar, chronic drunk . . . and deader than his credit rating.

Accidental death, according to the cops. But Kinsey finds a long line of could-be killers. Long-suffering wife and daughter; a lady who *thought* she was his wife (and had the bruises to prove it); out of pocket drug dealers; and the families of five victims of horror death crashes . . .

. . . a roll call of hatred that only Daggett's death could avenge . . .

'Classy . . . D is for deft and diverting' THE GUARDIAN

'Kinsey Millhone has a lot more than the alphabet going for her'
THE OBSERVER

Sue Grafton
'C' is for Corpse £5.99

A KINSEY MILLHONE MYSTERY

'Violent death is like a monster. The closer you get to it, the more damage you sustain . . .'

The doctors could do something about the damage to Bobby Callahan's body – but not for the broken bits of his brain. The car crash was no accident. Somebody wanted him dead and he can't remember who or why . . .

Three days later, whoever was trying to kill Bobby Callahan came up with the winning ticket. Kinsey Millhone had never worked for a dead man before, and she didn't need the money. But she cared . . .

. . . Cared enough to try and make sense of the whole savage joke . . .

'Quiveringly alive' THE DAILY TELEGRAPH

'C is for classy, strong characterisation and a tough cookie heroine' TIME OUT

'Private Eye-ette Kinsey Millhone gets more interesting by the book' THE TIMES

All Pan Books are available at your local bookshop or newsagent, or can be ordered direct from the publisher. Indicate the number of copies required and fill in the form below.

Send to: Macmillan General Books C.S.
                Book Service By Post
                PO Box 29, Douglas I-O-M
                IM99 1BQ

or phone: 01624 675137, quoting title, author and credit card number.

or fax: 01624 670923, quoting title, author, and credit card number.

or Internet: http://www.bookpost.co.uk

Please enclose a remittance* to the value of the cover price plus 75 pence per book for post and packing. Overseas customers please allow £1.00 per copy for post and packing.

*Payment may be made in sterling by UK personal cheque, Eurocheque, postal order, sterling draft or international money order, made payable to Book Service By Post.

Alternatively by Access/Visa/MasterCard

Card No. ☐☐☐☐☐☐☐☐☐☐☐☐☐☐☐☐☐☐☐☐

Expiry Date ☐☐☐☐☐☐☐☐☐☐☐☐☐☐☐☐☐☐☐☐

Signature   _____

Applicable only in the UK and BFPO addresses.

While every effort is made to keep prices low, it is sometimes necessary to increase prices at short notice. Pan Books reserve the right to show on covers and charge new retail prices which may differ from those advertised in the text or elsewhere.

NAME AND ADDRESS IN BLOCK CAPITAL LETTERS PLEASE

Name _____

Address _____

_____

_____

_____

8/95

Please allow 28 days for delivery.
Please tick box if you do not wish to receive any additional information. ☐